The

Shadow Garden

Nightfall Gardens: Book Two

ALLEN HOUSTON

COVER ILLUSTRATION: ANTHONY ROBERTS

The Shadow Garden
Nightfall Gardens: Book Two
Copyright © 2013 Allen Houston
This is a work of fiction. Any resemblance to living
people, places or events is purely coincidental.
All rights reserved.
ISBN-10: 0615909779
ISBN-13: 978-0615909776

For my brother Grant

CONTENTS

The
Shadow Garden

1

THE WITCH'S SURROGATE

Silas Blackwood was splashing cold, clear water from a woodland spring on his face and salivating over the smell of rabbit from the nearby campfire when he saw the body at the bottom of the stream.

A few months earlier he would have fled in terror at the sight of the swollen figure, bound by ropes, gently rocking beneath the water's surface. Nightfall Gardens had changed that. He and his sister, Lily, had lived through so much that finding a dead body no longer surprised him. There were worse things stirring in the Gardens.

Quarreling voices drifted to him as he examined the person in the stream. His uncle, Jonquil, and Larkspur were arguing once again. They had only left Nightfall Gardens three days before, but the way Larkspur complained, you would have thought they'd been on the road for years.

"I don't see the point," the dusk rider protested. "If we find Eldritch, what are we going to do? He's already proven he's more than capable of taking on the lot of us."

"We can't leave the villagers to die. We're honor bound to protect them, or have you forgotten that?" Jonquil responded.

Silas ignored them. Ropes of fog obscured his vision. They had been riding deeper into the mist land, and with each mile, the fog grew thicker and blotted out the dim sunlight overhead. Ghostly fingers caressed tree branches and distorted the sounds coming from the white-shrouded wilderness. An occasional empty pocket opened long enough to see the damp landscape and then it closed again like a magician swiping his hand over a coin.

A patch of fog floated over the stream, temporarily hiding the body. When it passed Silas could see that the man in front of him had been dead for some time. His face was bloated to twice its normal size. Minnows nibbled at where his eyes used to be. The skin of his face was so swollen that Silas wondered how it kept from bursting.

As Silas watched, the man's neck bulged and something started pushing through its side. Fear tickled his veins and the acidic taste of vomit filled Silas's mouth. A black fish, no bigger than his hand, thrust through the side of the man's fleshy throat. The fish swam against the current for a moment and then was off downstream.

He was still in shock over what he'd seen when he heard a rustling in the underbrush and Dan Trainer appeared.

"Well, what is it then?" Trainer asked noting the concern darkening Silas's face. At the same moment, he saw the body in the stream. The dusk rider kneeled by the bank and gazed at the figure that was tied to rocks under the surface.

"This isn't good. This isn't good at all," Trainer said, shaking his head. He was sallow-faced with thin lips and ears that hung like pendulums to his chin. He spoke little but observed much. Silas had tried chatting with him earlier that day, but Trainer had only spurred his horse faster, pulling ahead of everyone.

"What do you think happened?" Silas asked.

"Why, he was killed, boy. Simple as the nose on me face," Trainer said.

Silas felt a bite of irritation at the condescending tone in the rider's voice. "I *know* that. Why do you think he was weighed down with stones?"

"Well that's a different question completely," Trainer said, spitting into the water. The squadron of minnows eating the dead man's skin rushed to the surface and devoured the fresh spittle. "Looks like 'twere the work of witches."

"Witches?"

"Nothing wrong with your hearing then," Trainer said. He wrapped his wolf cloak – the kind worn by all dusk riders – tightly around himself.

The chill was increasing with the coming dark.

Dusk and dark were the only times in Nightfall Gardens. Daylight hardly made a difference in the ever-present gloom. Sunny days were an illusion that Silas daydreamed about before he fell asleep. He clung to memories of his old life with Lily as the Amazing Blackwoods, his father and mother, Thomas and Moira, traveling from town to town performing at third-rate theaters or anywhere that would take them. That innocent life was shattered the night Uncle Jonquil kidnapped Lily. Silas stowed away inside of the carriage to help his sister escape. Instead they were brought to Nightfall Gardens, the Blackwood ancestral home, to meet Deiva, their dying grandmother. She told them their tragic family history, of how their ancestor Pandora nearly set loose all of the evil in existence upon the world. In payment for her deed, the old god Prometheus created Nightfall Gardens, binding her and future Blackwoods to this place and making them caretakers of the three gardens — the White Garden, the Shadow Garden and the Labyrinth — where all the evil of the world was imprisoned. Before she passed, Deiva warned that when the last female of the family died, all of the monstrosities contained in the Gardens would be free to work their sinister magic on the world and enslave humankind once again.

They were on the trail of one of those monsters now. Eldritch, an old god, had freed himself from the Labyrinth and fled into the mist. The dusk riders who protected the Gardens thought he was gone forever. Recently though, strange reports had come from the mist land, of villagers who had been found with their skin turned inside out and the life drained from them. Jonquil and some other riders had gone north to investigate. One month later, they returned wounded and poisoned by Eldritch. Jonquil was the only one to survive, though he remembered little of what had happened.

"No time for daydreaming, boy," Trainer said, rising from his haunches. "We need to make sure the fire has plenty of fuel before dark comes. Don't want to be fumbling around in the woods when day is gone, especially if there are witches waiting."

"Shouldn't we bury him?" Silas asked. He felt for the dagger that he kept tucked in his belt.

"Nay, lad!" Trainer said grabbing his arm. The dusk rider was close enough that Silas could see the pits on his cheeks and hollows of his eyes. "He's had a water burial for a reason. The rushing water keeps him from coming back to life."

Silas looked at the tethered body, bumping on the creek bottom. Fear threaded through his heart. How could this eyeless corpse come back from the dead? He must have been under the water for weeks.

"So he's not dead then?" Silas asked, pulling his arm free.

"Oh, he's dead all right, but moving water binds a person who's been marked by a witch. Didn't your uncle teach you anything?"

"With all the other things trying to kill me, the subject never came up," Silas said. Up the hill, Jonquil and Larkspur continued their argument. The coming night turned the fog translucent in the gloom.

"It's a wonder you've made it as far as you have," Trainer said, shaking his head. "First, there are as many types of witches as trees in the forest. Most are harmless. They spend their time brewing healing poultices and love potions or think they have powers that they don't. Those are the ones that live in the world we come from. Then there is the other kind of witch: filthy fiends that drink human blood and are apt to snatch a baby from its crib. They are wretched creatures that worship the dark and all it brings. The most malevolent have lost their souls and no longer look human, so they need surrogates that can walk among people. These witches control their hosts, body and mind."

"Don't the people fight back?" Silas asked. The fog was rolling in ever thicker, up and down the banks. He could no longer see the water or the body hidden there.

"These people *want* the witches to control them," Trainer said, tapping his skull.

"Why?" Silas asked. The thought of something manipulating him, like a puppet yanked on strings, made him sick to his stomach.

"Power. It always comes to that, doesn't it? A true witch can find the kernel of envy, vanity, pride or lust in a person and pry until it's no longer a small thing but something that roars like the water at our feet. When that happens, the person belongs to the witch until they are corrupted to the point of madness. When the last of their humanity is drained, the witch buries them in rushing water so their soulless body won't come back and track them down. Then the witch finds a new surrogate. The worst witches go through people like Larkspur through a calfskin of wine. Now come, we must alert your uncle and prepare for the long night ahead."

Jonquil was turning a rabbit on the spit and arguing with Larkspur when they climbed into view. The hood of his cloak was thrown back and greasy hair flowed around his neck. The scar that ran from his lip to ear pulsated with an eerie glow in the firelight. Ever since returning from the fight with Eldritch, his uncle was leaner and frailer. There was a haunted look about his eyes, and the flesh had tightened around his cheekbones. His strength was erratic, and he used a walking stick to get around.

Larkspur, a tremendous glutton of a man, sprawled on the other side of the fire with a fallen log for a pillow. The rider must have weighed twenty stones and his jerkin and breeches creaked and groaned with the pressure of his flesh. His moon face was covered in patchy ginger hair and his owl-like eyes were at half-mast as he chugged the remnants of a bottle of wine and tossed it into the woods.

"If you ask me, we should have come here with all the power of the dusk riders," Larkspur said.

"Luckily for you, no one asked," Jonquil bandied.

"On occasion, someone likes to proffer their opinion," the giant said.

"And on occasion, someone wishes you would shut up," Jonquil replied testily. He noted the trouble on Silas and Trainer's faces as they came close to the fire.

"What is it?" he demanded.

"The type of bad news that always seems to follow us," Trainer said. By the time he finished telling Jonquil about the body in the river, Jonquil was on his feet, leaning on the gnarled stick he'd carved from a strangler fig in the Gardens.

"Aye, we need to collect as much wood as we can. Witches can't abide fire. If we keep it stoked, that'll keep us safe 'til first light."

Silas scoured the woods near the river. There was no shortage of fallen limbs, but most were soggy and useless from constant exposure to the mist. He finally found a good supply that had collected beneath an overhang and carried them to the camp, an armload at a time. He heard his uncle and Dan Trainer gathering more branches. Larkspur prodded the fire with a stick, and the flames licked at the sides of the charring rabbit. Sweat beaded on the big man's forehead, and Silas saw his hand tremble as he stirred the collapsed logs. The gregarious giant caught him looking.

"Something on my face, boy?" Larkspur scowled, displaying a mouth of wine-stained teeth. "Or do you make a habit of staring at everyone you meet?"

"N — no," Silas stammered, caught off guard.

"Good. Then stop looking at me and get more wood before night settles."

Silas brought two more armloads back. Between the three of them, they managed to gather a mound of firewood more than big enough to last until morning. Jonquil finally carved the rabbit, and the silence was broken by only the occasional snort or smack as they ate.

"Witches," Trainer said when they finished. "Been a while since we dealt with one of those."

"Not long enough if you ask me," Larkspur said. The sweat was pouring down his face now. He wiped his forehead with his sleeve.

"Seems more and more things are breaking free from the Gardens. It's almost more than we can do to put them back," Trainer said, eyeing Jonquil across the flames.

"We always do though. That's our lot, to hold back the evil that lives here and keep it from escaping into the world," Jonquil said.

"You think there'd be more of us though, wouldn't you?" Trainer said. "What are there? Thirty of us against the countless demons that prowl the Gardens. Hardly seems fair, does it?"

"And yet we beat them back each time and will

continue to do so," Jonquil said.

As they talked, it grew darker until nothing was visible beyond the light around the fire. The temperature dropped and a chilly wind ruffled Silas's neck and crept up his arms. Treetops stirred with the night breeze in the darkness far above their heads. Patches of fog continued to roll in, obscuring their vision further.

A strange sound caused Jonquil to stiffen. Was it a branch creaking? A wild animal? A voice in the forest? He threw his cloak back to reveal the blunderbuss and sword at his hip. He cocked the rifle and raised one hand, making a "shhh" motion. Dan Trainer drew a rapier and peered into the gloom. Larkspur appeared to be the most rattled of the three. The giant muttered and rubbed his face as though trying to wake from a bad dream. The calfskin of wine he was drinking fell gurgling onto the earth. A new breeze blew through the camp, and on it came a whispering voice so faint that Silas strained to make out what it was saying. "*Take your dagger and plunge it into your uncle's neck,*" the malignant voice croaked. "*Walk away from the fire and come to me.*"

"Stoke the flames, lad," Jonquil said, as if he too could hear what the witch was saying. "Ignore her. The crone only has power over those who are prone to corruption."

Silas got to work rebuilding the fire. With each new log, it grew warmer and brighter, and soon the tickle in his ear was gone. Jonquil and Trainer kept their weapons out as if prepared for an attack. The color returned to Larkspur's face.

"She's a powerful one," Trainer said. The sour-faced rider scanned the woods for movement.

"Imagine if she and Eldritch joined forces. What would we do then?" Larkspur licked his lips.

"Whoever she is, she'll die like any other witch," Jonquil said.

With the flames crackling and a full stomach, Silas thought that they must all be mad. Less than five months ago this scene would have seemed like the ravings of a laudanum addict to him.

"Is it possible for a witch to have more than one surrogate at a time?" Silas asked during the quiet.

"Mayhap. A powerful witch can have several. All of 'em dancing to the devil's tune until there's nothing human left," Trainer said.

"And when they die, the witch buries them in rushing water so they won't come back to try and kill them?" Silas gestured toward the stream murmuring in the night.

"Or anyone else that gets in their way," Larkspur said. He picked up the wineskin and took a draught. "The undead aren't too particular about whose life they take."

Jonquil stroked his blunderbuss and stared into the dark. " 'Tis true though that they are drawn to their old masters like moths to flame."

Another hour passed. Silas got up once again to fuel the fire. Larkspur and Dan Trainer lay spread on the ground with their eyes closed, though neither slept. The slightest sound of a bird or branch snapping, and both were up, swords in hand. Jonquil and Silas sat near the fire and watched visions capering in the flames.

"Tomorrow we arrive in Priortage, largest of the mist villages," Jonquil said. "It's also home to your ma's people. Hopefully, we'll find some answers about what happened when I came north last."

"Ma's people?" His mother told him that she'd met his father at an orphanage, that they didn't have family.

"Aye, crafty Fyodor, your grandda' and Lucretia, your grandmum. You've got aunts, uncles and more cousins than the Gardens have will-o'-wisps."

"Why didn't she tell us any of this?" Silas said, bitterness welling inside of him. For the longest time, he and Lily thought they were alone in the world.

"Trying to protect you is all. They thought if they ran away that this place would cease to be, like a bad dream disappears in the light of morning. But Nightfall Gardens doesn't forget. It waits until you smell the fresh dawn and then it yanks it away from you. It kills your spirit, long before your heart stops beating."

"But how could she leave her family?" Silas asked. He'd give up his life to protect his family — and by following his sister to Nightfall Gardens, he might yet have to do so.

"The people of the mist have strange customs.

You'll learn that soon enough," Jonquil said. "If you pick a different path than the one chosen at birth, then they cut off all contact with you. You're dead in their eyes. All of us — I mean everybody loved Moira. She was the prettiest girl in the village. Half-blind old men would prattle on about the springtime of their youth when they caught sight of her in the market. When she fell in love with your dad, it didn't sit well with Fyodor at all. You see, he'd already promised her to another."

Before Silas could ask who, a wolf howled so close in the woods that his ears rang. Trainer scrambled to his feet with his sword drawn. Larkspur pulled his considerable bulk up a second later.

"Sounds like he's almost on us," Trainer said.

"Should be fine if we stay near the fire," Larkspur added. "He won't fight us alone."

"Aarrrrrooouuggghhh," another wolf called from the woods. Silas saw glowing red eyes flash in the fog. That howl was returned by a half dozen others.

"Mayhap the crone is calling them to do what she can't," Jonquil said. His gun was leveled into the ghostly shroud that surrounded them. His top lip was pulled back in a sneer. Whatever gentleness there had been before was gone. "Stay close and steel yourself for a fight."

The air chilled and Silas felt the itch of a voice trying to find its way into his head. *Take your dagger and kill him. Slice his throat open,* the witch croaked. Silas grabbed for an image to push her away. For some reason his mind settled on Cassandra, the gardener's daughter. She was smiling, the same as the last time he'd seen her, the gargoyle Osbold flapping about the green girl's shoulders. The crone's voice popped like a bubble and was gone.

"Form a circle," Jonquil commanded. Another wolf howled, this one closer than ever.

Silas backed up to them, his dagger drawn. Larkspur was muttering under his breath. "Keep out o' my head. Leave me be," he cried.

"Stand tall," Jonquil said, slapping him in the face. "She only has the power you give her."

At that moment, a wolf growled, low and clear, at the edge of the trees. Silas saw first one, two and then three wolves step into the firelight. They were dirty, ragged animals with bared fangs and hungry expressions.

"There's more over here," Trainer called.

Four more shapes stepped from the mist.

"And here too," Larkspur said. More wolves came from the trees on his side.

The growls came from all around them now. Silas felt Jonquil tense next to him. A hideous cackling came from one of the trees. Silas glanced up and saw a putrefied face so vile that he had to turn away before he was sick.

Everything happened at once. Jonquil's blunderbuss went off with an earth-shattering roar and a wolf was torn in half by its power; blood and guts sprayed in the air. Silas pressed against the dusk riders as the wolves attacked. He had barely readied himself before a wolf launched in the air, sinking its fangs into his wrist and jerking him to the ground. Silas swung wildly with his knife and felt it slide into the wolf's throat but still the animal continued dragging him toward the woods and the twisted figure of the crone waiting with outstretched arms.

2
GRAVE SIGNS UNDER THE MANOR

"Are you sure this is necessary?" Cassandra Hawthorne asked.

"What's the matter — *scared*?" Lily Blackwood replied, giving her best angelic smile.

The green girl gritted her teeth and stared into the opening in the basement floor. The heavy smell of earth and trapped air wafted out of the hole. A flagstone, pried loose, was shoved to the side. Lily held her candle over the pit, and the flame sputtered and died.

"Who said anything about being scared?" Cassandra said.

"I mean, if you want to stay behind, I'd understand. No one would judge you for being afraid," Lily said, trying to suppress a smile.

"Give me your bleeding taper," Cassandra growled, re-lighting Lily's candle, while being careful not to touch her friend. The groundskeeper's daughter became angry if anyone tried to make contact with her. It was an odd quirk, but no odder than anything else in Nightfall Gardens.

The sounds of the kitchen came from above: dishes clattering, pots bubbling and a murmur of voices as the servants prepared lunch. Lily still found this hard to believe. Five months ago, she had been playing to audiences at the Golden Bough in New Amsterdam. That was before she found out a curse had been laid on the females of her family. When the last female Blackwood died, the curse would be broken and the evils contained in the Gardens would escape into a world that had long ago relegated monsters to myths and fairy tales. Lily was the last of the line of females in her family. Her fate was intimately woven with this house. In one of the rooms, moving images in the wallpaper showed her the bloody story of humankind before Prometheus trapped those nightmares. It was a dark time for the human race. They were hunted nearly to extinction and served as slaves to the old gods. Lily's ancestor Pandora opened Prometheus's trap out of greed, and the horrors ensnared within started to escape. With the last of his power, Prometheus created Nightfall Gardens and bound the frightening terrors there, along with the Blackwood family. The box itself was hidden somewhere on the grounds, the worst of the old gods still trapped within. She and Cassandra were searching for that box, because they were certain it could break the curse and destroy this place once and for all.

"Well, are you planning to stand there all day, or are we going?" Cassandra sniped.

Lily set her candle on the ground and dangled her legs into the opening until her feet found the top rung of a ladder. "Watch your step," she said, climbing into the gloom.

"Don't worry about me," Cassandra said, following after her.

At the bottom, Lily held her candle out so the buttery light reflected off the walls of the passage. A banging came from far away as if some great machine was working overtime, deep within the house. Cassandra dropped next to her.

"Are you sure it's down here?" the green girl asked.

"I'm sure of nothing, but that's what Abby's diary said," Lily responded. Abigail was Lily's great aunt. She had vanished while searching for Pandora's Box. Sometimes, Lily saw her ghost in the house. Not long ago, Lily discovered her diary, which contained maps of the house as well as a record of her search to find the box.

They followed the passage until they found themselves facing a stone door inset with an iron ring. The green girl grabbed the ring and yanked her hand back just as quickly. "Ouch. It burned me," she said, wincing in pain and sucking on her fingers.

"Let me try," Lily said, touching the ring and feeling cool iron. *'It's the house,'* she thought. *'It knows that I'm a Blackwood.'*

Lily pulled the ring, and the massive door swung open as though it weighed no more than a feather plucked from a pillow. They entered a vast chamber that disappeared into shadows. Worn steps led to the sunken floor. The walls were ancient and dripping with lichen. Unlit torches were lined up at intervals along the walls. The room was filled by row after row of sarcophagi. The coffins were all shapes and sizes. The only thing they had in common was that each contained a long, square opening cut into the top. Names were etched onto the lids in a language Lily couldn't decipher.

"Latin," Cassandra told her. "My father taught me."

"What's this say?" Lily ran her hand across the first coffin that she came to. The stone lid looked as though it weighed several hundred pounds. Carved on its surface was the name Corrie Blackwood as well as the phrase "Accepit animo malo hortis."

Cassandra chewed her lips and said, "The evil of the Gardens took her heart."

Lily's candle flicked as a breeze blew through the crypt. Invisible fingers marched down her spine and her skin tingled with goosebumps. A fissure, several inches long and wide, was cut into the stone. Lily held the candle to the opening. She jerked away in surprise when she saw closed eyes and desiccated flesh on the other side. When nothing happened, she moved the candle closer. Every bit of moisture had been sucked from the corpse's gray skin and gaping sockets.

Lily stepped away, glad not to look at the body anymore. Cassandra stopped at another sarcophagus. This one looked much older. The tomb was crumbling and pieces of it had fallen to the floor. The name Avery Blackwood was followed by the expression: Illa aperuit cor ad tenebras."

"She opened her heart to darkness," Cassandra said. The anger was gone from her voice and was replaced with dread.

By candlelight, they saw the oddly preserved remains of an arm where the sepulcher was broken. The corpse's hand was balled into a fist. The skin was torn from the knuckles and dull bone shone from splintered remains.

As they ventured further into the crypt, the coffins grew more ancient. Their candles cast halos on the wall before being enveloped by darkness. Lily stopped at another tomb. The lid had been pushed to the floor. Cassandra read from a fragment. "Desdemona Blackwood: Betrayer of all that was good." The green girl looked at Lily. "What does it mean?"

Lily looked into the vault and saw Desdemona's remains. The elements had whittled her to little more than bone and scraps of skin. The dress she wore had disintegrated, and parts of a rib cage and pelvic bone poked through the remaining fabric.

Without a word, Lily headed to the back of the room, where the ceiling sloped and the floor was uneven. This was the oldest part of the burial chamber. The tomb located there was little more than four pieces of stone crudely stacked together.

"Are you going to tell me what's going on?" Cassandra asked miffed.

"Later," Lily said distractedly. "I need you to read this."

Cassandra held her candle over the tomb and said, "Pandora Blackwood —" The green girl mouthed the rest of the words and turned to Lily, one eyebrow arched, "— Mother of Nightfall Gardens."

"So it's true," Lily said softly.

"What is?" Cassandra asked.

"Abigail's diary," Lily said. "She found this place. They haven't buried any Blackwoods down here in ages."

Cassandra looked nervously up and down the vast chamber. "Did you hear that?"

"What?" Lily asked, feeling the surface of the tomb.

"Nothing," Cassandra said, puzzled. "I thought I heard a scraping sound."

"Well you didn't. Now help me with this." Lily got on one side of the coffin and began to shove.

"You're opening Pandora's tomb?"

"Trying to. Now, help me push."

At first, the lid didn't want to budge. Who knew how many thousands of years it had sat there undisturbed? But after a couple of minutes, there was a terrible grinding noise and the top gave way and fell crashing to the floor. The deafening sound reverberated throughout the crypt.

"I hope this was worth it," Cassandra said as Lily leaned over the tomb. "I don't make a habit of grave robbing."

Lily hissed between her teeth.

"What is it?" Cassandra asked, moving to the other side of the coffin.

"Nothing," Lily said sounding disappointed. She held the candle so Cassandra could see that it was empty. "The body's gone. Someone must have moved it a long time ago."

"But why?" Cassandra asked.

"Who knows? Maybe they were looking for it the same as Abigail was …and we are now. Blast it! That was our last lead."

"Blast it? You've been hanging around Skuld too much," Cassandra said. She searched the tomb and found nothing but the letters XXIII etched into one of the walls.

"Twenty three? Do you have any idea what that means?"

"No," Lily said. She felt the amethyst necklace her grandmother Deiva gave her before she died. It had supposedly belonged to Pandora and been passed down through the generations. The stone might even have saved her from one of the Smiling

Ladies when the emissaries from the Gardens came to pay their respects after Deiva died. Esmeret, one of the Smiling Ladies, was preparing to tear Lily's throat open when she accidentally grazed the stone and went howling back into the Shadow Garden. The stone glowed a smoky purple in the light from the candles. Something made a sound at the other end of the room.

"Now don't tell me that you didn't hear that," Cassandra said.

"No, I heard it," Lily said, feeling the hairs rise on her arm.

The scraping sound came again, this time from different places — a sound like something scratching at a window.

"We should probably …" Cassandra started.

"…Get out of here," Lily finished.

The two made their way down the rows. The scraping sound seemed to come from all around them now. It was only as they neared Desdemona's tomb that Lily finally identified what it was. The noise was the sound of bone scratching against stone.

"Run!" Lily shouted, fear flooding her body.

The girls took off down the aisle, Lily cursing the dress she wore. The scratching grew louder. Somewhere in the room, a lid scraped open. To the side, she glimpsed Desdemona's tomb and gasped when she saw the empty space where a body had been.

"On the wall," Cassandra shouted, pointing

toward the ceiling. Desdemona was scuttling crab-like along its surface. The remnants of her hair hung limp around the pits of her eyes. At some point in the past her bottom jaw had fallen off.

A ragged moaning came from all around as though someone were trying to speak for the first time in hundreds of years. Lily saw another skeletal figure thrashing free of its tomb. It came to her then what the fissures on the sepulchers were for. They weren't so people could look from outside in; they were so that the women buried inside could see out.

No sooner had she thought this than something leapt from the gloom and landed on Cassandra. Lily caught a glimpse of a monstrosity in a tattered dress struggling with the green girl just as bony fingers yanked her arm so hard that she lost her balance and toppled into a freshly opened tomb. There was a nightmarish moment where Lily didn't realize where she was and then she felt the withered remains of a body beneath her. In the pitch black, the body stirred. Somewhere Cassandra was calling for help. The corpse's mouth pressed against Lily's ears trying to speak. "…*Adow …arden … adow …arden …adow …arden …*," it said, repeating the words as though they were a psalm.

"Shut — up!" Lily said, throwing herself backward. The hands loosened on her throat. Lily spun and swung the heel of her hand forward, driving it through the bottom of the skull and tearing the head loose from the body.

She jumped out of the coffin as the headless body snatched for her. More coffins opened as slumbering nightmares awakened from the centuries. The creature that had pushed her into the tomb stumbled stutter-step toward her. The corpse was moving its mouth but the only sound it made was a dry clicking.

When the dead body charged her, Lily swiped its ankles with such force that one of the legs broke off at the knee. Cassandra screamed again, and Lily turned to see the green girl being dragged away by a dozen of the corpses.

She needed something to use as a weapon. The dagger Jonquil had given her was useless against what she faced. There was nothing but the rubble of the crypts and the undead which were increasing with every moment that she wasted. Lily's eyes lit on a snapped leg bone and she tittered hysterically. She scooped up the leg by the ankle and lofted it on her shoulder as she made her way toward her friend.

Lily swung as the first of her ancestors shuffled from the dark at her. With the second blow she tore its head from its shoulders and with a kick sent it flying in to the dark.

Ahead, the corpses pinned Cassandra to the floor and were crawling over her like a swarm of locusts. One of the monstrosities crouched with a fist-sized rock in its hand.

"No!" Lily shouted. The corpse pulled its arm

back to drive the rock into Cassandra's skull. Lily charged into them, swinging the remains of the leg, shattering bones and loosening heads from bodies. Cassandra tore the arm from the corpse that was about to brain her with the rock. Hands and teeth that clawed and snapped besieged Lily. She smelled the dry stench of their flesh and stared into a dozen dead faces moving by some magic she couldn't understand.

"Ugly lot, you Blackwoods," Cassandra said, appearing next to her. "I think I've seen enough of your family for one day. Want to get out of here?"

"Been ready for a while now," Lily said, relieved that her friend was okay.

"Let's go then," Cassandra said.

Lily was never quite certain how they got out of the chamber alive. All she remembered was the corpses of her ancestors shambling after her, always one step away from overwhelming the two of them. By the time they reached the entrance, Lily's arms were so tired that she could barely lift them.

"Shut the door," Cassandra yelled as a fresh surge of undead streamed toward them.

Lily grabbed the iron ring and the door swung closed. They collapsed, exhausted. Furious fists pounded on the other side of the wall.

"Remind me never to come to your family reunion," Cassandra kidded.

"Do you think they can get out?" Lily asked, dragging herself to her feet.

"I think if they could, they would have done it by now. There's magic here, I smell it," Cassandra said.

They made their way back down the tunnel. The sound of the pounding grew fainter until they couldn't hear it at all.

"What I want to know is how your ancestors came back to life? Why are there openings on their tombs?" Cassandra asked.

"I —," Lily started and took a deep breath. "Part of it's in Abigail's diary," she said.

"What! You knew those undead were down there?"

"It's not like that," Lily said.

"Well, what's it like then?"

Lily opened her mouth to speak when a scuttling sound came from the dark.

The girls froze. Lily lifted the nub of the candle. Desdemona was hanging like a spider from the ceiling. What remained of her hair hung in her face. Her jawless mouth made her look even more like an arachnid. The ancient Blackwood watched them silently and then fled down one of the myriad tunnels that led to the underbelly of the house.

"She must have crawled out while the door was open," Cassandra said, after she was gone. "What do we do?"

"Let her be for now," Lily said. "Our candle will burn down soon. Who knows what else is lurking here."

They climbed up the ladder into the basement.

No sooner had their feet touched the floor than a squelching hand grabbed Lily by the ear and twisted until she cried out in shock.

"And what kind of naughties have you been up to?" Polly asked. The housemaid's shiny skin glistened in the light cast from the candle. Her eyes were milky orbs that reflected flame and were fathomless to read. Her bald head jiggled with movement and a trail of ooze ran down her forehead like sweat. "Warned you about poking around in places you don't belong, didn't I, Miss?"

Lily's shoulders loosened. Polly was one of the caretakers of the house. Like all the servants of the house, Polly was a reformed spirit that came from one of the Gardens.

"With Mrs. Deiva gone, you can't just run off everywhere that you like. You're the last female Blackwood, Miss, and I don't dare think what would happen if you was to die."

"I'm okay, Polly. We were just poking around in the tunnels to see where they lead," Lily lied.

"Is that it, is it? Some of those tunnels lead places you don't want to go. Believe me on that, Miss. They go dark places indeed. Now let's go, Master Skuld is waiting on you for your lessons."

Lily smacked herself in the forehead. She'd forgotten he was coming early today. Things were growing more unpredictable in the Gardens, according to the dusk rider. The only time he could spare to train her was in the afternoon when the things that lived in the Gardens were at their weakest.

The three made their way to the main entrance, where Lily said goodbye to Cassandra.

"I promise I'll tell you everything when I see you next," Lily whispered as they parted. The green girl gave her a wary glance as she left. Lily wished she could tell her friend what little she knew but there was no time.

Lily sighed as she entered her training room. Skuld was waiting to practice, wooden sword in hand. The dusk rider smacked her a good half dozen times during the practice and she tried not to cry out in pain as he heaped bruise on top of bruise. Moves that she normally blocked with little problem were beyond her.

"Your mind's not here, lass," the one-armed man said. "A warrior must always concentrate on the battle he's about to face or he will die."

'My mind is somewhere else,' Lily thought. It was on what she had just seen in the ancestral Blackwood tomb and on the curse that haunted her family.

3

THE BLOODY ROAD TO PRIORTAGE

Fiery pain shot through Silas's arm as the snarling wolf dragged him toward the witch. The crone's thoughts seeped into his head, telling him to stop fighting, that it would all be over in a moment. *"You wouldn't fault an old woman for taking your hot blood on a cold night, would you? Close your eyes and this world of torment will be but a memory."* Her fetid spirit was an all-powerful presence that threatened to envelop him. The further he was pulled from the light, the stronger she became.

'No,' he thought. *'I have to remember what Jonquil said, she only has the power I give her.'*

In seconds he would be in the woods where the witch capered and rubbed her hands with glee. Silas saw her through patches of mist. Her face was a mask of putrescence, and he had never sensed such a raging torrent of evil as that which flowed from her.

Silas recoiled from her presence, scrambling backward. The wolf bit down harder until he cried in agony. His uncle's blunderbuss fired in the background. Larkspur yelled for help in the fog. The wolf that pulled him was a rangy beast with a gray-peppered coat and the mad look of an animal that hadn't eaten in a long time. It was not nearly as big as the one that chased him through the woods not long after he'd come to Nightfall Gardens. Silas's dagger stuck out from the wolf's neck.

He lunged, snatching at the knife. For one horrendous moment the bloodied dagger slipped through his palm and then he caught the handle, twisting it free of the wolf's neck. The animal's jaw slackened and Silas plunged again, driving the blade through the wolf's throat and into its skull. The beast fell dead on the ground. Silas was only feet from the edge of the firelight, and the witch prowled the light as though it were a fence she couldn't pass.

"Anything, I'll give you anything you want," the crone's voice tempted. *"I can save your sister. I can make you the most powerful man in the world."*

He ignored her, crawling toward the fire where the battle was grinding to a halt. All but two of the wolves had been dispensed with, and his uncle and Trainer now made short work of those. When the last wolf was killed, a terrible soul-quaking shriek came from the woods. Silas looked back to see the witch leap into a tree and swing off into the night.

31

"Only the worst of them can do such a thing," Jonquil said. "A witch that moves like her can also fly short distances. That means she has done great evil."

His uncle looked pale and ashen; the fight had robbed much of his strength. He leaned on his walking stick and trembled with exhaustion. *'He must rest or he'll soon be back in a bed,'* Silas thought.

"The wineskin, lad — fetch me the wineskin," Larkspur said. The great giant was soaked in blood. He held one hand up to show where two fingers had been snapped off by a wolf. "The hairy bitch got a bite out of me. Surely, the best meal she's had in many a red moon." He laughed.

Silas found the wineskin and tossed it to Larkspur, who snagged it with his good hand. He uncapped it with his mouth and drained the skin with one long pull. "Ahhh, Skuld will have merry with me after all the grief I've given him for his lost arm," he said.

Trainer dragged the wolves to the edge of the fire as Jonquil applied salve and bandages to his nephew and Larkspur. A horse cried out in pain and terror in the dark.

"The witch!" Jonquil said cursing. "She's found the horses." Another horse whinnied in fear, followed shortly by two others.

"I'll take care of it," Trainer said, drawing his sword.

"No," Jonquil commanded. "None of us alone is powerful enough to fight her. She'll pick off any that leave the safety of the light. We'll stay here until dawn and walk the rest of the way to Priortage. We'll get some villagers to help us."

The dusk riders stoked the fire anew and huddled as closely as they could, though sleep came to none of them. Silas closed his eyes and drifted near slumber, never able to find it. He thought of his father and mother, trapped on the other side of the wall, outside of Nightfall Gardens. He could only imagine how worried they must be. They fled this place to raise their children in a world where horror didn't lurk around every corner. It hadn't been easy. His family never stayed in one town for long. The Amazing Blackwoods played vaudeville halls and third-rate theaters, living hand to mouth. Despite their struggles, they had been happy, a happiness taken away the day he found out about Nightfall Gardens.

A great log spit and crackled as it was consumed by hungry flames. Larkspur breathed heavily near him. Silas opened his eyes only once during that long night, to find Jonquil keeping watch over the three of them. His blunderbuss lay across his knees and he scanned the darkness for movement.

Dawn came an eternity later. Trainer, Silas and Larkspur packed their bags for the day's journey. The sky was giving up dark for the dismal gray of day's approach.

"A man my age should be asleep on a featherbed with a wench to bring him breakfast,"

Larkspur said, cracking his neck. His injured hand was wrapped in a bandage and he scratched it with his sword handle.

"You should have chosen another path then," Jonquil said. His face was pale and he seemed to have aged a decade overnight.

"I should have ignored the dreams that called me here," Larkspur said. "I'd be a robber baron in New Amsterdam if I had."

"Or a gulley man cleaning out troughs in slaughterhouses," Trainer said sharply.

"What do you know of my past, Trainer? When was the last time you smiled? It kills a man early to be as miserable as you are."

"I'd almost rather face the witch than hear the two of you prattle," Jonquil said. "Now put out the fire because we soon set off for Priortage."

Not long after, they found the remains of the horses tied where they had left them. Silas had to look away out of fear he would faint. He caught a glimpse of the dappled horse that Skuld lent him. It lay on its side, the horse's glassy eyes staring at the sky and a large gash on its neck where the witch had torn its throat open and drunk its blood.

"I swear she'll pay for this," Larkspur said as he bent over his horse.

Jonquil seemed hardest hit. His white mare had been with him many years, and the witch had spent the most time desecrating his horse. Parts of it were strewn to the riverbank.

"Aye," Jonquil said. "I'll wring her neck for this

34

if I get my hands on her."

The mist was so thick that it was impossible to see as they forded the creek. The fog weighed heavily upon them, and soon their damp clothes pressed against their flesh. Larkspur's usual jovial banter was gone. They made their way through the woods until they came to the most well-worn trail they had seen since leaving Nightfall Gardens.

"The road to Priortage," Larkspur said. "We'll quaff fresh pints of ale and sup on roasted goose tonight, lads!"

If the giant had expected to lighten their mood, he was wrong. Soon, rain began falling, chilling them to the bone and making the road a slippery skim of mud. The fog grew so thick that they may as well have been walking blind.

"It's the witch's doing," Jonquil said. "She's trying to keep us from reaching town before night."

Late that afternoon, they reached the outskirts of the village. They were marching through mud, rain pelting their heads, as Larkspur told Silas how many roasted pigs he was going to eat when a house appeared out of the mist. The cottage was made entirely of vines and seemed an extension of the woods rather than separate from it.

"The mist people believe that if a person's soul is out of tune with nature, it is damned to wander the earth forever," Jonquil said.

"While they huddle in huts and commune with the trees, the world progresses," Larkspur said mockingly. "I hear great steamships plow the ocean and that there is even a new device that can make photographs move."

Jonquil made his way up to the porch of the house and pushed the door open with his walking stick. "Someone left the door unlatched," he said. "Hello, is anybody home?"

As Silas watched, Jonquil hobbled into the cottage. The rain beat down around them, and then his uncle called, "Trainer, come here."

Dan Trainer disappeared into the house a moment later.

"I don't like the look of this, lad," Larkspur said. He was rubbing his sore hand and looking in all directions about them. "There's something rank in the air, I can feel it in my bones."

Jonquil and Trainer left the house and, without a word, set off in the direction of the village. Silas hurried to catch up with his uncle.

"What is it?" he asked.

"No one has called that place home in a while. There was blood about the floor and walls. Someone had drawn the mark of Eldritch over the fireplace."

"Mark of Eldritch?"

"All the old gods have their symbols. It's how worshipers recognize each other." Jonquil stopped and drew a symbol of a figure with antlers in the mud. "That's his. I tell you it makes me nervous. I thought my memory would start to come back the closer we came to the village, but it's still as blank as this mist. Well, hopefully Aiden Cogden can fill in some of those holes."

"Who's he?" Silas asked.

"Aiden Cogden," Trainer said, spitting on the ground. "Why are you talking about that daft loon?"

"Sour-faced Trainer," Larkspur said from behind. "Why do you despise Cogden so much?"

"He's a man without convictions, not unlike another glutton that I know," Trainer said, taking off at a fast clip ahead of the group.

"Watch it, you dour jacksnipe. I may be two fingers down, but I still have more than enough in my good sword hand to take care of a crab apple like you," Larkspur threatened.

"So who is he?" Silas asked his uncle.

"Cogden used to be a dusk rider, but abandoned it to live with the mist people. He's a musician, an artist and a man who likes to make merry," Jonquil said.

"He takes after my own heart," Larkspur said. "I prefer a man with a smile to the unhappy storm that rides Trainer's face. There's something wrong with a person who finds no joy in life."

"Even though he left the dusk riders, he still acts as our eyes and ears in the village," Jonquil said.

"That's when he's not chasing after a woman or playing songs at the tavern," Larkspur said.

The milky fog plumed as they entered Priortage. Silas was disappointed in his first glimpse of the town where his mother was raised. A wide muddy track made up the main road of the village. Silas took a few steps and sank to his ankles. The businesses and houses along the street were all built out of the same twisting vines as the house they'd passed earlier. Some homes were larger than others, and some were rounded with natural openings that were blocked by curtains. A hitching post was outside of one of the largest buildings. A few horses and a scraggly mule were tied up in front. As they passed, Silas heard shouting and laughter, alien sounds in the bleak landscape in which they walked.

"The Barn Swallow," Larkspur said. "I'll be returning there for a pint or ten later on tonight."

Two girls came along the sidewalk holding a parasol over their heads to keep the rain from falling on them. They had curly red hair and green eyes and wore white dresses. Silas almost did a double take; one of them looked so much like his own mother and Lily.

Larkspur bowed low as they passed. The girls examined the four strangers and leaned in whispering to each other. One of them seemed keenly interested in Silas, and her eyes followed him until they passed. He felt his face flush.

"You could go to the netherworld and back and never find women as beautiful as those that live here. That's why I don't blame Cogden. Some men have a weakness for the bottle, some have a weakness for the pipe, some have a weakness for their own mad dreams, and some have a weakness for women," Larkspur said.

At the end of the street, they came to a house larger than the others. It was a rabbit's warren of vines and trees that towered three stories above the ground and didn't end so much as melded into the woods.

"Your grandfather Fyodor lives here," Jonquil said. "As well as your gran Lucretia and your aunts and uncles. They say he's a holy man, but the only thing I've ever known him to be holy about is his pursuit of accumulating more wealth."

Silas watched the house until they were out of sight. It was exciting to discover he had another family here, one that he didn't know existed. At the same time, if Jonquil was to be believed, his mother had fled the village and had been disowned by them.

Aiden Cogden lived in the bottoms outside of town, in a ravine filled with gigantic old firs that housed one-room cocoons of vines and foliage for the poorest villagers. Jonquil stopped under one of the largest trees and pulled on a rope. A bell rang up above, and a moment later a dowdy red-haired woman stuck her head out from one of the windows. Her top was undone and she seemed drunk on wine or something stronger.

"What do ya want?" she asked suspiciously.

"Information and a room for the night," Jonquil said.

"Dusk riders," she said, as though disgusted. "Come from Nightfall Gardens to forget your woes. You can do that, but it'll cost ya. What kind of information do ya seek?"

"Just the whereabouts of a dear friend, Aiden Cogden. Is he home?"

"Layabout is more like it," she said. "A sassier man, I've never met in my life. He has a voice like honey and works magic with words, but ask him to clean his pigsty of a room, and he'll disappear quicker than the red moon in the fog. Nay, he left a while ago to play at a wedding. A wise person would find a seat at The Barn Swallow, for he'll be there to wet his thirst as soon as he's finished. Now, about those rooms …"

A rope ladder dropped down, and the four of them climbed up the tree to where the innkeeper waited to show them their lodgings.

"They're nothing fancy, but the rooms are comfortable, and I promise ya a good night's sleep," she said.

Each room had a hammock and window that opened to the outside. Silas dropped his pack and switched into dry clothes. He pulled his plain black cloak on and went out to where the dusk riders and innkeeper waited. The three wore their wolf cloaks that signaled they were dusk riders. Larkspur ran a comb through his thick hair.

"Don't worry," Larkspur said, slapping the boy on his shoulder. "You'll have your own cloak soon enough. Your uncle skinned that whelp you killed last eve. When we return and he cures it, you'll be like us in everything but name."

Silas looked as his uncle. "Is that true?"

Jonquil looked away sheepishly. "Aye, lad, you've earned it. You still have many years before you become one of us, but you've killed your first wolf, and that's the first step in joining our ranks."

The innkeeper tut-tutted. "Ya dusk riders are full of yourselves. Ya should learn how to enjoy the finer things in life, rather than swaggering around bragging about who has killed the biggest beastie. Ya don't hear that talk from Cogden. It's all love with him."

"And it's all love with me as well," Larkspur said winking at her.

"I bet it is at that," she said with a laugh. The innkeeper walked them to the landing. "I'll leave the ladder tied to the rope so it'll fall when ya come back. I'll be long in slumber. I don't want to be wakened by your drunken revelry."

Jonquil bristled at that but said nothing. "I have one more question," he said. "Have you heard anything about a witch in the woods?"

A troubled look crossed the woman's face and was gone so quickly that Silas didn't know if he had imagined it or not. "'A witch,' he says," the innkeeper said, chuckling. "No, the village is fine, it's better than ever. We people of the mist have our own belief in the divinity of nature and of one person's connectedness to another. We have no belief in those things that ya talk of and no worship for the likes of Eldritch or any of the old gods. Ya should enjoy your fill of drink and talk and of the women here. Put your crude superstitions away."

Jonquil nodded at her, and the four of them climbed down the ladder to the ground. His uncle led the way leaning on his staff for support.

"Is something wrong?" Silas asked his uncle as they approached the village.

As Jonquil turned to reply, the mist obscured his face and then cleared away. "I never mentioned Eldritch to her," he said.

4
LILY TOURS THE GARDENS

"Absolutely not! I forbid it," Polly said. The housekeeper would have stomped her feet if she had any, but instead she oozed in front of Lily, trying to block her from going out the door.

"Polly, I understand your concern, but I'll be with Skuld. He'll keep me safe," Lily said. The girl was dressed in a loose white shirt with riding pants and knee-high boots with a sword strapped to her side. She stepped to the side of the housemaid to go around her. "Besides, as mistress of Nightfall Gardens, don't you think I should see them with my own eyes?"

"But your gran Deiva never left the house," Polly countered.

"I'm not my grandmother," Lily said. "I'm tired of not knowing what I'm up against."

"Didn't you get a taste of that when one of the

garden's emissaries almost killed you?" Polly said. Her white face formed a pout; bubble skin furrowed at the temples.

"There are mysteries piled on mysteries here," Lily said, her temper rising. "How can I protect myself against what I don't understand?"

The housemaid opened her gelatinous maw to speak when an ancient rasp came from the dining room.

"You can't," Ozy said, a cloud of dust pluming from his mouth. The butler was a dried husk in a tuxedo. Bandages hung from his shirtsleeves and collar. His skin was yellowed parchment and his forehead was covered in egg-sized liver spots. Like all of the servants in the house, the butler was a reformed evil from the Gardens. He used to be a mummy whose job was to protect the pharaoh's tomb from looters, but then he caught a teenager who was stealing to feed his little brother and sister. After that, he no longer had an appetite for his duty. One day he ended up outside of the Gardens and was taken in by the Blackwood family.

"What would you have her do, then? Go to her doom?" Polly asked.

"Need I remind you of Miss Abigail or Deiva's mother Ramona?" Ozy said. There was a regal tone to his voice. "They both used to ride the trails."

Polly grumbled and pointed one dripping finger at Ozy. "Aye, and neither was the last female Blackwood either."

Lily took a deep breath to calm herself. In the past, anger and vanity often controlled her emotions. She needed a clear head if she was going to face whatever waited outside.

"I appreciate you thinking of my safety, Polly. But I'm going out, and neither you nor anyone else in this house can stop me. I'm mistress of Nightfall Gardens. Whatever rules my grandmother made are just that, rules. I will always listen to your wise guidance, but I have to make the best decisions to protect the house and Gardens."

Polly swallowed and shook her head. "As you wish," she said. "They tell you that they grow up. They just never tell you how quickly. I only ask that you do whatever Skuld says and come back before dark."

Lily nodded her consent and went out the front door, entering the dismal gray light for the first time since she and Cassandra had visited Raga the witch. Skuld and Arfast were waiting on horseback for her. The one-armed man's cloak was thrown back. The same hard expression chiseled his features as usual. Arfast was not much older than her. A smile played about his lips as he saw her come from the house. He was leading a white horse with ashy spots on its back.

"For you," he said with a mock bow.

"Thank you," she said, taking the reins and pulling herself onto the animal.

"You don't have to do this, if you don't want to," Skuld said. "It's been so long since a

Blackwood woman rode the trails, I don't fair know what to expect."

"Then we'll find out together," she said as they moved down the hill.

"What news of my brother and uncle?" she asked, pulling up next to Skuld.

"Still no word from the mist lands. I have a bad feeling," he said.

"Are you sure that isn't Ezekiel's stew we ate last night?" Arfast joked.

"Laugh while you can. I just hope you don't die with that laugh on your lips. This is serious business. There aren't enough dusk riders to protect the Gardens. With each passing day my men grow busier chasing down the creatures that are escaping. Mr. Hawthorne is working overtime to keep the plants around the house stocked to repel intruders, and every day their magical protection is worn away and he has to start again."

They approached the Labyrinth with its 20-foot-tall walls that kept anyone from looking in or out. It was the most secretive of the Gardens, where the old gods dwelled as well as beings from the myths that Lily read as a little girl. They rode single file along the outside of the Garden. On the other side, there was nothing but mist that drifted into the woods. They came to the end of the Labyrinth and followed its wall around to the backside. When they had ridden a few minutes more, Arfast held his hand up to stop them.

"What is it?" Skuld barked, looking for danger.

"Something I'd like to show the girl," Arfast said.

"Be fast about it then," Skuld said. "It's not wise to stop in the Gardens with her."

Arfast dismounted. "My lady," he said, putting his hand out. "Would you care to peek into the Labyrinth?"

"I would," Lily said. She felt her heart pounding rapidly in her chest as Arfast took her hand and helped her to the ground.

"The Labyrinth is a puzzle even to the dusk riders," he said. Arfast stood a head taller than her. "No rider that's ever gone in has ever come out; such is the puzzle of the maze that lies within. The walls are so thick that it's impossible to see inside, save a few precious places. This is one of them."

Arfast showed her an opening in the wall that was slightly wider than a fist. Lily sucked in her breath at what lay on the other side. Through a tangle of thorns, she saw a temple that looked older than time itself. The temple soared so high, it should have been visible for many miles around, yet she wouldn't have known it existed if the evidence wasn't in front of her. Marble colonnades, each as big as Nightfall manor, buttressed the building. A thousand steps ran toward the entrance of the temple. Gigantic urns burned with fire at the main doors. Crumbling statues of the old gods lined the temple. Each statue was a good ten stories tall. One of the statues was of a pregnant woman carrying a bag full of stars. Another showed a thin whip of a monster with tree bark for skin and antlers coming from its forehead. There was a statue of a horse creature and a Cyclops, others of gods that were almost too beautiful to behold and one of a monster that resembled a jellyfish from the deepest sea. There were water spirits and wizened old men in clouds and women with snakes in their hair. There were eight-armed gods and fat gods and gods who carried the weight of the world on their backs. For every idea ever thought, there was a god, and each of them was represented in the parade of statues that stretched to infinity.

"It's not possible," she said.

"Anything is possible within the Gardens," Arfast said.

"What is this place?" she asked.

"The hall of the old gods," Arfast said. "The ones humans worshiped when humanity was in its infancy and still had need of such things. Prometheus captured them in trickery to this place. It's said that when they walked, humankind trembled. The old gods were fickle with their love and demanded a high price for their benevolence. They asked hungry people to burn their crops and parents to sacrifice their first-born children, all without a blink of their eternal eyes. While some of them were good, many were beyond good and evil. They existed only to be worshiped and revered."

Arfast gestured at the statue of the woodland creature with antlers on its head. "That's Eldritch, the one your uncle and brother seek. He's no more a god than you or I. What he is, is power beyond comprehension. The fragments written about him claim that he has been here since the world was formed. When the Earth was young he lived deep in the forest, where the mountain folk worshipped him and brought him human sacrifices. The poison from his antlers can kill on contact, but distilled into water or alcohol it creates a drink of euphoric rapture that causes hallucinations and binds the worshipers through their addiction to him."

Lily shuddered at the thought of her brother, out there somewhere in the mist, tracking such a being. "How did he get free of the Labyrinth?"

"None know for certain," Arfast said. "Jonquil and the dusk riders chased him so far north that they couldn't see beyond their hands. Eldritch killed several villagers along the way."

"So they left him to roam free?" Lily said incredulously. As she watched, something stirred in the shadows of the temple.

"You make it sound as if the riders got bored," Arfast said. "They followed him further than any humans have ever traveled and returned. The ground disappeared in places from under their horses' hooves. It's the place of undoing, the borderland between our world and what lies beyond. It's said great white things with red eyes live there and eat anything that strays too far. To go further would have been certain death."

Movement on the portico caught her attention again and she saw a figure walking down the steps, but its head was bent low and she couldn't make out its face. Wings suddenly fanned out from behind his robes, more colorful than any peacock that had ever lived. The color of the old god's wings ran the gamut from supple reds to piercing blues and every shade in between. At that moment, the creature raised its head and Lily saw a beak and avian eyes. The old god opened its mouth and let out one of the most mournful sounds she'd ever heard. *'He's come to see if he has any worshippers,'* Lily thought. The bird god waited for a response. When nothing came, his wings folded back under him and he walked with his head down back into the temple.

"Enough," Skuld said. "It's not good to tarry here, especially with the precious cargo that we have."

The three continued alongside the Labyrinth wall and then followed a path to the bunkhouse so Lily could see where the dusk riders lived. A hard-looking man was packing a horse as they approached.

"What news?" Skuld said pulling to a halt.

"Heard Farragut caught a nestler up by the White Garden," the man said. "Nasty little buggers."

Skuld nodded and they continued on their journey. The mist was thin on this day and Lily could see all the way past the rambling gardens back to the house. As she watched, a turret grew out of the roof. Everyday, the house added and subtracted features like a person taking a deep breath. Ahead on the path, Lily saw a dusk rider bent over something pinned by ropes. He was holding a whip in his hand. With a snap, the dusk rider drew his arm back and cracked the whip against the creature, causing it to cry out in a buzz of pain.

"Blast it! What's that hothead doing?" Skuld said, kicking his horse forward.

When they were closer, Lily was able to make out what was tied to the ground. It was no larger than a small child and was covered in coarse black fur and ichor. Instead of arms and legs, it had hundreds of cilia that writhed underneath it, like the legs of a millipede, and its eyes were green multifaceted mirrors that reflected the world around them.

As they rode up, the whip came cracking down against the creatures back, and it emitted a howling buzz of pain in response.

Skuld slipped down off his horse and marched toward the rider. His face was livid. "By the gods, Farragut, you'd better tell me what you are doing," he said, gripping his sword handle.

"I was just having a little fun," Farragut said defensively. The dusk rider's cloak was raised and his face was smeared with dirt. A fresh trail of snot led from his nose to his upper lip. His eyes were small and mean.

"Fun is it? Perhaps you'd like me to lay that whip across your back and see how it feels," Skuld said.

As the two argued, Lily leaned over to Arfast. "What is that thing?" she asked.

"It's a nestler," Arfast said with disdain. "And from the looks of it, a baby."

"A nestler?"

"Old fairy-tale nightmares. They sneak up on people while they are asleep and lay their eggs inside their ears. It kills the victim and hatches a new brood that repeats the cycle. There's almost nothing so foul and loathsome."

While Skuld and the dusk rider yelled at each other, Lily rode up close enough to get a better look at the nestler. What a nightmarish existence, to cause nothing but misery, she thought. And here it was, just a child.

"What will happen to it?" she asked, her voice bringing the argument to a halt. Skuld and Farragut looked as though she'd sprouted a third eye.

"Can't allow a nestler to live even if it is a little one," Farragut said. "You got to kill him is what you got to do."

Lily turned toward Skuld. "Is that true?"

"Aye, my lady, a quick clean death. Dusk riders don't draw out suffering and torment for their own pleasure," Skuld said glaring at the whip that Farragut was holding.

"And where do nestlers live?" Lily asked, her horse cantering beneath her.

"In the Shadow Garden," Skuld replied.

"Fine. Then that's where we will take him," she said.

"We can't just let this thing go," Farragut said. "You never know what trouble they'll cause later."

"That's something I'll deal with," Lily said. "For now, this creature is a child, and it's scared and abused and it wants to go home."

"I don't take orders from no girl," the rider said, tossing the whip from hand to hand.

"I'm glad you said that, Farragut," Skuld said. He grinned at Lily. "With your approval of course."

Lily nodded her consent as Skuld stepped forward with his sword drawn. There was a savage grin on his face.

Farragut drew his whip back. "I'd been wondering how long before one of us took you down one arm."

"I can see I'm going to have to teach you manners," Skuld said, circling the dusk rider.

"Your tears will taste sweet on the end of my whip," Farragut said, striking with the weapon. It cracked forward and caught Skuld's blade, wrapping itself tight around the steel. Farragut yanked backward trying to pull it from the old rider's hand. Skuld moved then with astonishing speed. What he lacked in an arm, he made up for with his right foot. He kicked Farragut square in the chest and sent him stumbling backward toward the edge of the White Garden. Everything might have ended there, except Farragut tripped, losing his balance and tumbling over the line dividing the Garden from the paths. Before there was time to comprehend what was happening, two black shadows shot from the trees and snatched the rider, dragging him into the undergrowth until an echoing scream was all that could be heard.

"Blast it," Skuld said. "I should have never fought him. Least not here."

"What — what happened?" Lily asked.

"Shades," Arfast said. "They wait for anything that strays into the White Garden."

"And all for a nestler," Skuld said in disgust.

Arfast roped the creature to his horse so they could take it to the Shadow Garden. Lily couldn't believe what had just taken place. She was only trying to do the right thing. At that moment, a voice came from the White Garden.

"Lily, over here," Francois Villon was standing where the White Garden and the path intersected. He had an arm around Farragut who was bloody but still breathing. "I stopped them before they could do too much damage."

Villon was tall and lean with jet-black hair and skin so pale it looked translucent. His cheekbones were hollows and his eyes were as dark as his hair. A black doublet and cloak came down to his knees.

"Who is he?" Arfast said drawing his sword.

"The emissary from the White Garden, the one that saved my life," she said.

"Be careful. It could be a shade. You're a much meatier prize than some low-born rider," Skuld said.

"A gesture of good will," Villon said, pushing Farragut on to the path and stepping further into the Garden. "Now can I talk with you for a moment?"

"Stay clear of the Garden," Skuld warned.

Lily steered her horse over to Villon but stayed well on the other side of the path. "What is it?"

Villon smiled. "Not even a 'Hello, how are you?' after saving your life?"

"I've thanked you once, though I still don't understand your reasons for helping me," she said.

"You'll have to trust that I do have a reason and that it will become clear in time," he said.

"I'm sure it will, though I'm not a patient person."

The smile left Villon's face. "I can see that women still haven't changed in all the centuries I've been imprisoned here."

"I'll take that as a compliment," she said.

"I saw what you did for the Nestler," he said. "You do understand that, if the roles were reversed, it would have killed you without compunction."

"What's your point?" she asked, growing angry.

"My point is that you shouldn't expect mercy for the good acts that you do. The Gardens are full of terrible beauty and terrible things that will kill you if they have the chance. The only way to keep them in line is to make them feel pain. Mercy is a weakness," Villon said.

"It's also what makes me human," Lily said.

Villon threw his head back and laughed. Lily's face reddened. "You find that funny, I suppose," she said.

"I — I'm sorry," he said, trying to stifle the laughter. "It's just that humans always say that, as though mercy were the *only* thing that made them what they are. Hate, anger, loneliness, envy, greed and violence also make people human, but it's always mercy, compassion and love of which they speak. In all the history of humankind there has been more war waged than love and there have been more people who have lived lives of fear than of kindness."

"That's not true," Lily said.

"If its not, then why is the world in the shape that it's in? Even with us imprisoned here, people continue to kill one another. People die of famine and plague and the rich take more for themselves while the poor dream that one day they will be able to walk on the backs of their neighbors and live among those with too much. Good people are stricken by diseases that kill them in the spring of life. Meanwhile, dictators manipulate the levers of power and the world's leaders trample on those they are charged to represent. For some people, every living moment is one spent in torment and you, you want to talk about *goodness*," Villon said, sneering.

Lily was taken aback with the fury of his words. To live in such a world as he described would be unimaginable.

"Perhaps you've been away from humanity too long," Lily said. "For you forget the nobler parts of us, such as our love, generosity and ability to make sacrifices — and yes, our mercy."

"Ah, I only wish I could be away from humankind," Villon said, staring at the ground. "It's quite impossible though."

"Why?"

"Because I used to be human," he said, his voice falling to a whisper.

"What are you two talking about over there," Skuld growled. "Whispering voices in the Gardens jangle my nerves."

"What do you mean you used to be a person?" Lily asked.

"In Paris. I was there when the first city wall was constructed. My people worshiped the old ones," he said.

"How did you end up here?" she asked.

"It's a long story, one that there's no time to tell now," Villon said. "I came to warn you that a great upheaval is coming — strange forces are massing, and the wolves are acting as couriers between the Gardens. Something will happen soon; another attempt will be made on your life and you have to be ready."

"What attempt? What have you heard?"

"Watch your back," Villon said, stepping toward the trees.

"If what you say is true, what can I do?"

"Tell only those you trust completely and have them swear to secrecy."

Villon was merging into the shadows under the trees. He seemed to lose definition the farther away he went. "I have to go now, for if those that lived in the White Garden knew that I told you ..."

There was much more that Lily wanted to ask him, but Villon was gone.

"What did he say?" Skuld asked when Lily rode her horse over to him.

"Nothing," she said. "He was up to the same trickery as all the beings here."

Lily's tour of the Gardens ended shortly after that with a heavy rain that came as they released the nestler into the Shadow Garden.

"It's a mistake, I tell ya," Farragut said as Arfast cut the ropes and the creature skittered on its rolling antenna into the safety of the garden.

"You would have us kill a child who is still harmless for what it *might* do," Lily said.

"Aye, if I knew that it would grow up to murder those that I loved," Farragut said as the rain washed the dirt and grime from his face.

"None of us even knows what the morrow will bring," Lily said.

"I know what today will bring," Arfast said. "A hot cup of tea and a place by the fire until this rain passes."

"My lady," Skuld said. "It's time to get you back before you catch your death of cold."

"Yes," Lily said distractedly. In truth, she hardly

felt the rain because she was thinking of what Villon told her. Who was he? Was it true that some attack was being planned?

As they moved away from the Shadow Garden toward the house, none of them saw the three women with odd smiles that watched from beneath a tree. The Smiling Ladies held old-fashioned parasols over their heads, and their lifeless eyes followed Lily with hunger until she was out of sight.

5

BETRAYAL AT THE BARN SWALLOW

"Another pint, barmaid," Larkspur said, slamming his empty stein down on the rough wooden table.

Silas wasn't sure how the big man could hold any more liquid. A collection of drained mugs littered the table in front of him. The barmaid swept them all onto a serving tray and headed toward the busy bar.

"Mayhap you should slow down," Jonquil said. He had barely taken a sip of his drink and kept scanning the room for trouble.

"A man of my girth has an appetite for life that you couldn't understand, Blackwood," Larkspur slurred. "You and your family are too dour for my tastes, except for the boy here." Larkspur tousled Silas's hair before he could move away. "Don't let them take that from you, lad. All this talk of being the protectors of the Gardens will have you jumping at shadows."

Silas ignored him and took in the strange confines. The Barn Swallow was dome-shaped, its walls and ceiling made out of thick vines and richly colored leaves. The roots of nearby trees pushed up through the floor. White and yellow flowers bloomed on the walls. The tables were packed with men and women. The heart of the establishment was a polished bar where the barkeep, toothless and nearly blind, served up drinks as fast as he could make them. The barmaids were all young women with either red or blond hair in identical cornflower dresses and jauntily cocked hats which Silas quickly realized, were actually bird nests. The nests provided a place for the hundreds of swallows that swarmed near the ceiling to light for a rest. The tiny swallows, with their white breasts, would land in the nests, strut back and forth a while, and then fly back into the cloud of birds above.

The night was growing late. With each passing hour, people became more intoxicated. Voices grew louder, jokes were bawdier. A man grabbed one of the barmaids, pulling her to his lap, before she slapped him hard across the face. The men were towering and muscular with alabaster skin and, like the women, all had blond or red hair.

"If Cogden's coming, it should be any time now," Trainer said. He sat in the shadows with his arms crossed, his drink untouched.

"Patience," Larkspur said. "Good things come to

those who wait and to those who have a good time in the meanwhile." No sooner had he said those words than a commotion at the doors erupted as Aiden Cogden entered. The former dusk rider looked as different as night and day from the mist folk. He was short and thick around the haunches with black hair peppered gray. An old well-strummed guitar was slung over his shoulders.

As he entered, the patrons called out to him. Cogden smiled a warm hello and stopped to trade gossip on his way to the bar. He froze momentarily when he saw Jonquil and the others, but came over soon after carrying a frothing mug of beer so full that it threatened to top the stein.

"Jonquil!" he said and slapped Silas's uncle on the shoulder. "Good to see you. Larkspur, you old dog, already in your cups, I see." Cogden passed over Trainer and caught sight of Silas. "This must be the nephew you told me so much about. I have to admit, after the last time, I didn't think I'd see you so soon."

Jonquil sat forward tensely in his chair. "That's exactly why I came. I don't remember anything of what happened when I came north."

"Don't remember ... I don't understand," Cogden said. He leaned his guitar against the table and drained half of his pint in one gulp.

"It's as though my memory has been wiped," Jonquil said. "I have a few flashes but the rest is gone."

Cogden rubbed his chin. "You mean you don't

remember anything? What about the others that were with you?"

"Dead," Jonquil said. "Poisoned by Eldritch. I barely survived myself."

"You don't recall anything that happened the last time you were here?" Cogden asked again. Silas noticed that a worried look filled the former dusk rider's face.

"He's said it twice," Trainer said impatiently. "Would it help if he wrote it down and shoved it under your nose?"

Cogden leveled a cool eye at the sour-faced man. "When did the dusk riders start hiring such wretched ilk?"

Jonquil raised a hand between the two. "No offense, Aiden. It's been a long journey for the four of us, and we had a nasty run-in with a witch last night."

The next table fell quiet as if they'd heard what Jonquil said. Silas saw that the three men and two women there were staring at them with hatred in their eyes. So far, the rest of the bar seemed as boisterous as ever.

"A witch you say?" Cogden asked. Running his tongue across his lips, he looked around the bar and made a quick decision. "We need to get out of here."

"But now that you're here, the party's just getting started," Larkspur said. He stood and bellowed up to the rafters, sending the birds into a frenzy and causing people to clap, laugh and call out at him.

"Sit down, you ass!" Cogden said, a subtle tremor to his voice. "Gods. How long have you been here?"

"A few hours," Jonquil said picking up on his fear. "What is it, Aiden? Speak true."

"I'm surprised they haven't arrested you yet," Cogden said. He slung his guitar back over his shoulder.

"Arrest me? For what?" Jonquil said.

"Follow me, now!" Cogden said. Without another word, he walked out of the bar. The dusk riders followed. A growing sense of apprehension gnawed at Silas. Something wasn't right. Why hadn't he picked up on that before? He felt it as they walked toward the doors. There was a bottleneck of energy in the room that was about to burst free. The laughter was loud and jagged. A man fell backward from a bench and lay on the floor mumbling. A woman near his mother's age pointed at him, her eyes seized by madness. As Silas watched, they turned from blue to black and back again. "Demon child!" she said. "Filthy Blackwood." One of the barmaids convulsed and would have collapsed, except that a man caught her as she fainted. *'What's happening?'* Silas thought, and then he was out the swinging doors of The Barn Swallow and into the damp night air.

Cogden was waiting on the other side of the muddy road. He lit a pipe and took a drag, puffing a sweet-smelling aroma into the air. "Where are you staying?" he asked perturbed.

"We rented rooms from your landlady," Jonquil said. "What's wrong? I've never seen you so upset."

"It's worse than when you were here last," Cogden said. He paced as if trying to put his thoughts into words.

"What has?" Jonquil asked.

"Eldritch, the witch, all of it. No one wanted to believe, but only a fool would ignore it now."

"Tell it from the beginning," Jonquil said.

"All right, but we have to get out of here. If Fyodor finds out you are back in town, he'll have you thrown in the stockade. Come on. I'll tell you on the way. I should have my head examined for getting involved in this, but once a rider, always one, I suppose," Cogden said.

The red moon drifted in and out of the fog as they made their way. Silas wouldn't have been able to see where they were going if he didn't have Trainer's lanky figure right in front of him. Aiden Cogden's disembodied voice seemed to float from everywhere at once.

"It took place little by little so that when I finally saw what was happening it was already too late," Cogden said.

"What did, Aiden?" Jonquil asked again. Silas caught a glimpse of his uncle hobbling on his walking stick next to Cogden, and then the mist swallowed them again.

"Whispers of Eldritch. It started with a trickle. A

family of woodcutters found flayed in their cabin, a hunter spotting the rambling figure of a man with antlers and green eyes in the far north; little dollops that add up to nothing in the mist. Many things that escape the Gardens call this place home. The villagers dispatch those that they can and send for the dusk riders when it's something beyond their power. One of the village children went missing and was found tied to a tree in the woods. What was done to him ...," Cogden faltered. "He'd been made a sacrifice. The charred remains that were left showed the signs of some ancient ritual. I was the one who found the sign of Eldritch carved into the soft bark of the tree. It was shortly afterwards that we sent word to you. Little did I know how late it was."

Shimmering bands of light bounced on the mist ahead. The fog cleared just long enough for Silas to see that it was coming from the home of his grandparents, and then it was gone again.

"But, I don't see the mist people giving themselves over to a cruel earth spirit like Eldritch," Jonquil said.

"Nature is the mist folk's religion; each person in harmony with the world around them. They aren't a fussy, prudish lot like the Evangels back in New Amsterdam. They don't believe in Old Nick with a pitchfork and tail. They have only one rule: 'Harm no others'." After that, you have one life to live as you see fit. Which is why I came here," Cogden said.

"And how you ended up warming more than your fair share of beds," Larkspur said howling with drunken laughter.

"So how did he make headway with them?" Jonquil asked, ignoring the drunken giant.

"I'm getting to that," Cogden said. "It's my belief Eldritch wouldn't have recruited more than a handful of worshipers among the outcasts of the mist people, if it weren't for the witch."

"Who — who is she?" Silas asked, surprised to hear his voice in the dark.

"Her name is Bemisch. She appeared one day to a pair of young brothers who were chasing a wild boar. Her power is so great that she took control of one of them and made him attack the other. We'd never have known if the brother who had been left for dead hadn't been discovered by a search party and told them everything before he passed away."

"Bemisch," Jonquil repeated, as if the word left a sour taste in his mouth. "This is worse than I thought. She's one of the most evil crones in existence. It's said she had wickedness in her heart from the day of her birth and she learned to bend people to her will before she learned to walk. The older she grew, the more hideous she was to behold. Even still, she managed to possess the heart of a weak-willed king and made herself master of his lands and people. Many an innocent victim was plied on the rack. It's claimed that she liked to bathe in the fresh blood of maidens. Eventually the people revolted, and the king was hung from his castle walls. Bemisch had been imprisoned in the Shadow Garden all of these many long years. How she could have escaped without us knowing it is beyond me," Jonquil said.

"There was no time to send word about the witch before you arrived," Cogden said. "And I have my doubts about what good it would have done. They must have met in the mist. It's the only thing that explains how quickly the village fell."

"How quickly the village fell?" Jonquil replied.

"Aye. Who runs this town? For all the talk of equality and how possessions don't matter, which villager has accumulated more wealth than any of the others?"

"Fyodor," Jonquil said through gritted teeth.

"Aye, again. If you control him, you control half o' this town," Cogden said. "So who do you think the witch set her wiles on day and night?"

"But surely his wife and children must have known," Jonquil said.

"The witch had him under her bony thumb 'fore anyone caught wind. First, he stopped sending his men to patrol the forest and village. He threatened to close down his granary and let the food perish. He preached that if the villagers worshiped nature, then they must also worship old gods like Eldritch. Not many people believed it, but the most simpleminded did, and more worshipers were drawn to the dark. That was when you rode into town."

They approached the hollow where they were

staying for the night. The mist hung like shrouds of ghosts in the air. The rope hung from the gnarled tree where their rooms were. Cogden gave it a yank, and a ladder dropped and unfurled in front of them.

"We met up at The Barn Swallow and I told you what I knew," Cogden said as he began to climb. "Another child had disappeared. The villagers begged you to save them from Eldritch. In front of everyone, you promised to return after you captured him and arrest Fyodor and stop the madness that threatened to overtake us."

Silas was the last one on the ladder. He was halfway up when he thought he saw something leaping from one tree to another, a human-sized body frozen in a cloud of mist and then gone, leaving him blinking at dots where he'd been staring. Coldness flooded his veins. His heart seemed to stop for one moment. What had he just seen?

Cogden was inside the hatch and giving Jonquil a hand. "So you set off the next morning with your band and went north, following instructions a hunter gave you on where he'd spotted Eldritch's tracks."

Larkspur and Trainer crawled inside the hatch. Silas hung for a moment at the top of the ladder looking into the dark. He didn't see anything, but he could have sworn he heard a whisper in his mind that was lost in the wind. "*Almost,*" the voice seemed to say. Silas reached into the dark and a hand yanked him inside. The trapdoor closed behind him.

"What you didn't know was that we were sending you on a wild goose chase. And that we'd spiked the water we gave you with Eldritch's blood," Cogden said.

A match struck in the dark. Candlelight filled the room. Silas froze at the sight in front of him. The room was filled with men from the village. One had a knife pressed against Jonquil's throat. Larkspur was on the ground with a boot in his back, and a sword was pushed against Trainer's chest.

"I thought that would be the last of you. What I can't believe is that you fell for it again," Cogden said, his eyes turning from green to black.

6
GREAT WHITE WOLF

Lily dreamt of performing Shakespeare's *As You Like It*. "All the world's a stage, and all the men and women merely players ...." In her dream, the audience hung on her every word. A powder flash went off as a photographer snapped her photo for the *Parisian Star*. "Last scene of all, that ends this strange eventful history, is second childishness and mere oblivion, sans teeth, sans eyes, sans taste, sans everything." She finished the monologue and bowed as applause echoed off the walls. The audience gave her a standing ovation, their figures silhouetted by flames from the gas jets. Then the lights came up and Lily saw the audience. A scream lodged in her throat at the hundreds of charred corpses that stood clapping. In the front row, Villon stood, dressed in tuxedo with red cravat. "Bravo," he cried. "Bravo, Lily." For the first time she noticed the scratching so subtle that it was almost hidden in the boisterous applause coming from the legion of dead. The sound was fingernails, gently, oh so gently scratching brass. It grew louder, until with one last look at Villon, she rushed back to the land of consciousness.

Lily was used to the strange noises that came from the manor: bumps and moans as she passed closed doors that she was never to open; bloodcurdling shrieks that sent her bolting upright in bed, only to be followed by dreadful quiet and the sound of rats or something worse in the walls; calliope music drifting down empty halls; or ghostly footsteps. These were all noises that her ears were well acquainted with. But she'd never heard anything like the noise that ripped her from her dream.

'What was that about?' she thought, pulling the blankets tightly around her. Nightfall Manor was chilly at the best of times, but during the hours before night switched to day, it was downright frigid. The blood moon shone the length of the room from a crack in the drapes. All was silent as Lily turned over to sleep. And that was when she heard it again, a scratching coming from her bedroom door, like a cat that wanted to be let in for the night. She lay there listening as the noise continued unabated, and then she climbed out of bed, careful not to make a sound. As she watched in horror, the doorknob turned ever so slightly. The Lily from five months ago would have fled in

terror, but no more. Taking a deep breath, Lily grabbed her practice sword and threw open the door.

A nightmare stared back from the open doorway. Desdemona was inches away, her empty sockets watching Lily as if she could still see. The last wisps of hair hung from her peeling scalp. Where her lower jaw should have been, there was nothing but a gaping hole. The tattered shroud of her dress hung off one shoulder, revealing dull bone. They froze, Blackwoods separated by centuries, and then Desdemona lunged with a manic fury that Lily hadn't expected.

She barely raised her weapon as Desdemona drove her halfway across the room. Slashing skeletal fingers grabbed at the sword and tried to yank it from Lily's grasp. Lily kicked in response, shoving her dead ancestor away and preparing for the next attack. Desdemona threw her head back. An angry rasp came from the remnants of her voice box. With one movement, she took to the walls, scrabbling onto the ceiling, perched on the chandelier and then leaped across the room where she landed on the dresser and began furiously rooting through Lily's jewelry box.

Desdemona found what she was looking for and held it aloft, mesmerized. The amethyst necklace that supposedly belonged to Pandora glinted purple in the moonlight. Lily swung the blade, severing Desdemona's hand from her arm. The necklace dropped with the hand to the floor. Lily's ancestor spun with a hiss and head-butted her, and she slammed backward into a wall. Something crashed to the floor. Lily tried to parry, but the weapon was no good up close. Her hand found one of Desdemona's ribs and broke it free, thrusting the bone through the carcass of her ancestor's body. Desdemona's good hand raked Lily's face, and then she scuttled across the floor toward the severed hand that clutched the necklace.

"Put — it — down!" Lily said angrily. All she wanted was a full night's sleep without monsters trying to kill her at all hours, but apparently that was impossible. *'Take a deep breath. Remember what Skuld taught you.'* Lily stepped between the dismembered hand and its owner. She noticed the projection mirror had fallen on its side. The mirror showed grotesque reflections of the people who came near it. With Lily, it showed her decomposing; something that truly frightened her when she'd come to Nightfall Gardens but now seemed like a parlor trick. The mirror was facing them and reflected in its surface was Desdemona, not as the skeletal horror she had become, but as the beautiful young woman she used to be. Chestnut-brown hair framed an oval face and swan-like neck. Soulful green eyes blinked from above a pert nose. Lily snatched the necklace from the hand and tossed it in front of the mirror. Desdemona followed the necklace and froze at her reflection. A horrible rattling sob came from her as she touched bony fingers to her skeletal face. In the mirror, an elegant hand caressed the full bloom of youth. As Desdemona turned her face, side to side, to examine her newfound beauty, Lily came up behind her with the sword. She felt sad for the grotesquerie that studied itself in the mirror. Was her ancestor remembering when she walked Nightfall Manor or how the dusk riders turned to follow when she rode past? As Lily watched, the mirror fogged and the youthful Desdemona melted away leaving only a skeletal husk staring at its own dead face. Desdemona howled in anguish once her true self was revealed.

Lily hesitated too long. Desdemona turned as she swung the sword and the spell was broken. The scuttling creature leapt to the wall and with one last mournful look at the mirror fled the room. Lily raced to the door in time to see Desdemona turning a corner in the hallway.

'I should have finished her when I had the chance,' Lily thought. She straightened her room and lay down, but sleep wouldn't come. Her heart was racing from battle and she couldn't stop thinking about what would have happened if she hadn't awakened before her ancestor snuck into her room. She built a fire and burned Desdemona's curled hand in the flames.

Lily lay in a fitful doze until she heard off-key whistling coming along the hall. Cheerily unpleasant was the best way to describe the shrill whine of the tune. *'Oh no,'* Lily thought. She jumped out of bed and made for the changing screen where she slipped out of her nightgown and into riding pants, a white blouse and gray jacket. She was pulling on her boots when the door opened and Ursula entered.

The cleaning woman stood no more than five feet tall with a unibrow and widely placed eyes that were twice as large as a normal person's.

"Good morning, Miss, beautiful day. Looks to be gray and overcast with a good chance of a long miserable rain. How I do love it," the glumpog said as she turned the bed.

Lily came from behind the screen. Her mood dropped with every step closer to the strange little woman making her bed. Tears welled in her eyes as she started crying uncontrollably at how hopeless and forlorn life was. She'd been a fool to think that she could defeat all of the dark forces aligned against her. Better to just walk into the Gardens and let them do what they wanted. It would be over soon and she wouldn't have to try anymore.

'No,' she thought, wiping the tears from her eyes. *'It's all in my mind. I just need to get away from Ursula.'*

It was the unfortunate fate of the glumpog that no matter how cheery or pleasant, they sent every living creature into a tailspin of depression and hopelessness whenever they were near. Lily tried to be out of the room whenever Ursula came, not because she didn't like her, but because of the dark feelings that came over her when the glumpog was around.

"Going for a ride, eh, Miss?" Ursula said, dusting the room. "Be careful. Me old gran used to say 'Never trust a horse.' They can throw you sky-high and then you'd break your neck. Where'd you be after that?"

"Uh, thanks Ursula," Lily said, feeling the chains of depression pull her down further. She stepped past her to the door, which seemed a thousand miles away.

The glumpog put her nose in the air and began to sniff. "Something don't seem right, Miss," she said. The little woman got down on her hands and knees and crawled to the fireplace as if following a scent. "What's this then?" she said, drawing Desdemona's charred fingers from the grate. "Knew I smelled something funny. We glumpogs got a sense o' smell that can't be beat. Which is good and bad. Ever smell an arpblaster? Believe me, you don't want to."

Lily felt so forlorn at this point that she could do nothing more than tell the truth about what had happened the night before. When she was finished, Ursula responded. "Oh, no good, my lady, no good. You shouldn't have gone poking around in that cellar. This old house is full of secrets that it does no good to know. Many a person has disappeared here over the years. Think of your own dear aunt Abby who haunts these halls. Have you told Polly or Mr. Ozy?"

By now, Lily felt as if she wanted nothing more than to lie down and cry herself back to sleep, but she took a deep breath and said, "No, and you mustn't either. Not until I know more about what's happening."

"All right, Miss. You can count on me," Ursula said. "Heed my words though. There's places it don't pay to go poking around inside o' here."

Lily stopped at the door and looked back at the housemaid scrubbing the fireplace. "Ursula, the number 23 doesn't mean anything to you, does it?"

The glumpog waggled her unibrow in concentration. "No, miss. Can't say it does. Beautiful age, though. Old enough to be an adult, but not old enough to realize how difficult things can be."

After breakfast, Skuld showed up for their morning weapons class. The dusk rider was in an unusually irritable mood. He attacked her with extra ferociousness, striking her twice on the arms with the wooden practice sword, hard enough to leave bruises.

"Put your arms up and defend yourself," he barked. "Or do you think the Smiling Ladies will give you a second chance?"

The morning weariness dissipated as Skuld struck at her again. Lily pivoted and spun, blocking his sword and drawing close to find a weakness in his defenses.

"You're getting faster," he said in approval. "But you're holding yourself back. You do that in real life, and it'll be the death of you. What's the matter? You afraid of hurting an old one-armed man?"

Lily opened her mouth to tell him that wasn't the case when Skuld came in fast and low, driving the practice sword into Lily's stomach and knocking the breath from her. She fell to her knees gasping for air.

"You're a weak little girl. Now if you'll excuse me, I've got a *real* job I must attend to," Skuld said as he stalked towards the door. "Maybe tomorrow you'll be in better form."

Lily sprang to her feet and wiped the tears from her eyes.

"Stand down, child, before—." Skuld barely had time to get his sword up before she was on him, driving him backward, parrying his thrusts and smacking him hard enough in the wrist that he winced.

"Aye, that's better," he said with a hard grin. "Remember what I told you about not letting emotion overtake you though."

The dusk rider came in low again, but this time Lily was ready. She blocked his blow and spun letting Skuld's momentum drive him past her. As he stumbled forward, she wound up and struck his backside with all the force of a cricketer letting loose on a ball. Skuld grunted with pain. "That's what I wanted to see. What have you been holding back for?"

When it was finished, both of them were covered in sweat. Lily's body was so sore from the bruises that she was afraid she wouldn't be able to get out of bed the next morning.

"You're getting better, I'll give you that," Skuld said, slipping on his wolf-hide cloak.

"That's only thanks to you," Lily said.

Skuld squirmed, uncomfortable with compliments. "Well, the teacher is only as good as his pupil."

"What news of my brother and uncle?" she asked, making her way to the window where she could see the dreamlike Gardens obscured by bands of thin mist.

"Too early to say. I'm sure they'll be fine. You're uncle is hard as obsidian. I've been in many a hairy situation with him, and he always got us out. There's no one else I'd want at my back."

Lily nodded, but she didn't like it. Nothing was ever simple in the Gardens, and a person who was fine one minute could be dead the next. She watched as Skuld cinched a sword to his belt. The ragged stump of his arm was white with scars and puckered to a tip at the end.

"Skuld, how — how did you lose your arm?" Lily knew it had something to do with the wolves that prowled the Gardens, but she'd never heard the full story. For a moment, she thought he wasn't going to answer. Instead he came to the window and stared out toward the grounds.

"You know that dusk riders don't talk about their pasts before they came to the Gardens?" he asked. "There are people I've ridden next to for 20 years and for whom I've risked my life that I know less about than I do you. Once you come through the gates, the past no longer matters. You are reborn."

"I'm sorry. I didn't mean to offend," Lily said.

"You didn't," Skuld said. "They say the past no longer matters. I've not found it such a simple matter to forget where a person comes from. Do you know Beantown?"

Lily nodded. "My family spent a month performing at the Rickety Moon in the center of Old Town." She recalled very little of Beantown other than the squalid filth of the shanty where the theatre had been and the fact that the front page of the local broadsheets seemed to lead with a murder every morning. It was one of the few towns that their mother and father hadn't let them walk the streets alone.

"Good, then you know what a cesspool it is. Horse dung piled ten feet high on the streets. Pestilence in every standing puddle of water. Taverns and brothels on every street corner. Half of the town was a slum that went up like a tinderbox when an old woman's lantern broke and lit a pile of straw on fire. The mayor was owned by the local mob bosses. The coppers always had a hand out, and the streets were full of orphans."

"It sounds terrible," Lily said, taking a seat on the windowsill.

"The first thing I remember is my brother, Roger. Not my parents, they died of the plague when I was a wee bairn. Roger was the only parent

I ever knew and the only hero I ever had. He was a
big lad with black hair and twinkling blue eyes. He
was always ready with a laugh, not that there was
much for us to laugh about. We lived where the
night took us. Sometimes we worked in the stables,
mucking out the animal stalls and sleeping in the
great haylofts. Other times, we found shelter in old
basements or boarded-up houses. I never went
hungry, though. There was always food for us.
'Just stay here and I'll be back,' Roger used to say,
and then he'd disappear and come back later with
salted meat and fresh bread or sometimes pies that
were still cooling. I wish now I'd asked where that
food came from. One day Roger didn't come back. I
waited until dark, but eventually I left the shed
where we'd been hiding and started searching. I
remember the bright lights of the saloon windows
and the wooden sidewalks that creaked underfoot.
There were so many people: men in suits and
women in long dresses with frilly edges and
workers with worn-out hats and ripped coats. I
thought I might look forever until I saw the paddy
wagon ahead. It was the scourge of all orphans, for
to be picked up by it meant a one-way ticket to the
workhouse on the edge of town. The workhouse
was a horrible disease-ridden place, where children
slaved from sunup until late in the eve. It was
dangerous working the machines, and most
children were maimed or killed before they
reached the age where they could leave. *'Please
don't let him be in there,'* I thought, but I looked

through the bars of the wagon and there was no mistake. Among the handful of dirty children locked up in back was my brother. Roger came to the bars when I saw him. There were tracks on his face where he'd been crying. 'Well, they nabbed me fair and honest for trying to nick some fresh salami for us. You're going to have to be strong now. We'll get through this,' he told me. I don't know if he believed a word of what he said, but I didn't. I followed the wagon, all the way to the iron gates of the prison. My brother waved at me through the bars as it disappeared inside. I never saw him alive again."

Lily felt a lump in her throat. "What happened?"

"I waited every day outside of the gates for the priest who visited the children. He was a kindly man with spectacles and sharp eyes. 'You see my brother today, Father?' I'd call, and he'd give me a grin. 'He's right as rain, boy-o,' he'd say and wink before heading on his way. One day, I was waiting and the priest came through the gates. 'You see my brother today, Father?' I asked. Only this time he didn't smile. He looked deflated, and there was a terrible weariness in his features. He bent down in front of me. 'I'm sorry lad, but your brother has gone to the Lord's kingdom.' 'What's that mean?' I asked. The priest sighed, 'One of the machines got stuck, and the foreman made your brother crawl inside to fix it … and the machine started again. He never had a chance.' I ran then, far from town into the mountains, and made my living as I could,

working on farms, almost starving to death. I never stayed anywhere longer than a few days. Always, I kept moving. Though I didn't know it, this place was drawing me close. I began to dream of the Gardens. The closer I came, the stronger the dreams were, until one day I found myself outside of the open gates. Dark was coming and I could see Nightfall Manor, shifting and moving, like it always has since the moment it was born. I walked through the gates and up the drive, unaware that I was being followed by a pair of wolves. I heard them before I saw them, howling in the fog. It was a terrifying sound that shook me to the holes in the bottoms of my boots. Then, I saw them: male and female white wolves, bigger than I'd imagined such creatures could be. They bared their teeth and moved in, one step at a time. I was defenseless and the house was too far to run for. I had little time to think about this before the animals were on me. The next moments are horrible to recall. One of the wolves bit through my arm to the bone. I almost lost consciousness, but somewhere, I heard a person yelling and a horse galloping. The next second, the animal was releasing my arm. I somehow climbed to my feet, my useless right arm hanging at my side. Indeed, there was a man on a horse. That was the first time I saw Jonquil. Back then he was little more than a lad himself. His hair was still black and he was still courting Moi —."
Skuld caught himself. He rubbed the nub of his arm as he finished the tale. "He tossed me a sword

and drew his own weapon. 'Fight for your life,' he said. The female wolf came at me again, teeth snapping as I jabbed to keep her away. The pain in my arm was so unbearable I don't know how I managed to stay on my feet. When your life hangs in the balance, though, you can do more than you ever believed. I finally drew close enough to drive the blade home. I pierced her heart and she fell dead at my feet. In that moment, the male wolf howled with dismay. That was enough for Jonquil to cleave half of its face away. The male wolf was no fool. He ran into the mist with a long howl and was never seen again. Now if you're through with wasting my time, that's the story of how I came to Nightfall Gardens." Skuld walked to the door. "I'll see you tomorrow. Make sure you ice down those bruises. We don't want Polly getting angry at me."

It wasn't so easy to fool the housekeeper, though. Polly tut-tutted when she saw the bruises on Lily's arm and scratches on her face. "Mr. Skuld is too rough on you, he is. It's not proper for the lady of the house to be playing swords like some common saddle tramp."

"I'd rather know how to defend myself than be helpless," Lily argued.

"The house will protect you," Polly said, gathering a bowl of water to clean the wounds.

"You mean like it did last time," Lily snipped.

Polly froze as if the words stung. Lily found it difficult to tell what emotions lay behind the smooth exterior of the housekeeper's face. She slid across the floor leaving a gigantic slug trail in her wake. Her bald head glistened with the light that came through the window. Her back was humped and there were patches of slime where her hands accidentally touched her uniform. The housekeeper was the glue holding the manor together, but they were in uncharted territory. Lily was the last female Blackwood. If she were to die, there would be no one left to keep the ancient beasts in check, the Gardens would empty and darkness would reign over the world once again.

A feeling of pity for the gigantic slug overtook Lily, and she walked back her words. "I'm sorry, Polly. That was uncalled for. I'm sure you've done all you can to protect me. Only, I need to be able to defend myself if the situation arises."

"You're as pigheaded as your grandmother," Polly said, washing the cuts on Lily's face. "The difference is Mrs. Deiva never gave what was out there the chance to get to her. She stayed locked in this room, waiting for a husband who never returned. I began to think that was normal, but its not. It's a terrible, short life that most Blackwoods live, and you are right, you should be prepared, because if the time comes and you are not, woe to us all."

Polly slithered out of the room and left Lily to clean her weapons. Not long after, there was a knock on the door and Lily looked up to see a man with bushy hair and a thick mustache, wearing a checkered vest over a blue shirt and workpants.

The man was wringing his hands as if uncomfortable in her presence. There was a sadness about him that she sensed before he spoke.

"Mr. Hawthorne, milady. You called for me," he said.

Lily smiled and asked him to have a seat. "Cassandra's told me so much about you."

The groundskeeper perked up. "Oh my Cassie's a good kid. I hope she hasn't been filling your head with a bunch of nonsense."

"No, not at all. It's not because of her that I've asked you here," she said. "I need help of a sort."

"Say no more. What can I do?"

"I suppose you've heard about what happened when the emissaries of the Gardens came to the house after my grandmother died," Lily said.

"Aye," Mr. Hawthorne replied. "I looked through my father and granddad's records but never saw anything like it in the history of Nightfall Gardens. For one of the emissaries to attack you like they did is unprecedented."

"And I've heard about the protections you place around the house every night. That they are wearing out more quickly than before?"

Mr. Hawthorne hung his head as if ashamed. "Aye, the dragonflower, nightsbreath and witch vine have to be replaced every week now. The walls holding everything back are growing weaker."

"Speak freely with me," Lily said.

The groundskeeper sighed. "I can't maintain it

much longer. I'm running through my stock as fast as I can raise them. Without your brother to help, I'm working 14 hours a day to maintain what defenses there are. The dusk riders have taken bad losses over the past year and their ranks are in disarray, what with your uncle being gone. I worry dark powers are beginning to infiltrate them."

"That's what I feared," Lily said. A light rain was falling in the gardens now. A strong wind blew against the windows. "I need some help from you."

"Name it. If I can, I will," Mr. Hawthorne said.

"I need some enchantments to place around my room at night. I don't trust that the house will be able to hold out intruders much longer. I want something that will keep out everyone that wishes to harm me."

The groundskeeper pulled his mustache in contemplation. "I think I've got just what you need. Golgotha extract. It's powerful stuff. Put a few drops around your door and windows and no one that wishes you ill can get inside."

Mr. Hawthorne bowed and backed toward the door. "Begging your pardon, milady, but I should get back to work."

"Of course," Lily said.

"I'll have Cassie run some up to you later," the groundskeeper said. He looked at the floor as if there was something he wanted to add. The silence went on so long that Lily finally spoke. "Is something the matter?"

"I'm not sure how to phrase this, but I wanted to ask a favor," Mr. Hawthorne said shyly.

"Of course. What is it?"

"It's about my daughter. I — it's just that — well, tomorrow is the anniversary of her mother's death…"

"I'm sorry to hear that. Cassandra told me how she was dragged into the Shadow Garden by the vindictous root," Lily said.

Tears welled in Mr. Hawthorne's eyes. "Aye, that's it all right. Got her and there was nothing I could do. It's just that tomorrow is the thirteenth anniversary of her death and I need some time to be alone. I wondered — that is — I wondered if Cassie might be able to spend the night in the Manor. She doesn't need to see her old dad sniffling and sobbing about."

Lily was puzzled. That was all he wanted? It felt like the groundskeeper was hiding something, that there was more behind his words than his simple request. Cassandra had never given her reason to believe it before, but Lily sensed her friend's father was deeply troubled.

"It'd be a pleasure to have company. Time passes so much more quickly with a friend," she said.

Mr. Hawthorne grinned. "Aye, indeed it does. I'll send her up with the Golgotha extract later."

"And tell her to pack her bag for tomorrow. We're having a sleepover," Lily said.

When the groundskeeper left, Lily went to the

window and looked into the Gardens. They were windswept and empty as if even the creatures inside had hidden to get out of the elements. A moment later, Mr. Hawthorne appeared and stalked away. Lily felt confused and unsure of what to tell her friend when she arrived. Her sword skills weren't the only thing that had gotten sharper in the last month. She had also learned how to read people. Mr. Hawthorne wasn't just sending Cassandra to the house so he could celebrate the anniversary of his wife's death alone. He was also trying to get her out of the way because he didn't want her to know something that he was doing.

7

JAIL OF LIVING WOOD

"You should have known better than to come back, Jonquil, for you've signed your death warrant," Fyodor said. Silas's grandfather was sitting on a throne made from interlocking vines growing out of the wall. He was tall and broad-chested with a beard the color of frost. The violet robes that marked him as an elder billowed to the floor. In one hand he clacked a pair of petrified hydra eggs out of habit.

This was not how Silas envisioned meeting his grandfather. The dusk riders were on their knees, stripped of weapons. The banquet hall was filled with his aunts, uncles and cousins. A dozen men with long blades surrounded them. In the galley, Silas glimpsed men with crossbows, ready to fire at any unexpected movement. A woman who must be his grandmother with the same silver hair as her husband sat in a chair made of hydrangea. A sweet, sickly smell filled the banquet hall. The woman locked eyes with Silas, giving him a troubled look.

His grandfather stood surveying the room. "We have traitors in our midst," he said, his voice echoing across the hall. "The once noble dusk riders are a shadow of what they were. There was a time we worked together for mutual protection, but no more. They are lapdogs that drink at the same trough as the spiritual filth that they are meant to protect us from. Aye, they commune with the beasts of the Gardens now. They've turned their backs on the natural order. They've joined forces with false gods and threaten the peaceful way of life we have here."

Fyodor stopped in front of Jonquil. "This is the worst of the lot. He came to me in good stead many a moon ago to ask for the hand of my youngest daughter, Moira; a blessing I freely gave him. And what happened? His brother stole her away and they fled through the gates. He wasn't man enough to protect what was his, and he dares call himself the leader of the dusk riders. It's a slap in the face to all the good men who've worn that cloak before. They used to be a proud band, and now their ranks are filled with thieves, liars, gluttons and boys."

Silas's grandfather addressed the hall. "I warned Jonquil the last time. If he ever came to this village again, he'd hang from the highest tree, and yet here he is in front of me. The others seek to sow rebellion and unsettle our town. So I ask, what should we do? Would the winds blow mercy or would they blow death?"

"Death!" Someone cried out.

"Kill them!" another voice called, and this one Silas thought had the same cackling quality as Bemisch's.

"Hang them!"

"No, put them on the rack and stretch them," a female screeched with excitement.

Silas chanced a look behind him. What he saw froze him to the marrow. The faces of the soldiers and his family were filled with looks of religious ecstasy. These were people no longer in control of themselves. Some of their eyes changed from normal to black as he watched. Only a few of the people wore uneasy expressions at what was taking place. He noticed the girl in the white dress with red hair who had been staring at him so intently before. She pulled back from the crowd and left the room. Had Jonquil really asked for his mother's hand in marriage? That was too much to think about right now.

"Split them in half!"

"Maim them!"

"Enough!" Fyodor said, raising a hand. "These three shall dance on the end of a rope. As for Jonquil, he'll be placed in the stocks for the world to see his shame. What say you to that?"

Jonquil looked up and spoke for the first time. "With what are we being charged?"

"Oh ho, he wants to speak of charges," Fyodor

said. One of his eyes swirled black and then blue. "You're being charged with murder. More than a dozen villagers have gone missing or turned up dead in the last few months. You were seen leaving the house of one of the families."

Jonquil laughed. "You've gone mad. You called us here to investigate. These three weren't even with me"

"Lies!" Fyodor roared.

"Don't you see," Jonquil said loudly enough for the room to hear. "You're all under the influence of the witch Bemisch and Eldritch."

A woman moaned in fear and the room fell silent. Fyodor's face contorted with shock, and something else, as if he was fighting to control himself. He lost, though; for a second later, he spoke. The first words from his mouth came out in Bemisch's voice. *"You dare speak of the old god? You'll meet the lord of death soon but not before you beg.* Take — take them away."

A sword was pressed in his back, and Silas was told to stand. His grandfather had already turned away. He was conferring with a group of men in identical robes. His grandmother was watching him with the same uneasy expression as before. The room parted to make way for the riders. He saw many people with the same red hair and green eyes as his mother. Cogden was waiting by the door of the banquet hall, strumming his guitar. "Sorry about that mate," he told Jonquil. "Nothing personal. A new day is coming, innit?"

Jonquil sneered. "The end of yours and all of ours is coming if Eldritch grows in power. What purpose will you or any of the villagers serve once he is free?"

"Trying to plant doubt in my mind? You can't tell when you're beaten. It'll make for a good ballad, though. *The Fall of the Dusk Riders.*" Cogden plucked out a tune on his guitar.

They were marched into a courtyard with a babbling fountain. A wall of bamboo hid this place from the outside world. The mist hung heavy on the trees. A frog croaked in the woods. Chilled fingers stirred a breeze and the cold weighed on him as Silas felt the presence of the witch. He thought of Cassandra and of his family as the first awful probe penetrated his mind. *"Join us. It's pointless to fight. I can give you anything you want and all you've been too afraid to take."* The crone tried to dig out his memories and uproot his secrets. Tears washed his eyes at the thought of the cruel japes he'd made, of the countless times he'd passed the starving in the streets of New Amsterdam and done nothing to help, and of the envy in his heart when he'd climbed a wrought iron gate to peer into one of the houses on Millionaires' Row. How he'd coveted their opulent possessions and the wealth that allowed them to live as gods. He could have all that now, if he would allow the witch to control him as she had the rest of the villagers. It would be the easiest thing in the world. But then what would happen? What would she make him do? *"Nothing*

you don't want to, nothing you haven't wanted to,"
Bemisch whispered. An image of Cassandra came
to his mind again: the green girl with her blond
green hair tucked behind her ears breaking into
laughter at a joke he made.

Each of the other dusk riders was fighting his
own battle. Jonquil bit his lower lip with grim
determination. Trainer muttered under his breath
while sweat beaded his forehead. Larkspur was in
the worst shape. The great man trembled with fear.
His eyes were closed and his face was bright red as
if he were holding his breath. Veins bulged in his
forehead as he stumbled blindly at the point of a
sword. At that moment Silas looked back at the
great house and froze. Standing at an upstairs
window in plain view was Bemisch. She was even
more horrible to behold in the light. Her skin was
the color of moss that grows on gravestones and
her hair was full of twigs and hung down to her
breasts. She was bent and bloated, and her arms
were outstretched as if she were conducting a
chorus of the damned.

A commotion to his right made him look away
from her. A guard flew past him and struck a tree
hard. Larkspur was struggling with another guard
for a sword. "She won't get me, she won't," the big
man said. He delivered a blow to one of the men
and wrested the sword free. The other guard
managed to get his blade up as Larkspur swung
and sparks shot into the air.

"Move and you're dead, boy," a whiskey-drenched voice said in his ear. A blade pressed into Silas's back.

Larkspur fought like a man possessed. His massive bulk moved with a quickness that surprised Silas. The guard barely had time to get his sword up before the giant was feinting at him from a different angle. "I — won't — go!" Larkspur said. Each word was punctuated with a ring of the sword against steel. The guard kept moving backward with no chance to set his feet. Soon they were halfway across the yard. The second guard moved in stealthily with his sword at his side.

That might have been the end of the big man, but Silas yelled "Behind you!" as the second guard lunged, and Larkspur dodged and swung with his sword. Blood exploded into the air as his sword took the man's hand off at the wrist. The guard screamed and held his arm outstretched; the hand was attached by only a few tendons. The other guard froze long enough that Larkspur smote him in the face with the sword handle. Bone crunched as the man's nose shattered, and the guard collapsed in a heap.

"Take one step towards us and we'll kill your friends, fat man," the guard watching Jonquil said.

Larkspur gave them a wild-eyed look. His nostrils flared to the size of pence pieces then he ran into the dark. A bell from the house rang seconds later. More guards, carrying torches, streamed out and headed off in the same direction as the escaped dusk rider.

Replacements came to escort the remaining dusk riders and to make sure that they didn't break free. They were marched down the streets of Priortage. Mud sucked at their boots and the mist hung in gossamer waves that dampened their skin. The only light came from The Barn Swallow where voices were raised in merriment. Silas saw a woman in a tight corset step through the swinging doors to light a smoke from a cigarette holder. The other homes and businesses were dark.

A guard came running as they reached the town jail. "We've trapped the fat man," he said gasping for air. "He only made it as far as the ale cellar before we caught up with him."

"Did you make an end of him?" asked another of the guards.

"Well, no," the other guard said, chagrined. "He fought off three of us and made it down the stairs. There's no other way in or out of the cellar. The first guard that rushed him gained a prick for his trouble that he won't soon forget. The second was carried out on a stretcher. Don't worry though. We have him trapped. There's nothing down there but crates of ale and meat so old it would poison him if he tried to eat it. All men must sleep, and when he does we'll make sure he never wakes."

Stocks that were made from the same twisting vines as everything else in town stood in front of the jail as an ominous sign of the mist people's justice. Jonquil was marched to the device, and the stocks were opened with a clasp on the side.

"Take the others inside. Fyodor decreed that this one will serve as a warning," a guard said.

As Silas watched, his uncle was placed in the stocks and the gate was swung shut and locked. Jonquil looked up in time to take a fist across the face from one of their captors. His uncle grunted, but showed no other reaction. "That's for bringing ill to our peaceful town," the guard said.

"The only ill comes from the old god Eldritch and his lackey Bemisch," Jonquil said. He spit blood on to the ground. How long he could last with his head and arms through the torture device was a bet Silas wouldn't want to wager.

"Don't — mention — his — name," the guard said with a quiver of fear. He turned to the others and barked. "Why do you stand there? I told you to take them inside!"

The jail consisted of one room with a desk and a cot where the sheriff slept. The old man who was sitting behind the desk stood to attention when the guards led Silas and Trainer into the room. Behind him were two cells whose bars were made from sand-colored wood.

"We brought you some house guests, Blix," a guard said. He eyeballed the jailer. "You been dipping into honey hooch again? Last thing we need is for you to start hallucinating while you're watching these two."

"I look like I been?" Blix said defiantly. The sheriff's face was peppered with stubble. One of his blue eyes bulged larger than the other. He didn't have teeth and kept sucking on his lower lip. A battered tin star was pinned to a gray shirt that used to be white. He moved with a bow-legged gait. When he got closer, Silas smelled unwashed armpits and sweat.

"What in the name o' the mist have we got here?" Blix said, eying Silas. He turned to the guards. "This one ain't more than a boy."

"Riders. Fyodor wants them locked up until he decides what to do with them. Now no more questions, old man. You're to put them in a cell and forget they are here until we come back in the morning," the guard said.

"Always giving me orders," Blix muttered under his breath. He fumbled out a ring of keys and went to one of the cells. He opened it and turned to the guards. "Well stop your jilly-jabbering and bring 'em here. They ain't gonna lock themselves up."

Silas and Trainer were shoved into the cell, and the door locked behind them.

"Save yourselves some effort, boys," Blix said. "These bars are made from living wood. 'Tain't nothing stronger in this sorrowful world. Regrow thicker than the eyes of a gili worm if you manage to break or saw through. And believe me; you don't want to try that. You don't want to try that at all. Mind your cellmate as well. He's got teeth." The old man chuckled and wiped his nose with his sleeve.

"Quit your yapping, old man," the guard said as

they prepared to leave. "And remember what I said about the honey hooch."

The guards streamed back out of the jail. Once they were gone, Blix took a pot from under his desk and poured a shot of golden liquid into a glass and tossed it down in a gulp. He put his feet up on the desk and began mumbling. "Been doing my job longer than that boy's been alive," he said.

Trainer sat on one of the cots in the room. Ruby moonlight came through chinks in the walls of the jail cell. Silas tested one of the bars but it felt harder than steel.

"Forget it, boy," Trainer said. "Do you think they would have built a cell of something so easily broken? The mist people learned to tame the living wood back when this place was new. There's no way out except the key that old reprobate carries around his neck."

"So what are we to do?" Silas asked.

"Do? Well, we sit right here until Fyodor calls us back before him. How long do you think we'll last then? With the witch prying into every crevice of our minds and fanning all the dark thoughts we've ever had?"

"Jonquil said Bemisch could only control a person if they were corrupted," Silas said pacing the cell.

"Aye and we all are. It's only a matter of degree. Believe me, if she pokes and prods you long enough, your mind and all its secrets will unravel. Why do you think Larkspur fled like a wee child?

She was cracking him like an egg against a pan."

"We can't just sit here. We have to warn the others," Silas said.

"When you find a way out let me know," Trainer replied. He laid on the cot and put his hands behind his head. A crack of moonlight hit his face and Silas saw the scowl written across his features.

Silas paced the earthen floor, his thoughts racing. Trainer was right. There was no way out but the old man's keys. If they didn't get help soon though, none of it would matter. Eldritch and the witch controlled everyone in the town. And that raised another question: Where was the old god? If the witch felt comfortable enough making her presence known, why hadn't they seen Eldritch? Where was he? Silas grasped the bars and stared out at the sheriff. He had never known such despair in all his 12 years of life. How had the Blackwoods handled the burden they carried for so many centuries? Surely, other members of his family had been in tighter spots and persevered.

Blix poured himself another shot of the honey-colored liquor and slurped it down. When he was finished he sang:

"My Jennie of the valley
I met you in the mist
Where the sweet vine grows
And the clear water flows
And love how it sparkled
Like the morning dew

Upon our first kiss."

The sheriff leaned his head back and fell asleep. His snores sounded like the rattle of a train piston.

Something shifted in the next cell, and for the first time Silas noticed a figure curled on one of the cots.

"Blaaaaaaaccccckkkkwwwooooooodddd," said the voice in a silky whisper.

Silas jumped and his pulse quickened. As he watched, a blanket slid from the figure on the cot and a spindly bat-like figure stood on clawed feet. The creature was covered in coarse fur with inky eyes and v-shaped holes instead of a nose. With an unfolding motion, wings shot from behind the monstrosity spanning the width of the cell. The wings made a rattling motion like an animal about to strike. "I smell Blaaaaaaaccccckkkkwwwooooooodddd."

"Step away from the bars, boy," Trainer said. "That thing must be what the sheriff was talking about when he said to watch our cellmate."

The winged figure came close enough that Silas could see its needlelike nose and black orb eyes. Malformed ears jutted from the top of its head like antennae. It tilted its head back and forth watching Silas.

"What is it?" Silas asked.

"How should I know?" Trainer said irritably. "There are thousands of entities living in the Gardens, and people expect the dusk riders to remember each one."

"I'll tell you what it is," Blix said. His eyes were still closed and his head was tilted back. He spoke from a drugged stupor. "One of the strays that escaped from Nightfall Gardens. Ain't nothing nice about it at all. Watch out if the nasty bugger wraps its wings around ya. Caught it at the Widow Shamus's. Its wings were drawn tight around a full-grown heifer. 'Tweren't nothing more than a pile o' bones by the time we pried it loose. I'll be glad when they burn it so I won't feel those black eyes watchin' me no more."

With that, Blix tailed back off into slumber. He muttered and twitched, his body convulsing as if he were possessed, until his chin dropped on his chest and he began snoring again.

"What's wrong with him?" Silas asked.

"Honey hooch," Trainer said sourly. "The man's a weak fool. It floods your body with pleasure and makes you forget pain and misery. The moment you're sober though, it all comes back worse than ever. When you grow older you'll learn it's not so easy to forget the memories that torment a man."

The bat-like creature in the other cell rattled its wings and continued watching Silas and the dusk rider. It opened its mouth exposing a pink tongue. "Blaaaaaaaccccckkkkwwwwoooooooodddd, sooooo hungryyyyy."

"I'll Blackwood you," Trainer said, exploding from the cot. "If you don't shut your gaping maw of a mouth, I swear to the old gods I'll drive a blade right through that pea brain of yours and scatter your ashes until not even the wind can find them."

The bat-like creature screeched a challenge in response, its wings rattling so fast that they were a blur. As quickly as it began it stopped, and the creature went back to its cot and folded its wings back over itself.

"It'll shut up for now," Trainer said. His face was gray and haggard. "Dawn is coming soon, and those from the Gardens are at their weakest then."

"Thank you," Silas said.

"Don't thank me," Trainer sneered. "It's a dusk rider's job to keep you precious Blackwoods alive. God knows why. Just keep your yap shut and let me sleep. If anything, tomorrow will be worse than today." On that negative sentiment, the dusk rider curled up in his cloak and went to sleep.

Sleep wouldn't come for Silas though. He listened to Blix in his honey hooch slumber and the almost imperceptible breathing of Trainer. From the other cell there was no noise at all. Silas got the distinct impression the bat creature was awake, brooding. Red moonlight turned rust as the coming gray dawn approached. It was then that he heard footsteps approach from the other side of the wall. They stopped just outside of where he was jailed.

"Silas?" a female asked. The voice was surprisingly young and lilting.

"Yes," he whispered, shifting on the cot so he was closer to the wall of vines.

"Thank the spirits," the girl said. "After I saw your uncle in the stocks I didn't know what they might have done with you."

"Who are you?" Silas asked, keeping his voice low. He pressed one of his eyes against a chink in the vines and saw fiery red hair and milky pale skin.

"I'm your cousin, Mirabelle," the girl said. "I know you have a lot of questions but you'll have to be patient. It's not safe to speak here. What's important is that you listen right now."

"Okay," Silas said sitting up on the cot.

"Good," the girl said relieved. "Not all of us are under the spell of the witch or the old one. Our grandfather Fyodor is under their sway as are most of those in positions of power. They plan on holding a council meeting later to decide your fate. The witch has commanded them to burn you at the stake. I heard her foul and evil plan as she conferred with grandda' in his study. Fear not though, there are still friends on the council. He is going to delay the vote until the following day. So you must be ready tomorrow night. We'll come for you late in the eve when the witch is hunting and Blix is deep in a honey slumber."

The cold gray of dawn penetrated the cell now. Silas peered through the crack again. He saw rose lips on the other side. She couldn't have been much older than him.

"I have to go," Mirabelle said. "It's not safe to be out this early. Bemisch has many eyes in the village now. Oh, I almost forgot. Grandmother said to tell you to be strong."

Before Silas could respond, his cousin was gone and he was left listening to the sounds of Priortage starting its day. A cart rattled past the prison walls and a horse whinnied. Soon after that, a bell rang and a group of men passed as another work morning started in the village.

It was a long time before Silas fell asleep.

8

BLACKWOOD RITES OF PASSAGE

A sleepover was so unlike her "normal" duties as mistress of Nightfall Gardens that Lily was surprised the next morning when she realized how excited she was about her friend spending the night.

Even before Jonquil brought her here, Lily and Silas had lived unusual lives. Life on the road in a traveling theater troupe meant that they were regularly uprooted and seldom made friends. At some point she formed a shell around herself, and when one of the local children reached out with a gesture of companionship, Lily icily ignored it … and soon The Amazing Blackwoods would be off to the next town.

'I never got to be a child,' Lily thought as she made her way to breakfast. *'I never made friends; our mother was our schoolteacher and the road was our*

home.'

Ozy was setting a plate of hot buttery croissants and a pot of tea on the table as she entered. One of the mummy's bandages drooped into the jam dish as he served her. When she first came here, Lily would have chastised him with no thought for his age or the countless eons he'd served the family. But like many things over the past several months, she'd changed and now felt sympathy for the ancient bedraggled butler.

"Can I ask a question?" Lily said putting jam on a steaming croissant.

"I've found that when humans say, 'Can I ask a question', they've already decided that they *are* going to ask one," Ozy intoned, dust puffing from his mouth.

Lily let that pass. "Were you ever a child?" She took a huge bite of croissant.

"Oh me, oh my, that was a long time ago," the butler said in a drawn-out rasp. "I suppose all things must be young at one time. Hmmm. No, I mean, yes, yes, I do recall it so very vaguely. Just flashes really. My mother and father were among the first death warriors to guard the pharaohs. Watching them suck the life out a person was a sight to behold. I played around the Sphinx and pyramids and the sand was my home. Those early days, when I was safe in my mother's withered arms, were the best of my life. Other than that, my childhood was horrible, really. My only acquaintances were the children of death warriors.

The best part of being a child is the part that comes before you are aware that the world has teeth."

'He has a point,' Lily thought. *'Now that I know about this place I can never go back to being the person I was. Too much depends on making sure that Nightfall Gardens remains, at least until I find a way to destroy Pandora's Box once and for all.'*

"You're smiling," Ozy said, a cough of dust coming from him.

"I suppose I am," Lily said. "You made me remember something I'd forgotten."

"Glad to be of service, even if I don't know what I did," Ozy said.

Cassandra arrived not long after, lugging a valise, with her pet gargoyle Osbold perched on her shoulder. Lily demanded that she be allowed to step on the back patio so she could meet her friend's pet. Nothing that came from the gardens was allowed inside without the permission of the house. The little gargoyle was just as the green girl had described. Osbold was the color of quarry rock and the size of a small dog. His leathery wings were filled with tiny veins. He squawked with joy and excitement when he saw Lily and flew about her, buzzing in circles, finally landing on her shoulder, cooing and picking at her hair.

"He likes you," Cassandra said, setting her valise on the ground. "Though, he likes your brother as well. I don't know what that says about his taste."

Lily sighed. Her friend had a crush on her

brother and, of course, that meant she took every chance she got to insult him, just to prove that she didn't.

"Well, I like him, too. Don't I, Osbold?" she said tickling the gargoyle's chin. Osbold shrieked at her in pleasure. A low mist was hanging over the grounds today. From the patio, Lily could see three paths diverging in different directions. Down the hill to the left was the path that led to the White Garden, the greenest of them all. In the center was the Shadow Garden, where everything except the rose bushes seemed bleached of color, and to the right was the wall of shrubbery that blocked from view what was happening in the Labyrinth.

Cassandra turned to the gargoyle. "I'm going inside now and I'll be home tomorrow. You keep an eye on dad, alright?"

Osbold seemed to understand everything that she was saying. He squawked back at her and then lifted into the air and soared away.

Cassandra watched him fly off over the Gardens. "I hope he'll be okay," she said. "I've not been away from him since the first night I found him on one of the paths."

"Sure he will," Lily said. She picked up Cassandra's valise. "Now let's go inside. I can feel Polly watching us. She doesn't like me being out here."

Inside, the housekeeper was waiting to scold her. "Scared me half to death you did, stepping out in broad daylight for all the gardens to see.

Unnecessary risk is what I call it."

"I can't stay cooped up in here for all my life," Lily said. "I'll go mad."

"Better that, than the gardens being your final resting place or something worse," Polly fumed and slithered away leaving a trail of slime in her wake.

The walk to Lily's room took twice as long that morning. The house had expanded and added extra rooms, growing in size since breakfast. Lily felt the floorboards groan under her feet as they reached the third-floor landing. They passed an open doorway and saw Ursula inside making the bed. The glumpog whistled an off-key tune as she straightened the sheets. As usual, Lily felt the urge to weep when she saw the maid.

"Ah, there you go Miss, just the person I was looking for," Ursula said. Her stringy hair fell limp around the pointed chin of her heart-shaped face. Her soft brown eyes looked amplified as though she were looking through magnifying glasses.

"Why's that?" Lily asked, a heavy gloom falling over her.

"I just finished cleaning this room for your friend," Ursula said. "Miss Polly's instructions. Thought she'd be right comfortable here, she did."

The room was on the other side of the hall from Lily. It was small and tidy with faded silver wallpaper that bulged loose in places. A window looked out on the massive expanse of front lawn stretching to the main gates and the nothingness that existed beyond. The window was partially open and a faint breeze cleared the room of its musty odor.

Before Lily could say anything, the green girl was thanking Ursula. "This will do very well."

"My pleasure," Ursula said, giving a smile that made Lily's mood sink further. The heavy weight of existence pressed upon her. She stifled the urge to throw herself head-first through the window to the ground below. "I love going into those rooms ain't been opened in a long while. This one was nicer than most. Only nasties lurking here was a bunch of chatterbugs." The maid held up a bulging sack that writhed in her hands.

"What are *those*?" Cassandra asked, an eyebrow rising quizzically at the chattering sound coming from the sack.

"Got 'em out of the mattress," Ursula said. "Chatterbugs like to hide inside the stuffing and sneak out at night after a person's asleep. They'll eat your nose and fingers and bleed you dry. Silly little buggers." The glumpog giggled as though she were discussing kittens rather than nasty bloodsucking parasites. "Anyway, I got 'em all. Put a piece of raw meat inside of a sack on top of the mattress and they couldn't resist. You should have a right comfortable sleep now."

"Are you sure you don't want to stay in my room?" Lily asked. Right now she wanted nothing more than to curl up somewhere and cry until her tear ducts ran dry.

"No, I need my space. I can't — I don't like people near me when I'm not awake," Cassandra said.

If Lily hadn't been on the verge of tears, she would have asked why, but instead she swallowed. Her lips quivered with sadness.

"Right as rain then," Ursula said. "Enjoy your chinwag." With that, the maid picked up the bag of chatterbugs and left the room.

The mood lightened with each step that the glumpog took, until Lily felt like her old self.

"Well what do you want to do?" Cassandra asked when they were alone. "See if we can track down Desdemona? Try and uncover what the number 23 means?"

Lily took a deep breath. She'd been trying to avoid this moment for days. She finally spoke. "There's something I need to tell you about the Blackwoods that I learned while reading Abby's diary. I couldn't bring myself to believe it until we went into the catacombs and I saw it for myself."

"What is it?" Cassandra asked.

"It's a long story, better told with hot tea; someplace more comfortable than this room," Lily said.

A roaring fire crackled in the fireplace of the study. They took seats near the window that overlooked the Shadow Garden. As if Polly had read her mind, a silver teapot was waiting with finely patterned china cups.

Lily poured tea and watched the steam rise.

Outside, the day was the same drab gray as usual. Bruised storm clouds waited in the distance to deliver their payload.

"How much do you know about Blackwood history?" Lily asked, as they drank their tea.

"Only what you told me about Pandora's Box," Cassandra said. "You Blackwoods always been the ones in charge of the Gardens. The women rule from inside the house, while the men are put to work as dusk riders. Always to be separated."

"That's what I thought as well. That's what Deiva told me. And then I found my great aunt Abby's diary," Lily said. She pulled the slim, cracked leather volume from a pocket in her dress and set it on the table. "And you helped me crack the code when we went to visit Raga, the witch. But I wasn't completely honest about what I found inside."

"What do you mean?" Cassandra asked, her eyes narrowing.

"I need to start from when I opened the book and the words revealed themselves," Lily said.

"Okay," Cassandra said, waiting for Lily to drop a cannonball on her.

"You have to promise this won't change the way you think of me or my brother," Lily said.

"I doubt my opinion could be swayed from what I already think," Cassandra said.

Lily nodded and opened to the first page. "It all started on my grandmother Deiva's fourteenth birthday when Abby found her mother, my great-grandmother Ramona, sobbing inside her bedchamber."

She began to read from Abbey's diary.

"The sound of the party faded as I neared mother's bedchamber. As I climbed the stairs, I heard Deiva holding court over a group of dusk riders, telling them how she would be mistress of Nightfall Gardens one day. Oh, how she loves to preen, as though being cursed to this place is a great honor. I have to admit, though, my sister grows lovelier each day, while I seem destined to remain the bookish one, overshadowed by the great burden she bears.

I was passing my mother's room when I heard sobbing from behind her door.

"Mother, are you okay?" I asked entering.

"Not at all my little dove," she said, trying to regain her composure.

"Why?" I asked.

"Because I've tried to protect you from the terrors of what waits beyond childhood and, even though I've done my best, I can't stop the march of time," she said.

"I'm afraid I don't understand," I said.

"Come and sit," she said, patting the bed next to her. "I should have told you a long time ago, but as Blackwoods, our lives are already so difficult that I was hesitant to heap more misery on you."

By now, my curiosity overwhelmed my fear. I felt a tingle of cold fascination as my mother related the following story.

"We Blackwood women are the most cursed of the

cursed. From the time we're born we know our destiny is to live without feeling a moment of safety. It's a burden we've borne so long it's impossible for us to think of life beyond this dank house. Prometheus's punishment was so cruel that I think he must have been a demon from deepest hell. Or, perhaps, I'm wrong and this place is nothing more than a dream and we'll awake one day to laugh at those things we fear in the darkest hours of the night."

Mother removed an ivory-inlaid box from the mantle. "Did you know I used to have a sister?" she asked.

"I had an aunt?" I asked stunned.

"You did," mother said, opening the box. Inside was a sketch of a girl who could have passed as mother's double. She had the same raven hair and soft cheeks.

"Simone was my twin," she said. "In all things, we were the same, except for one."

"What was that?"

"She was braver than I was. And when the time came to take part in the rite of passage, it was she instead of me who went."

"Rite of passage?"

"The oldest Blackwood female in every family is called to enter the Shadow Garden at the age of 14, unless they can find another female family member to take her place."

"Your sister was the oldest?" I asked.

"No, I was by two minutes. By two minutes, my fate was sealed. From the day I came into this world that fact haunted my every waking moment. Each passing second was a torment until finally, I awoke on my fourteenth birthday. A huge banquet was held in the dining hall, only it was more of a wake. I wish I could claim that I was brave, but that couldn't be further from the truth.

I asked my father when I would have to go. Stony-faced, he said I must be patient; that this was a thing the Gardens decided.

"Weeks passed and I began to wonder if the moment was ever going to happen. One night I was told to come downstairs. My mother was waiting in the foyer with a black envelope clutched to her chest. 'It's come, at last,' she said. I wasn't sure whether to feel terrified or relieved that I no longer had to wait for the guillotine's blade to drop.

"With trembling hands, I opened the envelope. I swear I felt the cursed thing try and bite me. When the envelope was open, I clasped a piece of black paper with the most perfect white lettering I've ever seen. It said, 'Your attendance is requested in the Shadow Garden when the red moon rises. — The Smiling Ladies' Almost as a mocking afterthought, a caricature of three stick figures holding parasols was scrawled below.

"I was struck dumb with fright. Of all the monsters in the tangled briars of the Shadow Garden, none is as feared as those three porcelain characters who walk the paths in the cold, starless nights. (Mother was right. I've since scoured our library and much is written on the three skeletal females figures who seem to be at the impasse of every major tragedy since the dawn of humankind. The Mesopotamians and Egyptians have written about them, as well as the Celts and other inhabitants of old Europe. There's even a tale written of *"the Three Sisters" who visited the first emperor of China. They traveled only at night and were chased from the town by the palace guards after a series of mysterious deaths.)"*

"What did you do?" I asked.

"What could I do? I prepared for my demise. I said goodbye to the faithful servants including Ozy. The old mummy blubbered a regular dust storm. After that, father came from the Gardens, where he was on patrol. He was a hard man with no time for sentimental foolishness, but I saw sadness in his dark eyes.

"Finally, I went to visit my mother. Regal to the end, she tried to pretend nothing was happening. Only when the first red light mingled with dusk, did the tears flow from her eyes.

"Don't cry," I said. "For there's a good chance I'll be back before the cold knock of morning."

"It's not you I weep for," she said.

"Then who?" I asked, puzzled.

"For your sister," Mother said. She flung one hand at the windows as though she couldn't bear to see what was taking place outside.

I looked then, fear tearing at my heart. "Oh no," I exclaimed. "Oh no." But it was too late, Simone, my sister, was climbing into a black carriage pulled by a team of skeletal horses. A man in a black coat and top hat sat on the buckboard with his collar turned up and his features hidden in the shadows.

"You wouldn't survive," Mother said. "Your sister is stronger than you. I'm sorry, love."

All the cowardice I'd felt flooded me with shame, and

I did the only thing I could. I ran down the stairs and onto the lawn, but I was too late. The carriage was gone. By the time I raced to the Shadow Garden, only the trees stirred with the wind. From inside, I thought I heard gentle conversation and cruel laughter. Before I could do more, my father was dragging me away as I screamed Simone's name."

"Did you ever see her again?" I asked. Outside, Deiva and the party guests were oblivious to the tragic story Mother was sharing.

"Oh, she came back the next morning. They almost always come back," Mother said. "Some hardly seem the worse for the experience, while others are no more than a whisper of who they used to be."

Simone was different, Mother said. The brave, gregarious girl was lethargic and easily confused. She laughed hysterically for no reason and carried on conversations with people that weren't there.

"She began sleepwalking," Mother said. "I would hear her late in the night. Her bedroom door would open and I would slip out to follow after her and steer her back to bed. Most of the time, she went to the kitchen or the basement, where I would watch her crawl on the floor as if searching for an opening. Once, she tried to go out the front door. I pulled her back, but what I saw froze me to the marrow. Waiting at the edge of the Shadow Garden were three women."

"Another time when father was visiting, Simone hid behind a suit of armor on the second floor landing. When he passed, she gave him a shove that sent him tumbling down the stairs. Only by the grace of whatever force

runs this universe was he spared serious injury. No one would turn their backs on her after that. The babbling fits and periods of lunacy grew more frequent, until she was locked away in her room.

"The final glimpse I had of my sister is one that will haunt me until they carry my lifeless body to the pyre. The door to her room had been shut for months. Only my parents and the servants were allowed to see her. One afternoon, the door was left open a crack. It must have been a particularly difficult day or I'm sure that never would have happened. I peeked through the opening, and what I saw filled me with almighty horror. Simone was restrained on her bed with straps pinning her so she could barely move. The creature on the bed growled as my mother tried to feed her.

'You have to eat, darling or you'll never get better,' my mother said, but she knew that was a lie. Simone was never getting better. It was then that the maid spotted me at the door. Without so much as a word she slammed it shut. I never saw my sister again."

Mother finished her story as the laughter drifted up from below. The hour was growing late. I knew the dusk riders would soon head to the bunkhouse and Deiva and I would retire to our rooms.

"Shortly after that my sister died," Mother said. "At least that's what my parents told me. Now, I know the truth of what happened to Simone and the other Blackwood girls who've gone to the Shadow Garden."

"What is it?" I felt a dry lump of fear in my throat.

"They bury them; they bury them alive in the tombs. The ones that don't make it through whatever tests the

Smiling Ladies give them; they lock them inside the vaults where they sleep the sleep of the damned for all eternity."

"Why?" I said, my voice shaking.

"I don't know," Mother said. "To hide our shame? Perhaps they think a cure will be found one day. Perhaps, they can't bear to snuff the final flame of life from those whom they've loved so dearly. I know it's true though, because I've been there amongst the tombs below the kitchen. I've seen Simone's crypt with a slit cut on top so that she can see into the blackness. I saw and was too afraid to do anything. She saved me, and I was too terrified to save her. I couldn't tell either of you before now; it's too horrible. Better to grow up in ignorance."

"It's alright," I said, but already I was thinking of Deiva. She was one year older than me, but wasn't it true that she had always ignored what was happening around us, content to flirt with the dusk riders and take trips to the outside world when the gates were open? What chance would she stand against the Smiling Ladies? She made fun of me for reading the vast stack of moldering books about our family history in the library. Wouldn't that put me in better stead than her? I decided then that I would dedicate all my waking hours to finding Pandora's Box and breaking the curse that has loomed so long over my family. It is the only way to protect my sister. I must do it quickly as well, before a black envelope arrives bringing with it ill tidings.

Lily closed the book and looked at Cassandra,

who was enthralled by the story. She got up to stretch her legs and peered out of the same window that Abby and her mother might have looked out years before. She could see the rain squalls moving closer in the distance.

"There's much more that Abby wrote in her diary. Almost as many Blackwoods pass the test as are turned into whatever we found in the catacombs."

Cassandra noticed her friend was deep in contemplation. "What's wrong with you then? You look like you've seen a ghost."

Lily gave her the look of someone who has shouldered a massive burden only to find that there is more to come.

"My birthday is in a month," Lily said. "I'll be fourteen."

9
MIRABELLE AND THE GREAT ESCAPE

"Wake up, you louses. This ain't no inn with a feather bed where ya eat fresh fruit from a maiden's hand," Blix bellowed. He banged a tin cup against a silver tray outside of Silas's cell.

The boy lurched awake from a fitful sleep. The bruised light of morning filtered through chinks in the wall. By its color, he could tell he hadn't gotten more than three hours of sleep. Silas sat up and stretched. His muscles were tense and sore. His mind was murky and it was difficult to concentrate. It was shaping up to be a bad day.

"You heard me, ya pug-ugly son of a bat," Blix said, hammering the cup and tray with frantic insistence. The winged creature shifted in the next cell, but didn't unfold its wings.

"Stop your pounding, old man, or a doctor will have to remove that cup from your backside," Trainer growled. The dusk rider was sitting on his bunk with his knees under his chin. He didn't look amused.

"Tough one, eh?" Blix said. "We'll see how tough you are when the flames rend your flesh and your eyes pop and hiss like eggs on a hot skillet." The sheriff chuckled. "They'll be voting on what to do with you soon, and it won't be long before you meet your maker. All your sass won't help then, will it? And while your skin's bubbling like a sausage over a fire, old Blix will be cozy here with his feet up on his desk. So, think on that!"

The sheriff looked just as bedraggled as he had the night before, except that he'd wetted his hair and run his fingers through it, plastering it to his forehead. His face was stippled with whiskers, and crow's feet ran in jagged lines from around his eyes. He picked up a bucket with a ladle. The smell of oatmeal filled the jail.

"Now, why don't you hold your tongue and have some of Blix's famous morning oatmeal topped off with his secret recipe?" he said winking. "Take my word. It'll take the edge off and make your day more bearable."

"Aye and no doubt we'll see flying dragons and visions of our past loved ones as well if you've spiked it with what I think you have," Trainer said. He turned to Silas. "Don't touch it boy, he's poured honey hooch into it. You'd be no good after that.

Who knows what challenges we have to face. It'll be that much harder if we're unable to control our minds."

Blix frowned, the deep lines drooping to his chin. "He's a fool, lad. I'm offering you a chance to deaden the pain. You'll never even feel the flames until it's too late. One fella to another, I'm giving you the same compassion I'd hoped to be shown."

Silas shook his head. "No thanks."

"To the White Garden with both of you then," Blix said, waving a hand in disgust. "You can't say I didn't try and do anything for ya. Which is more than this soulless blighter can." The sheriff spit at the cell where the bat creature was yet to stir. "I don't know why Fyodor is makin' me keep this thing alive. In the old days, we'd have lopped its head off as soon as we caught it. I don't like it, I tell ya. I don't like it at all."

Blix shambled bowlegged over to the other cell and pushed a half-filled bowl through an opening with his foot. Silas didn't have time to see its contents before the bat-creature flapped out of the bed. In one fluid motion it was across the cell, its wings encircling the bowl. Slurping noises filled the cell.

"Makes a man sick to his stomach," Blix said. The sheriff closed his eyes as if he were being transported somewhere outside of the dingy cell.

"What is it?" Silas asked.

"Blood," Trainer said.

"Cow's blood," Blix said, popping his enlarged

eye open. "Let's get that straight. One of the guards brings it to me fresh every morning."

"You ever think to ask why?" Trainer said.

"Ain't my job," Blix said. He straightened the filthy shirt that contained his sheriff's badge. "Court wants me to keep that damnable thing alive, and that's what I'm gonna do."

"You look like the kind of man that takes orders," Trainer sneered. He flipped on his side and turned to the wall.

"Now see here," Blix said, but when it was obvious Trainer wasn't going to respond, he dropped it. The old sheriff's shoulders slumped. He doled out a big bowl of the oatmeal for himself. "Shame to let this go to waste," he said.

Silas watched in horror and fascination as the bat creature opened its wings and the bowl fell out and rolled on the floor. It was so shiny and clean that he could see his distorted reflection in the hammered tin. The creature found its way to the darkest corner of the cell and folded its wings over itself. It slept standing.

The rest of the morning Silas spent thinking about Mirabelle. Who was she? Could he trust her? What if the council vote was rigged, and he and Trainer were marched to the pyre later that afternoon? And what of his uncle? What torment was he enduring?

Blix started feeling the effects of the honey hooch. He put his buckled shoes up on the desk and sang "Jennie of the Mist" in his not altogether unpleasant voice. He was just finishing it for the dozenth time when two of the guards from the night before came into the jail.

"In it again, are you, old man?" a guard said angrily. "Fyodor isn't going to like it."

"The only reason he need know is if ya tell him," Blix said. A goofy grin lightened the harsh features of his face.

"Just see you don't get so far into your cups you begin to think you've got bugs crawling on your skin like the last time. If anything were to happen to these two, they wouldn't be the only ones burned on the pyre."

"Does it *look* like anything is going to happen to them?" Blix said. He pulled his feet off the desk and they smacked on the ground. "Rub your eyes and see what I do: one man and one boy snug as a cherry fox curled in a tree inside that yonder cell. Give the bars a shake. Go ahead, don't be shy. Try as ya might they won't move an inch. All is well taken care of. So, take your threat and walk it back across the muddy street. An old man is entitled to whatever pleasure he can find."

One of the guards snorted. "Aye, but pleasure can turn to pain if they should get free. Keep that in what remains of your poor besotted mind."

The guards left. The long afternoon dragged on. Silas tried to tell Trainer about Mirabelle, but the dusk rider waved him off.

"If I'm going to die, let me die in peace without you babbling in my ear," Trainer said.

Wagons rattled by outside of the cell. A bell rang. He heard children talking and the sound of laughter as women passed. Priortage was at the apex of its business day. The light began to dim inside the cell.

The guards came back when the red moon was peeking through the slits in the wall.

"They've postponed the vote until tomorrow," one of the guard said. "It looks like they're your problem for one more night."

"And what of the devilish creature?" Blix asked, nodding toward the other cell.

"No word. Fyodor wants you to keep it safe until he decides what to do with it," the guard said.

"I don't like it. I don't like it at all," Blix muttered.

"Nobody's asking for your opinion. Just keep them safe until the morrow," the guard said.

When the guards left, Blix was in a tizzy of anger. "I been sheriff here more years than that boy's been alive and he tells me, 'No one cares about your opinion.' Bah, to the Gardens with him."

He pulled the jug from under his desk and poured himself a glass of the golden liquid. "All three of ya heard what he said. Keep your yaps shut and enjoy the fact that ya live for one more day."

The sheriff must have been in a particularly sour mood, because he drank a second and then third glass of honey hooch. By then, the sounds had quieted outside and the last of the workers had gone home for the day. From far way, Silas could hear laughter and music. He wondered absently if Aiden Cogden was playing for patrons of The Barn Swallow.

Blix was spellbound by the honey hooch. He swatted at his face in a drunken stupor and spoke with a thick voice. "Get 'em off me. Let me be," he said. The sheriff placed his head on the desk, and soon the sound of snoring filled the jail.

Trainer came alive and sat up on his bunk. "What was it you wanted to tell me earlier then? The sheriff's a fool, but he must be a wily fool to have kept his job for so long. Go on, speak."

Silas told him about the conversation he had the night before with his cousin.

"This could be a cruel trick, the kind Bemisch would love to play. Then again, what other options are there?" Trainer said. "Every second we're here is one that we're closer to death. I've known your uncle many years, but, as strong as he is, one more day in the stocks will kill him. For that reason alone, let's hope she told the truth."

The hours drifted past, and with each second, Silas grew more fearful something had gone wrong. Maybe it wasn't safe for his cousin to be about? Maybe the plan had been uncovered? Or what if the witch finally gained control of her and his grandmother? Just when he thought he couldn't stand it any longer, there came a soft knock on the jail door. The knocking grew louder. Still Blix didn't wake from his drugged slumber. The front door opened and a slight figure entered, closing it quickly behind her. Silas sucked in a deep breath when he saw his cousin for the first time. She was one of the girls they had passed when they'd arrived in the village, the one who stared so intently at him.

Mirabelle wore a blue cloak that shrouded her face. She pushed it down and red hair spilled out. She had the same milky white skin as the rest of the people in the town, and her eyes were speckled green. She looked toward the sheriff, but Blix didn't stir. She came over to the cell.

"Hello cousin," she said, putting her fingers between the bars and grasping his hand. "How many cups did Blix drink?"

"Three that I counted," Silas said.

"Then he'll be in a deep slumber until well past dawn," she said. Mirabelle smiled at the dusk rider. "You must be Trainer."

"The time for introductions is when this jail is behind us," he said brusquely.

"Of course," Mirabelle said. She went to Blix's slumped figure and slid the key from around his neck. In another moment, the lock clicked and the door swung wide.

"Follow me," Mirabelle said, pulling the cloak back over her head.

"What will happen to the sheriff?" Silas asked following her.

"Who cares?" Trainer said.

131

"He'll likely be called before the council and punished," Mirabelle said.

"The pyre?" Silas asked.

"Could be," Mirabelle said, glancing at him, and there was a troubled look on her face. "But otherwise it would be death for the both of you."

"Put him in the cell," Silas said. "We can make it look as though someone jumped him and got the better of him."

"Frig that," Trainer said. "While you dally, I'll free your uncle from his shackles." The dusk rider pushed past Mirabelle and into the night.

"Help me," Silas pleaded.

"He would not do the same for you," Mirabelle said, but then she shrugged.

She and Silas looped their arms under Blix's shoulders, dragged him to the cell and dropped him onto one of the bunks. They locked the door and placed the keys on the desk.

"Okay, let's go," Silas said.

At that moment, the jailhouse door opened. They both turned expecting to see Trainer and Jonquil, but instead one of the guards faced them. He must have been on his nightly rounds. In one hand he held a lantern and in the other a spear.

"What do we have here?" he said sneering. "A dusk rider who isn't old enough to shave and a sweet treat of a wench. Fyodor will give me a promotion for this."

He lunged at Silas with the spear, but the boy jumped backward.

"You're quick, stripling, but my staff has a long reach," the guard growled. He lunged again, and this time Silas felt a burning pain as the tip of the spear punctured his arm.

"Mirabelle, run!" Silas said.

Had Silas known his cousin better he would have understood she had no intention of doing any such thing. A dagger flashed from her boot and was sticking from the guard's shoulder before Silas realized she'd thrown it. The guard screamed and stumbled against the cells.

"I'll kill you for that," he said, yanking the blade free. He was standing with his back against the bars of the cell when the bat creature struck. All day it had been immobile, asleep standing up with its wings folded, but the smell of blood brought it to life. Its wings unfolded through the bars and grasped the guard jerking him into a deadly embrace. The guard's muffled scream seemed to last forever. Before Silas or Mirabelle could react, they heard the creature feasting on rich crunching bones.

"Let's go," Mirabelle said grabbing Silas by the hand. "He's already dead."

They fled into the mist that swept the streets and obscured everything around them.

"I have to find my uncle," Silas said. The fog was so thick he couldn't see in either direction.

"This way," Mirabelle said leading him to the stocks. They arrived just as Trainer freed Jonquil. His uncle looked gaunt and exhausted. He tried to smile, but Silas could tell it was taking everything he could muster.

"About thought I was finished," Jonquil said. "My head took a few hard knocks from the stones that the village children threw at me, but otherwise I'm fine."

Trainer put his arm around Jonquil and helped hold the dusk rider upright. "Took you long enough. Now what's the second part of your grand plan?" He asked Mirabelle.

"There's a wagon waiting for us," she said.

They turned into an alley and followed it past a shop where a weary looking baker in a white smock was baking bread for the coming morning. When they came out the other end of the street, a wagon drawn by two horses awaited them. A hunched figure wearing a hood sat on the buckboard.

"Climb in," Mirabelle said. "I'll explain everything when we get away from here."

Silas and Trainer lifted Jonquil into the wagon, where he collapsed.

"What about Larkspur?" Silas asked as the horse started off into the mist.

"Your fat friend seems to have gone mad," Mirabelle said. "He's trapped himself in the ale cellar and skewers anyone who tries to get him. They say he must be superhuman to exist only on sour ale and the fetid meats down there."

"It's the perfect diet if you knew him," Trainer said.

"There's little we can do for him now," she said. "The important thing is to get you away. We know a cabin a few hours north where you should be safe. It's where your uncle went the last time he visited."

"What about my grandmother?" Silas asked as the wagon bumped out of the village into the thick black of night.

The woman on the buckboard turned and Silas saw her face clearly under the hood. "*She* can only go with you a bit of the way, as much as she wishes otherwise," his grandmother said.

10

AN ANEMOI'S DEADLY TIDINGS

The storm finally settled over Nightfall Manor. The rain drummed its fingers against the windows and ran in rivulets down the glass. A squall was building up over the Gardens. Outside, the trees whipped and gave a horrible moaning sound. The perpetual dusk turned the color of a bruise on a rotten fruit. Flashes of blue lightning left afterimages in the sky.

"Never seen it like this," Polly said, slithering into the room, leaving a glistening trail in her wake. She swept up the tea tray. "Best you stay here until I fetch you for dinner. Strange things are about tonight, strange things indeed."

Glass shattered inside the house, followed by pitiful wailing: *"My eyes. What happened to my eyes? Why can't I see?"* Terrible moaning came from somewhere else. The hair rose on Lily's arms. A tiger roared in a nearby room, sounding as if it were killing prey. Knocking started up one side of the wall and traveled down the other. Other noises were there as well: chains rattling, echoing footsteps, whispers that tickled their ears but emanated from nowhere at all, babbling voices of the damned. A huge boulder sounded like it was rolling down the hall outside of the room.

"What was *that*?" Cassandra asked when the noise faded.

"I can tell you what's causing it," a rasping voice said.

The three turned to discover Ozy, the ancient butler. He'd entered while they were distracted.

"Well, what is it?" Lily asked. She felt a spike of irritation that there was one more secret Nightfall Gardens had yet to play.

"An anemoi," the decrepit butler said, a wisp of dust exhaling from his parchment lips. "At least that was what Master Cornelius called it. I've only seen it twice before in all my long years here."

The house went wild with sound. Thousands of doors banged open and shut. Voices of the dead giggled in merriment. The overwhelming smell of jasmine filled Lily's nostrils, its sweetness almost suffocating her. At the same moment, a cold hand pressed against her chest and began pushing the air from her body. She gasped, trying to draw breath. That was when Polly screamed. "Oh no, you don't. Get out of here, you undead fiend." The air rushed back into Lily's lungs, and she gulped in oxygen.

The housekeeper was chasing the barely discernable form of a ghost toward the fireplace. The spirit looked back once before it disappeared into the fire and Lily saw the bearded features of a man as it merged with the flames.

"What is an anemoi?" Lily gasped when she could breathe again.

Ozy rubbed his sandpapery hands together. "It's a storm of sorts. Master Cornelius said they only come to Nightfall Gardens once every couple of hundred years when the energy of all the things here comes to a head. It's a safety valve for the well-being of this place. Otherwise, the anger, hatred and other negative emotions would explode. An anemoi only happens when the Gardens are at their most restless. When it passes, things are better for a while."

"How long do they last?" Lily spoke loudly to be heard over the sounds of the house.

"Sometimes hours, sometimes days," Ozy said laconically. "The first with Master Cornelius was over by the rise of the red moon. My second anemoi kept Mistress Vargitan in her chambers for a week. What a state the house and Gardens were in after that!"

"Are we supposed to just stay here until it's finished?" Cassandra asked. The rain was pounding on the glass with such force that the Gardens looked like little more than a sodden smudge. "My father and Osbold are out there somewhere."

"And he'd want you safe until this passes," Polly explained.

Cassandra gritted her teeth. "What he'd want and I want are two separate things. If I decide to walk out that door, no one best stop me."

"I'm afraid I couldn't allow that, Miss," Polly said. Her gelatinous eyes squeezed to the size of squashed grapes.

"Don't make me salt you, you slimy thing," Cassandra grumbled

Polly gasped. "I can hardly believe my ears. Thought you had better manners than that, I did. Once Polly's trussed you up like a Devonshire ham, we'll see how smart your mouth is."

"Both of you calm down," Lily commanded. Her head was throbbing from the incessant noises coming from every direction. "The last thing we need is to be at each other's throats."

Something crashed against the wall hard enough to unmount an oil painting of one of her ancestors. The painting fell and ripped on a chair. The door swung open, and Ursula entered with a luminous smile on her face. "What a party this is! I haven't had this much fun in ages."

She picked up the hem of her maid's uniform and twirled across the room. "I wish wot someone had told me beforehand though. I would have gussied myself up for the occasion."

"Glad to see someone is having fun," Cassandra groused.

All of the anger fled the room when the

glumpog entered and was replaced by a soul-crushing depression that saturated every fiber of Lily's being. What was the point of all of this? What was the point of anything?

If Polly felt the same dismal feelings as Lily, it didn't show on her blank face. "Why aren't you at your post?" she asked.

Ursula laughed warmly and waggled her unibrow. "Came to tell you there's a fire in the kitchen. Right beautiful it is as well. The way the flames are licking at everything. It's toasty down there, it is."

"Fire?" Polly said and cursed. "C'mon Ozy we have to —."

"I'm already with you, ma'am," the ancient butler said. He moved with an incredible slowness but the fact that he was already at the door meant that he took the threat seriously.

"You two stay in this room. No matter what happens," Polly said. "Can I count on you to do that?"

Both of the girls nodded yes, though Lily was so downhearted, she wondered why the servants didn't just let the whole place burn to the ground and them along with it.

Ursula followed the others to the door. "Do you think I can take off early and join the fun?" she asked as the door closed.

The two girls were alone in the room again. Lily felt her spirits lift as she always did when the glumpog was out of sight.

"You're not really going to go out in this?" Lily asked.

"I have to," Cassandra said. "What if something has happened to my father?"

"I'm sure he's fine," Lily said. She reached to touch her friend, and the green girl jerked away, a scowl mixed with fear on her face.

"I told you not to touch me. No one can ever do that. Don't you understand what would happen?"

"No, I — what are you talking about?"

"I can't tell you. I can't tell anyone. You wouldn't want to be my friend anymore. I was stupid to think I could ever have friends," Cassandra said.

'Why can't anyone touch her?' Lily thought. While she mulled over the question, the volume began to drop in the house. First, the doors stopped slamming, followed by the lowering of the ghostly voices until they were gone. The roaring, gibbering and all of the other noises that filled the house over the past hour dwindled.

"Do you hear that?" Lily asked when the sound was gone.

"What?" Cassandra asked.

"Exactly," Lily said. "It's stopped, the anemoi is dying down."

The green girl went to the window and looked out on the rain that steadily fell. The trees were no longer bending with the wind. The rainstorm continued but it was no worse than many others Lily had witnessed.

"Um, who's this?" Cassandra said, startled. A young girl with straight black hair and a black dress with white ruffled collar had appeared in the chair across from her. The ghostly girl had a serious look.

"Abigail," Lily said. "What are you doing here?" It was always a portent of something else when her great-aunt appeared.

As they watched, Abby began writing on a window beaded with perspiration.

"What's she writing," Cassandra asked.

Lily watched her aunt make the letter R on the glass and then U. Abigail continued to write, seemingly unaware that they were leaning so close. When she was finished, the ghost of Lily's great-aunt dropped from the chair.

Already the letters were fading, but there was no mistaking what they said: "R U N."

Lily and Cassandra saw the same alarmed look in each other's eyes. The flames in the fireplace flickered and dimmed as though something was drawing the air from the room. Someone was coming. An electric charge coursed through the clammy air of the house. An ill feeling seeped through them the way that the northern lights shimmered through the night sky on the other side of the gates. The sensation penetrated Lily to her core.

"We have to get out of here," Lily asserted.

"I know," Cassandra replied. Her friend's face revealed an emotion Lily had never seen in her before: fear.

There was no time to waste. Whatever was coming would be there soon. They fled into the hall. Candles burned low in their holders, the fat wax dripping down their sides. The dull yellow light cast circles on the wall. The wallpaper was a faded rose that made the hall look darker than normal. A frayed carpet ran the length of the floor. The girls instinctively turned the way they always went. A figure stood at the end of the long hall, so far away that he looked like an illusion. The creature's arms were spindly, and it was hunched like a toad. As they watched, the creature took one sliding step toward them. It made a wet burbling noise as it sucked air.

"This way," Lily said, darting in the opposite direction.

They ran past door after closed door, down the endless hallway, until a sharp pain into Lily's side and the two slowed to catch their breath.

"Where — are — we — going?" Cassandra asked, gasping for air.

Lily slipped Abby's diary from her pocket. A map inside showed some of the immovable features of the house as well as secret paths leading to the Gardens.

"There's a staircase ahead," Lily said. "If we get there, we can circle back to the dining room."

"It was a trap," Cassandra said, when they'd set off again.

"What was?" Lily asked.

"The storm, the fire in the kitchen. Don't ask me how, but the whole point was to draw Polly and the others away so you would be left alone."

Her friend's words reeked of the truth. All of her training over the past months, and she felt as helpless as the night the emissaries tried to kill her. She'd sworn that would never happen again, and yet here she was, as powerless as ever.

"What do you think it is?" Lily asked after they'd walked for a several minutes.

"An assassin of some sorts, no doubt. I wouldn't let the way he moved fool you. I've grown up in the Gardens, and often the most innocent seeming things are the most deadly," Cassandra said.

The hallway narrowed around them, subtly at first. The walls and ceiling closed in a little at a time. The rose wallpaper gave way to dirty marble. One second, the girls were surrounded by dripping candles; the next, torches hung along the walls. Up ahead was the last closed door. Beyond that, marble arches emptied into darkness.

"The stairs should be somewhere," Lily said.

The air smelled stale, like old earth and the rotten tang of overripe fruit. Faded frescoes adorned the walls. Lily gasped, as much at the contents of the work, as at their beauty. One section depicted a beautiful girl with white-blond hair standing like a giant over the three Gardens. In the Gardens, spirits twined along her legs as though they were enveloping her. She saw the Smiling Ladies, as well as shades, bogeys, witches, goblins, winged serpents, old gods and assorted evils she didn't know existed. There was so much detail that she could have studied the paintings for hours. Every being in the gardens was represented in the frescoes.

Cassandra traced her fingers over the wall. "It's you," she said. "You're the girl in the painting."

"Me?" Lily replied, dumbfounded. She stared closer. It was true that the girl resembled her, but how could it be? The fresco looked thousands of years old.

"Look," Cassandra said, pointing at a detail Lily would have missed, so subtly was it painted. Flaking away on the fresco was a mark that would have been illegible given more time. The numeral XXIII was painted over a black castle in the center of the Shadow Garden.

"The crypt!" Lily said. "It's what we saw written in Pandora's tomb."

The green girl smiled. "You Blackwoods are slow to learn, but once you get it, you don't forget."

"What's it mean though?" Lily pondered.

"It means the answer lies somewhere out there," Cassandra said, tapping the fresco.

Something gave one long dragging step behind them, and the torches flickered. Lily felt the same apprehension as she had in the study. The creature following them was drawing close. She looked down the hall but saw nothing but darkness stretching to infinity.

The two ran. The walls drew so close, Lily could

have touched them on either side. It gave her a claustrophobic feeling, as though she were being buried alive.

"Ahead," Cassandra said. The hall now widened, and they saw a fountain and spiral staircase. They came to a room where the clay tiles were cracked with age. The fountain was covered in the sculpted heads of sea horses, mermen and other creatures of the deep. Clear water trickled into the molded fountain.

As they passed the fountain, Lily saw movement in the water. Something mottled and black swam along the surface. Its back was riddled with green bumps, and a fin protruded from the water. The fish was no longer than her arm, and its face resembled that of a shrunken head that she'd seen once at a carnival. Mossy hair floated from its skull. There were no ears, only holes where its head merged with its body. Gills opened and she saw flashes of red as they expanded. The head formed a blunt point that merged with thick lips. The eyes were what troubled her most. They blinked as they followed the girls' progress across the room.

The two started up the winding stairs. They hadn't climbed more than a flight when an ear-piercing shriek echoed off the walls and ended abruptly. Lily looked over the railing and choked back tears. The humped creature with spindly arms was standing over the fountain. The fish thing was a dripping mass in its hands. The top half of the creature was gone. As she watched, the toad creature shoved the rest in his mouth and chewed. The assassin must have known it was being scrutinized. It looked up at Lily and pulled fish bones from its teeth.

"Gooooood," the being croaked smacking its lips.

Lily got a good look at what was trying to kill her and realized that she and Cassandra were wrong. Whatever was following them wasn't slow. It was playing with them, the way a cat might play with a bird that has a broken wing. In the weak light of the torches, Lily and the assassin locked eyes. The killer was a grotesquerie that she could have conjured in a nightmare. Its head was wide and flat, and its black eyes bulged far apart. Its nose tapered to a point and two slashes were all that marked it. The creature had no neck. Its head sat on top of a lily-covered breast, and its arms and legs ended in oversized webbed hands and feet.

"Go," Lily shouted. They set off up the stairs, taking them two at a time and not daring to look back. The stairs continued on and on, and still there didn't seem to be a way to get off of them. They ran so long that Lily's thighs burned and she grew lightheaded. She looked back and saw the toad creature dragging its bum leg up the stairs one at a time. All the while, it smiled revealing a mouthful of teeth that looked like arrowheads. She remembered then that Villon warned her someone was going to make an attempt on her life.

The top of the stairs finally loomed ahead. The

ceiling above was painted green and gold with stars, galaxies and constellations. Meteors ripped across the endless sky, and the old gods played in the patterns to those who could see them.

The floor looked like the galley of a ship. Burnished walls glowed with a dull sheen. The ground listed under them as though it swayed with waves. Lily even thought she smelled salt spray. The doors along the hall contained portholes. A rotting face with a gold earring, its head wrapped in a purple bandana, peered from one of the openings.

"Please run, this is such fun," the creature croaked behind them. The assassin hopped on its good leg, covering five feet at a time as he came after them. *'He'll be on us in a minute,'* Lily thought, as another stitch knifed her side.

"Ahead," Cassandra said. An open door lay no more than a dozen steps ahead of them. Lily stumbled after her into the room, and not a second too late. She had barely cleared the doorway when Cassandra swung the door shut and it came down hard on one webbed hand. Bones were crushed and green liquid sprayed from the wriggling fingers in the crack.

"H – e – l – p me," Cassandra said to Lily, shoving against the door as the frog creature bellowed and croaked on the other side.

"Out of the way," Lily commanded. She set herself against the door and felt the tremendous strength of the creature struggling to free its hand.

"Now!" She said. Cassandra let go and Lily loosened the door long enough for the assassin to yank his hand away, and then they slammed and bolted the door. It buckled as the monstrosity threw itself against the other side.

Lily searched the room. It looked like they were in a ship's cabin. A cot was pushed against one of the far walls and a small writing desk was covered in papers brittle with age. A ladder bolted to a wall, led upward.

"The desk," Lily said. The two dragged it over and lodged it against the door, which was splintering with every blow crashing on its ancient surface.

Cassandra looked at the ladder. "Ladies first," she said.

"You're never going to let me live my title down, are you?" Lily said.

"Nope," the green girl said.

Lily couldn't help but smile. Her friend was maddening, but there was no one she would rather have at her back. They scrambled up the ladder and into a crow's nest at the highest point of the house. This was the end of the line. There was nowhere else to go.

Cassandra leaned over the railing and whistled. "I wouldn't want to meet the ground from this height. The riders would have a wretched job picking up the pieces."

Lily looked over the edge and saw what her friend meant. The drop to the flagstones seemed impossibly far away. She drew in a sharp breath of misty air. The rain had slowed to little more than a drizzle. Was there ever such a view of the Nightfall Gardens as this? On one side, the Gardens were soaked and bedraggled with the sweeping tendrils of fog that coiled through them. The red moon was hidden behind rainclouds that moved quickly across the sky. Lantern light glowed from the bunkhouse where the dusk riders lived. Beyond that, the woods lurked, their branches reaching in every direction. On the other side was the wide magnificent lawn with a graveled path that led from the black iron gates that opened upon her world once a year. Past the high walls and the gate, there was nothingness.

The door in the room below shattered, and they could hear the toad creature gurgling and croaking. "I guess this is as good as any place for a last stand," Lily said.

The only sound in the crow's nest was the wind whipping the last of the rain against the house. Even the Gardens seemed to have fallen silent as if listening. The spell was broken when they heard the sound of the creature dragging its useless leg up the ladder.

"Get behind me," Cassandra said. The green girl rolled up the sleeves on her dress to expose graceful wrists.

"No," said Lily. "It's my fault he's after us."

"Stop thinking the world revolves around you, and trust me," Cassandra said. A blue flash of lightning illuminated her face. "There are things you don't know about me."

No sooner had she said that, than two bulbous eyes appeared above the edge of the trapdoor. The eyes were the size of ostrich eggs. The head came next, wide and flat, covered in bumps with scars crisscrossing its amphibian surface. Lily caught a whiff of pond scum as the rest of the assassin's head and shoulders appeared.

"Led me on a merry chase, you did," the toad creature croaked in a baritone. "No matter. I like to play with my food before I devour it."

The creature wriggled the rest of the way up the ladder and into the crow's nest. He opened his mouth in a loathsome smile when he stood before them.

"Always give Mugwump these sorts of jobs," the assassin gurgled. "The children of Bristly Bog used to tremble at the thought of me showing up at their window on a night like this." He sniffed the night air. "Many of their bones are still nestled there in the soft mud, where they're likely to stay until the final light burns out on this world. Not Mugwump though. No one remembers him anymore. He's not even a half-tale in Bristly Bog anymore. Nothing to show I ever existed except those bones and the sweet memory of their screams as I dragged them into the murk until their lungs filled with water."

Mugwump took another step toward them.

"But you won't forget, will you? I'll be the last

thing you see when your vision blurs and the final breath leaves your body. That's why they sent Mugwump. This is fun for him. The only warmth that burns in my blood is from knowing that one day the people of Bristly Bog will once more whisper my name in fear and barricade their doors at night because I might be lurking in the shadows to take their children. They won't forget me so easily then."

"Stay back and hold your tongue, you wart-bound monstrosity. We're not children who cringe in their beds with the coming of night," Cassandra said.

Mugwump dragged his lame foot across the floor of the crow's nest. The last of the anemoi moved off toward the nothingness beyond the gates. Thunder crashed. The ruby moon peeked from behind the rushing clouds and illuminated the rain-drenched Gardens.

"Don't mock Mugwump, green girl. There was a time when my name sent chills from one end of Bristly Bog to the other. Plowmen wouldn't walk the roads at nights and mothers kept candles burning in front of altars in the hopes that the old gods would protect their wee ones. But they didn't, no more than anyone can protect you."

Lily felt the railing against her back. She glanced down and in a flash of blue lightning saw Mr. Hawthorne standing on a path that led to the Shadow Garden. He was talking with a woman who was masked by the shadows. *'What's he doing?'* she wondered, but only for a fleeting instant. Suddenly; Mugwump sprang on his good foot and crossed the distance between them, landing so close to Cassandra that their lips could have touched.

"We'll see how well you mock with that pretty head torn from your body," he croaked.

"Well enough for you," Cassandra said, snatching the slimy flesh of the assassin's arm. It let out an anguished sound that was half croak, half squeal and jerked like a wriggling fish speared on a pole, but Cassandra was holding on with an iron grip. The assassin leapt across the crow's nest, dragging Cassandra with him. Still, she wouldn't relinquish her hold, even as she was pitched against the railing.

"What black art is this?" the toad creature croaked in agony. The smell of frying flesh wafted on the misty air. Wisps of smoke rose from where the green girl clenched his arm.

"You said you liked a jape, how does this suit you?" Cassandra jeered, clawing at its face with her other hand. Her fingers sank into the soft orb of its eye. A green flame burst from the socket, and Mugwump gave a grunt of terror.

'How can her touch burn as though acid were flung on flesh?' Lily thought.

"Its no wonder the people of Bristly Bog have forgotten you," Cassandra said. "You're forgettable. Not even worthy of a tale told on a cold winter's night."

"Don't — mock — me," Mugwump croaked as they grappled by the balcony. What happened next came so quickly that it left only an imprint on Lily's eyes. One second Cassandra and Mugwump were intertwined, and then the railing gave way with a tremendous crack and her friend disappeared with a scream into the night.

"Cassandra!" Lily yelled, but it was too late. Mugwump stood by the broken railing, his chest heaving up and down. The gristly socket of his burned eye drooled a viscous yellow liquid. He held his wrist at the same useless angle as his foot. He bellowed a tremendous victory croak.

"Warned her not to mock Mugwump," the assassin said. "Sent her right down, I did. Same as I'll do you."

Mugwump dragged his useless leg toward her. "Do you know why my foot is so twisted and broken?"

'Remember what Skuld told you,' Lily thought as she circled the crow's nest, facing him. *'Stay calm. Don't let him rattle you.'* She picked up a piece of shattered railing that was long enough to wield as a club. *'Keep him talking. Let him think you are nothing more than a little girl who can't defend herself.'*

"What happened then?" she asked, circling to where the moon shone into Mugwump's good eye.

"The good folk of Bristly Bottom set a trap for Mugwump. They grew tired of me taking their children, and a tired people are those to watch most closely. Why don't you put down your stick?

Wouldn't you like a nice long rest? One where you never have to stare upon the horrors of this world anymore?"

Lily *would* like a nice long sleep, but even with this creature gone, she knew the sound of her friend's scream would torment her forever. Best to keep him talking. "How did they trap you then?"

"With sweetmeats, the crying of a newborn baby. It drew me from the depths of the bog where I lived. I followed the sound through the night to a mud-covered hut with a straw roof where candlelight peeked between closed shutters. I waited until all was dark and crept quietly through the unlatched door. I should have known it was wrong then. I smelled no child, only the sweat and fear of men. I stepped into the room, peering at the tiny figure in the rough wooden cradle. I didn't notice the trap until my foot came down and it snapped with enough strength to take off the paw of a bear. Mugwump is no bear though. I pried it from my near-severed foot as the room lit with candlelight. I saw four village men with short axes and spears. In the crib was a wooden doll carved to look like a child."

Mugwump was circling closer to Lily, trying to lull her.

"They hacked and stabbed at me as best they could, but only one man escaped from that house, and him only to warn the others, scare them so they would never try such a thing again. Put down your weapon, child. We will sing songs of you in the Gardens, of how the last female Blackwood gave up without a whimper. The others will pay me well for this — oh yes, my broken body will be restored and the people of Bristly Bog will fall on their knees in front of me again."

"There's only one bit that you've got wrong," Lily said.

"What is that my sweet?" Mugwump said, inching closer.

"The part where you fail," Lily said. "No one will ever fear you again and they'll laugh when you come back empty-handed."

Mugwump came at her springing on his good foot, just the way that she imagined. Lily thrust upward with the splintered board and shoved it into the soft underbelly of the assassin as he came crashing down on top of her. The splinters tore her hands as she twisted the board into the spasming toad creature. Mugwump's wet and foul-smelling blood gushed over her dress and onto the floor of the crow's nest. The assassin kicked and clawed with his good arm as Lily wrenched the board that was buried deep in his belly. A series of weak guttural croaks came from his mouth. His weight was crushing the air from her and his foul skin, which had swum the deepest mires, pressed against her nose.

"You little fool," he croaked with a rattling wheeze. "I would have made your death easy. Others will come that won't be so kind."

Lily felt the last spasm of life leave Mugwump

and he collapsed on her. She would never have imagined that the beast weighed so much. *'Air,'* she thought as her mind began to grow cloudy, but whichever way she turned, the cold, damp flesh of the assassin filled her nostrils.

'Not like this,' Lily thought, and she gave one final shove. Her lungs burned, but panic was replaced with peace and a white light. Far away, she thought she heard voices as the last of her breath left her body. Something came closer in the whiteness, a figure that was undefined and then came into focus, a smooth face with worry lines buried into the soft folds of slug-colored flesh. *'Polly,'* Lily thought as she passed into unconsciousness.

11
COMING SIGNS OF ELDRITCH

The cabin stood high on a muddy hill, so far into the mist that Silas couldn't tell if he was awake or dreaming. The wagon creaked up the last of the trail as the first pale smudge of dawn appeared in the ghostly clouds that floated thick about them. Ancient pines marched down the hill in the direction they had come.

"You'll be safe here," Mirabelle said, looking back at Silas and the others. Jonquil was sprawled across the wagon-bed, his head on his nephew's lap. Trainer's legs dangled over the tailgate, and he looked as though he were chewing boiled leather.

His cousin pushed one red curl from her eyes. "Bemisch's power is weaker in the hills. Only the maker knows why."

"Maker?" Trainer said with a cruel laugh. "There's no maker, only the cold misery of life and an empty pit that awaits us all."

"You must have faith, good sir." Silas's grandmother spoke for the first time since they left Priortage hours before. "Not all of his plans are meant for us to understand."

"You keep your faith, and I'll keep my steel. We'll see which works better for us when Eldritch appears with poison dripping from his claws," Trainer said.

The cabin came into sight as they lurched up the stony path. Purple ivy cascaded from the roof, and yellow canaries moved among the vines as they flew from their nests. The cabin walls were made of live wood, and the cracks were patched with moss that glowed lime-colored in the light. The cabin appeared to sag under its own weight. A chimney made of river stones jutted from the top. Thorn bushes grew wild against the sides of the cabin; their white tips gleamed with malice.

"Homey," Trainer sneered.

He and Silas lifted Jonquil and carried him inside. The floor was warped, and no light reached into the interior. The fireplace took up one wall of the cabin. Its massive stones were charred black from centuries of use. Two straw-covered mattresses with dirty blankets and a rough-hewn table with benches were the only furnishings. An open doorway led into another smaller room outfitted with a third mattress.

"No reason for them to go to all this trouble for us," Trainer said sarcastically as they laid Jonquil on one of the beds in the living room.

"It was my father's hunting cabin," Mirabelle explained, standing in the doorway. "But no one has come here since he died, except for Jonquil and the others on their way to find Eldritch."

"So what are we to do then?" Silas asked. "We must get word back to the other riders. Lily has to know what's happening."

Mirabelle gave him a sympathetic look. "The woods aren't safe right now. The wolves are patrolling, looking for you, and Bemisch will send her mind far and wide to find us."

"There has to be something we can do," he said.

"There is," Mirabelle said. "Talk with our grandmother. She must leave quickly or all will be for naught."

"You're not going back?" Silas asked.

"I can no longer pretend. The witch would read my thoughts, and the other villagers have fallen so deeply under her sway, my life would be forfeit. There are few left like our grandmother who haven't been corrupted by Bemisch."

Silas's grandmother was waiting beside the wagon. She'd pulled her hood back so he could see her. The imprint of his mother was etched across the deep lines of her face. His grandmother's red hair had faded to a grayish brown, but her eyes burned with the same icy blue as his mother's. The high cheekbones and determined chin were the same.

She cupped his face gently with her hands and

turned it from side to side. "Yes, I see my daughter written on your features, but even more of your father," she said. "Is it true your sister takes more after her?"

"Yes," said Silas. Lily *did* look more like their mother.

"I would like to meet her one day when this is settled and there is peace in the Gardens," she said. "I'm afraid though, that hard times have fallen upon us and each must play their part in the tapestry unraveling in front of us. Do you know how to be brave?"

"I try," was the best Silas could answer.

"Good you did not say yes," his grandmother replied. "For men who believe they are brave are either arrogant or the first to run in a fight. You must try and be brave then for your sister, your family and those who live unknowing on the other side of the gates. You must steel your mind, for even here the witch will seek entry so she can catch flame in those dark places every human mind has. You must push back against any seductions Bemisch offers. She works for Eldritch, who poses an even greater threat. "

"Where is he?" Silas asked.

"In the birds, in the trees, in the water that rushes down the mountain," she said. "He's an old god, which means he has no use for human companionship, only the power of their worship. Some say he lives further north, where the land ends and mist becomes all, and only comes down to sate his blood thirst. He has the witch do his bidding, and for many months now there have been more and more creatures from the Gardens that are finding their way to him."

Silas found it hard to believe there could be a place where the fog grew thicker than it did here. He could barely make out the house through the impenetrable clouds that floated above the ground.

"So what do we do?" he asked.

"You must wait here until I'm able to send a message. I'm afraid we can only bring this situation to an end by taking bold and dangerous steps. You dusk riders must drag the witch back so that she is entrapped in the Garden again or she must be killed. Her power grows stronger every day. Before long, she will be able to read into the furthest crevice of every mind, and then no one will be able to stand against her. Even then, we must contend with Eldritch, but, as my mother used to say, 'You can only take one step at a time in the mist.'"

His grandmother climbed onto the wagon. "I must go now. Already I've tarried too long." Silas's grandmother looked down from the buckboard. "How is Moira?"

"Fine, the last time I saw her. I'm sure she's worried sick about Lily and me, but the gates will open one day and my parents will come back to Nightfall Gardens," Silas said.

"Let's hope," his grandmother said, drawing the hood back over her face. "Judge your grandfather not too harshly. Fyodor's a stubborn man, and his pride was injured when Moira refused his match of your uncle and left with Thomas."

There were many questions Silas wanted to ask, but there was no time. His grandmother cracked the reins and the horse moved slowly into the fog. "Draw a tight rein on your thoughts," she said, as the wagon disappeared. "Keep good memories close to your heart, and the witch cannot hold you."

Silas listened to the wagon creak away until the sound could be heard no more. Mirabelle was drawing sacks of food from a trapdoor in the center of the room when he entered.

"I stored these in case I should ever have to hide here," she said. "We've enough to last us for weeks. There's dry wood in the round house out back."

"Well, aren't you prepared?" Trainer said bitterly. He drew his wolf cloak about him and lashed his sword to his side.

"Where are you going?" Silas asked.

"Out," Trainer said. "It'll make me feel better to kill something. These woods have to be teeming with game. I'd like something hot and crackling with juices for dinner. What does the lady of the manor request? Roast rabbit, wild boar, duck, squirrel or perhaps delicious venison?"

"None," Mirabelle said. "I eat nothing stamped with the consciousness of life. I eat only the plants that grow on the land."

Trainer wrinkled his nose in disgust. "Don't worry, by the time I'm done with these animals there won't be any life left in them." He stormed out the front door into the mist.

"He's a very unhappy man," Mirabelle said when they were alone. "His soul is colored with the torment that he carries."

"How do you know that?" Silas asked, as they went out back to retrieve firewood.

"One need only look," she said. "It's the same way I know things about you and Jonquil and the villagers and the animals of the woods. It's why I wear the white; it marks me and the other Daughters."

"Daughters?" Silas asked, as he loaded up an armful of the dried wood.

Mirabelle laughed, pure and sweet. "I wouldn't expect you to know of us. There are so few and we are shunned except when needed for healing or reciting odes to the dying. It was one of the things our people brought with us when we came to Nightfall Gardens all of those years ago. The mist people believe in the spirit of the natural world. All things are part of nature: me, you, Lily, the animals in the forest, the trees, the sky, even malignant beings such as Bemisch and Eldritch — although they represent the worst and lowest of the spirit. Our creed is to injure as few as possible, to leave the world better than when we came into it. Daughters dedicate their lives to guiding people along the path. It's our job to tend the wounded and pave the way for those about to die. We learn many skills, including the ability to see into another's soul and the essence of their being. Your friend is an angry, hostile man. What made him that way, I don't know, but until he learns to come to peace with it, he will never be free."

They built a fire and soon the logs crackled.

"What do see you when you look at me?" Silas asked. They sat in front of the massive hearth, warming their chilled bones.

"You don't carry as many bruises as those who have lived longer. The older a person becomes, the more wounded their spirit, for people make compromises and have regrets that have hammered them in the forge of age," she said.

The chimney sucked the fire into a roaring blaze and it wasn't many minutes before the inside of the cabin was toasty. Jonquil shifted on the mat where he lay, but never uttered a word. His face looked waxy and yellow. Mirabelle's hair was such a deep red as to almost appear black in the flickering flames, while her eyes were blue stones that stared intently. A spate of freckles peppered each of her cheeks. The white shift she wore was spattered with dirt from carrying the firewood. She hardly looked like some devout nun.

"How did you become a Daughter?" Silas asked. It was early afternoon outside, yet here in the cabin, it might as well have been darkest night.

"It chose me," she said, scrunching her bobbed nose. "I was always able tell a person's true nature as long as I can recall. Once when I was a wee lassie, I remember my mum twisting my brother

Aaron's ear and asking if he'd been eating the fresh blackberry pie she'd made. He swore to nine heavens he hadn't, but as he gave his denial, I saw the white glow around his body darken and I knew he was lying. This is my earliest memory. I wasn't even able to walk yet."

Mirabelle explained that she grew used to knowing people's lies as well as their other secrets. "I knew the village baker, Mr. Coolidge, lusted after Widow Halsley because his aura burned bright red whenever she was around. I knew that, despite the way Randolph Teague laughed and slapped Comstock Wiley on the back, he hated his old childhood friend. I could see when people were angry, joyous, melancholic, envious, frightened and all the other emotional colors that make up human nature. One night, I saw a jittery man leave The Barn Swallow. He was following a woman who was heading toward the outskirts of town. His aura was so dark as to blot out his features. I could tell that he planned on killing her as soon as they were into the woods. I ran and told Blix, but at first he wouldn't believe me. I practically had to drag him out of the jailhouse. Finally, he deputized some men to come with us. We had barely traveled into the woods when we heard a woman screaming. We came upon the man as he stood over her with a rock, preparing to bring it down on her head. Blix and the others dragged him off and the woman lived to tell the tale. Word got around about me, though."

Mirabelle told Silas that she was preparing for bed one night, not long after, when her parents called her down. There was a visitor in the house, a woman with a maelstrom of wild gray hair, who was dressed all in white. She smiled when she saw Mirabelle at the top of the stairs, as if she were seeing a lost family member. Her aura glowed the same color as fresh cream.

"Her name was Edna, and she was one of the Daughters who lived together in a commune in the forest. 'Yes, I can see it about you,' Daughter Edna, said turning my face from side to side. 'You have the feel.' This was my first time seeing a Daughter up close. They lived in a rambling old house near the Blue Fin River and only came into town on the weekends. They were spoken of with reverence, but, as often as not, people crossed to the other side of the street if they saw one of them coming along. That's why I was so surprised when you and the others didn't turn away when you saw us on the street."

Mirabelle began studying with the Daughters, going to their house by the river and learning how to control her gift. "They taught me other things as well: how to make healing poultices and to tend for those about to depart for the shadowland. They made me understand that I have a gift that's not something to be ashamed of. The maker gave me this skill so I could comfort those afflicted by the sorrows of life."

"I won't be a proper daughter until I turn 16,"

she continued. "For now, I'm in training like Natasha, the girl who you saw me with. When that birthday comes, I'll take the vows and leave behind this world that chips away at the fragile matter of our spirits and dedicate myself to a life of succor and purity."

"What of your family or of having children?" Silas asked.

Mirabelle laughed. "The Daughters are my family. Helping others is the mission I serve."

"It sounds lonely," Silas said.

"No lonelier than some," she said. "Isn't there some purpose that you strive for?"

'To be away from here,' he thought. *'To pretend that this place never existed.'* "To protect my sister and keep the Gardens from falling," he finally said.

"Aye, we have the same ambition then, for the daughters will be able to do little good once the old gods walk again," Mirabelle said.

The two of them spent the rest of the day preparing the cabin. They brought in more firewood, scoured the cooking utensils, and traipsed out to the well and carried back fresh water. When they were finished, Silas lay on the mat next to his uncle while Mirabelle went into the other room. He fell into a deep sleep disturbed, by a nightmare: A snorting, snuffling creature chased him through the woods. The mist was so thick that Silas stumbled over tree roots and branches scrapped at him because he couldn't see which direction he was going, and still, whatever was chasing him came closer. Silas could hear its hooves thundering on the ground. The mist blinded him. Silas took one false step and his foot came down in a rabbit hole. His ankle snapped and he was thrown to the ground. He tried to pull himself up, but it was no good. A snout emerged from the mist, followed by evil burning eyes, whiskered cheeks and the mangled teeth of his opponent. The Jinkinki stood in front of him, a look of triumph on his face. "I told you I'd chase you through the seven hells for a taste of your sweet flesh," the creature oinked. His breath smelled of open graves and of rotting meat. "You can never run far enough to escape the Jinkinki."

Silas shot up in bed in a blind panic. He hadn't thought of the Jinkinki in a while. He had faced the monster that lived off dead flesh when he and Arfast braved the White Garden to find Fairy Bells to save Jonquil. The Jinkinki became enraged when Silas smashed a lantern holding two sprites that were his captives. The sprites escaped and the Jinkinki, naturally vengeful, swore he would chase him to the ends of the world. Hadn't Arfast said something about how Jinkinkis had the power to appear in people's dreams?

The door crashed open, dissipating that thought. Trainer stood in the entry holding the bodies of several skinned squirrels. Day had slipped away, and the rising moon's red light was mixed with the fog, giving it a shimmering, ruby appearance.

"Right, who wants a bit o' these munchers?"

Trainer asked. His mood had noticeably lifted with his time away from the group. Mirabelle came out of the next room, wiping sleep from her eyes. "Oh, that's right. The lady of the house doesn't eat beasts of the woods; leaves more for the men," he said.

Jonquil stirred. His face was as gray as the ashes in the fire, but his eyes burned and the white scar that ran along his cheek gleamed. "Where have you been?" he asked.

"Exploring our new home as much as a person can do in that pea-soup fog," Trainer said, taking off his boots cake with mud. He knelt by the fire and started to skin the squirrels. "I climbed into the hills until there was nothing but rocks and mist to keep me company."

"And what did you get for your troubles?" Jonquil asked.

"Sore feet," the rider said. "And lots of wolf tracks. I don't know what they eat for game, there be so many of them."

"The hills have always been heavy with dens. We've had no problems with them," Mirabelle said.

"But now the witch can control them," Jonquil said. The rider pulled himself up until he was standing. "Where's my walking stick?"

"Lost, I'm afraid," Trainer said. "Saving it was the last of our worries when we fled from Priortage. We barely escaped with our weapons."

Jonquil sighed. "I'll have to make a new one. Lad, would you help me?"

Silas's uncle leaned on him as they made their

way outside. The air was heavy with mist and Silas drew a wet mouthful into his lungs. Somewhere, a howler owl gave out a blood-piercing shriek, a sound like someone who was dying.

"She says I stayed here, but then why is it no more than a flash in my mind?" Jonquil asked. "None of this seems familiar."

"Eldritch's poison almost killed you," Silas said. "It makes sense that it would leave holes in your memory."

"Does it?" Jonquil asked. "I wonder. Keep your eyes open, lad, and if anything should happen, save yourself and tell the others. They need to know what's brewing in this darkness."

"We'll go back to Nightfall Gardens together," Silas said.

Jonquil laughed. "Always hopeful to the end. I would have figured this place would have beaten that out of you by now." He tousled his nephew's hair. "Being here reminds me of my first trip to the mist with your father."

"You were tracking a goblin," Silas said, remembering what his uncle had told him.

"Aye, that's a story we'll save for a long night," Jonquil said.

The next week passed uneventfully. The four of them settled into a routine with Trainer, heading out at first light to hunt and returning in the early evening, while Jonquil set out to walk the nearby hills, hoping to gain his strength back. The first two days he was gone little more than an hour before he was back and had to lie down, a fever burning on his brow. After that though, he seemed to get better and was gone two and then three hours. Because there was little else to do, Mirabelle took Silas into the woods and showed him which plants were poisonous, which ones could be eaten, and where to find the ones that could be used for healing. He was sure Mr. Hawthorne would have enjoyed picking her mind for scraps that he could put in his book about the plants of Nightfall Gardens. Mirabelle spent the hour before dawn on her knees, meditating in the little room in the cabin. Silas could see her outline in the white dress, hair spilling around her shoulders, hands clasped together, a beatific look on her face. She sat there immobile until the hour was up, and then she rose, smiling, and went about her day.

"Her time would be better spent making us breakfast," Trainer said the first day that they were there. Patchy stubble was beginning to grow on his pockmarked cheeks and he was looking more sallow than usual after the adventures of the last few days. "Praying is nothing more than wishful thinking. It doesn't fill the belly or put a roof over one's head. If there is a maker, it don't care hog spit for what we think."

"And yet they drew you to the Gardens to serve them," Mirabelle said.

"If I'm the best that they can do, then we're in trouble," Trainer sneered.

One afternoon, while Silas and Mirabelle walked

in a grove of pines, she told him about their family.

"Grandpa Fyodor is a man easy to rile. Before Eldritch and the witch, he was one of the most respected elders in the town. Shrewd — that's the word I always heard said about him. He built his fortune off his wits. He owns The Barn Swallow, you know, as well as most of the town. My dad says Fyodor collects money the same way a dog does fleas. Joining the council, preaching the word, all of it was one more way for him to make sure nothing happens to upset his grip on power."

Mirabelle picked a pine needle from the ground and began stripping the green shoots.

"I don't want you to think badly of him. He's fiercely loyal to his family. That's why he was so angry when your mother ran off with Thomas," she said.

"Why?" Silas asked. He remembered his grandfather's smoldering anger when the dusk riders were brought before him. Fyodor looked at Jonquil with particular disdain. *"He came to me in good stead many a moon ago to ask for the hand of my youngest daughter, Moira; a hand I freely gave him,"* his grandfather had said. But what did that mean?

"Best ask your uncle," Mirabelle said. "The details I know are so slender they could pass through the eye of a needle."

Silas resolved he would ask his uncle about their family history that night.

"You have a troubled glow about you," Mirabelle said. She touched his face with gentle fingers. "None of this has to do with you. This happened long before you were born. The maker made us with our faults and all. Daughter Edna says we all stumble blindly toward the truth."

Two things happened that afternoon that kept Silas from asking his uncle about his father and mother. As Silas and Mirabelle walked from the woods, they saw Jonquil hobbling in their direction with the new walking stick he'd carved. His wolf hood was pulled down, and his silver hair hung greasy around his face. His cheeks were hollowed, and his eyes stared from sockets that looked as though they'd peeked through death's door.

"What's wrong?" Silas asked, for he could see the trouble writ on his uncle's face.

"I found, fresh carved in a tree trunk, the Mark of Eldritch. Someone has been watching us," he said.

"Where?" Mirabelle asked. His cousin exuded calmness that Silas didn't think himself capable of at the moment.

"Down the trail," Jonquil said. "It wasn't there yesterday, I'm sure of it."

"That is troublesome," Mirabelle agreed. "The only one who lives near is Mad Abraham, and he's more scared of other people than they are of him."

"Perhaps it was someone passing through," Silas said.

"I've lived too long to believe in coincidence," Jonquil said. "Go and find Trainer. He said he was heading up to Snowy Point to search for game."

Silas looked up into the hills but all he could see was a rolling wall of fog so thick that it created a blanket. Snowy Point was a bluff more than an hour up in the hills where Trainer had discovered that a family of goats lived. Try as he might, he hadn't been able to catch one in the traps he set.

"Don't dawdle," Jonquil said. "We may have to leave before the red moon rises."

"And go where?" Silas asked.

But Jonquil didn't answer. "Just go, lad, and get back as soon as you can."

The climb to Snowy Point took Silas an hour and more than once he wasn't sure he was going in the right direction. The ground was hard and covered in loose boulders, some the size of a grown man. The earth slid out from under him at one point, but still he kept heading north. When he was above the pines the wind tore at his cloak and his hands stung with cold. The ground was craggy, and channels were etched into the soil where water ran down from the snowy hill. The pines grew smaller and were less sparse. Twisted runts of turquoise-colored trees dotted the hills above. The sky was its usual slate gray, heavy with the anticipation of rain. Snowy Point was close now, a stony peak covered in dirty snow.

Silas heard Trainer before he saw him. His voice was babbling on the wind. *'Who's he talking with?'* thought Silas. Fear flooded his belly. His instincts, which had grown sharp, sent warning signals. He stroked the dagger that hung from his belt and listened for more voices, but heard nothing. He climbed again, sure that every living being within a mile radius could hear the rocks sliding from under his boots.

"I'll trust you no more than I trust anyone else," he heard Trainer say, then his voice was snatched away again.

Silas looked up and saw the silhouette of the dusk rider on the hill ahead. Trainer had his blade drawn and it shone bright in the dull landscape. He was facing off against a black wolf with bared fangs. The wolf's fur rippled with the wind. The wolf growled something at the dusk rider that almost sounded like words.

"Dan!" Silas yelled. The word echoed from the surrounding hills. He started off at a run toward him.

The wolf and dusk rider came together with the black wolf launching itself in the air and Trainer thrusting his sword. Silas stumbled and lost his balance. When he looked up, the wolf was limping and Trainer was circling him. The wolf made another desperate lunge, but was no match for the dusk rider. With two more slashes the wolf's legs buckled and he fell dead. Silas arrived as the animal breathed its last. Blood flowed from its mouth and poured from deep wounds on its side. Trainer wiped his blade on a nearby rock.

"Are you all right? What happened?" Silas asked.

The dusk rider looked up at him. "Who gave

you permission to do that?" Trainer asked brimming with his usual cauldron of malice.

"What?" Silas asked.

"To use my first name. I never gave you call to use my birth name. Only my friends do that, and I have none of those," he said.

"The wolf —," Silas started.

"— came at me from those rocks," Trainer said, pointing. "Its den must be nearby. We need to get down from here, in case the pack returns. That one must have been ill, so they left it behind. Now what brings you here?"

Silas explained why he had come. When he finished, Trainer cursed under his breath. "Is there no place to find a moment's peace in this wretched world?"

The last light was fading as they approached the cabin. Smoke poured from the chimney and the night birds were starting their songs in the woods. Jonquil sat by the fire staring into the flames, as if they might hold answers to their problems. Mirabelle was meditating in the next room.

"There you are. Where in the blazes have you been?" Jonquil said, when they entered.

"A man can only walk so fast," Trainer snapped back. "We came as soon as the boy found me."

"Then you've heard of the mark I found," Jonquil said.

"Aye," Trainer said. "And we're sitting here defenseless."

Mirabelle entered. "Grandmother said she

would come with tidings for us tomorrow."

"And what if she brings more than tidings? What if she brings your grandfather's men with her?" Jonquil asked.

"She wouldn't do that," Mirabelle said.

"Not unless the witch has got to her," Trainer said.

"It hasn't. Not her," Mirabelle replied. She came and stood next to Silas.

"Even the strongest fall," Trainer said. He hadn't moved from the door since they entered. The rider stood out of the light, his face an imperceptible mask.

"So what do we do?" Silas asked. "Night has fallen and Bemisch is at her strongest. We have no horses or supplies. Eldritch — and those who worship him — may be in the woods."

Jonquil scratched his chin. "It would be suicide to set off down the hill now. We'll give your Gran one more day, but then we must leave this place."

"And tonight?" Trainer said.

"Aye, we're sitting with our throats bared, but we'll do the best we can," Jonquil said. "Do you still have that pack Mr. Hawthorne made, lad?"

Silas reached into his cloak and pulled out a velvet bag Mr. Hawthorne had made for him before they set off from Nightfall Gardens. He opened the sack; inside there were half a dozen pouches with different herbs mixed into them.

"Good," Jonquil said. "We'll sprinkle Dragon's Breath around the cabin. It's not much of a deterrent, but it should give us tidings if anything approaches in the fog."

Silas and Mirabelle walked the boundary of the cabin, sprinkling the pale blue powder onto the soil until it formed a circle. The mist was moving in so heavily now that, even though his cousin stood two feet from him, she was nothing more than a blur. When they finished pouring the last of the powder, the two watched the fog rolling in like plumes of smoke belching from a giant furnace.

"Something is amiss," Mirabelle said. "The mist doesn't become this thick for another day's ride north. This is not natural."

"The witch?" Silas asked.

"Or something worse, Eldritch may be stirring nearby," she said.

"If Gran doesn't come tomorrow, then we must set off for Nightfall Gardens," Silas said.

"And a hard journey it will be," Mirabelle said. "The woods will be watched all the way to the Gardens. We'll have to travel through the woods. It won't be safe to take roads or trails. It won't be safe to start a fire at night. We'll have to travel slowly and be alert, for if the villagers discover us, our lives will be short indeed."

There was little talk after that. The four ate without appetite, and a gloom fell over them. Trainer took the first shift, listening for the slightest stir in the yard. Silas tossed and was unable to sleep. Every time he started to doze, an image of the witch came to him or he imagined the Jinkinki sneaking up outside of the house. He lay that way until Jonquil took his turn at watch. His uncle pitched new logs on the fire and stirred them with a bent rod. Silas waited until his uncle was sitting in a chair with his sword across his lap and then tiptoed to him.

"What are you doing up, lad? You should be sleeping. You'll need all your strength for tomorrow," Jonquil said.

"I'm not tired," Silas lied.

"Too many things weigh on all of our minds," Jonquil said. "I'll be glad when we are out of this curse-bound place. Even the Gardens will be a welcome sight."

Silas cleared his throat. "I know about you and my mother being betrothed." His voice was a little more than a whisper.

Jonquil straightened up, stiff-backed. "What have you heard?"

"Little enough," Silas said. "I wanted to hear the tale from you, of the time you and my father rode into the mist after the escaped goblin, of how you met my mother."

Jonquil stared at the dark rafters of the cabin as if staring into the past and then spoke.

"We found the dusk rider, early one morning while we were on a ride. His throat had been slit and the blood drained many hours before. I bent to examine the ground and saw the three-pronged footprint leading into the mist that meant only one thing — a goblin had escaped from the Gardens."

12
POISONED BY THE ANGEL TRUMPET

Lily awoke to a feeling of impending doom and the stink of something cold and slimy against her nose. She opened her eyes. The ceiling formed a pattern of shifting shapes overhead. Her door was open, and she heard a spirit gibbering in one of the closed rooms down the hall. Candles burned along the mantle. Her throat burned, and a heavy melancholy pressed on her like a feral cat crouching on her chest.

"I think she's waking, Miss, her eyes are open," Ursula's voice said, speaking from somewhere out of sight, and Lily started to make sense of the soul-crushing numbness she felt. "Would you like me to sit with her for a while longer?"

"That won't be necessary," Polly said. "Go fetch

some tea. I think that would do her more good than us hovering over her."

"Understood, Miss, understood," Ursula said.

Lily heard the floorboards creak as the maid left the room, and immediately the weight lifted, though the depression didn't go away.

Polly came into view. Her face was covered by a membrane that looked as if it would burst at the slightest touch. Her eyes were white orbs that masked her emotions. The collar of her dress was hardened with mucus. She sat at the edge of the bed and stroked Lily's face, leaving behind a slimy substance on Lily's cheeks, which was clogging her nostrils when she tried to breathe.

"How's my Lily," Polly said. "Had a rough one, she has. Ozy is trying to figure out how Mugwump got into the house. That was a close one, the closest I've seen in all my years here."

Lily's throat was raw. "Cassandra?" she croaked. Her friend had tried to protect her, and paid for it with her life. *'She's the first to die for me, but not the last,'* Lily thought.

"Oh fine, fine, Miss. Cassandra's in the room across the way. She took a nasty spill, but will be up and about in no time at all. Same as you." Polly's response astonished Lily and began to lift the darkness that consumed her.

Lily sat up in bed, her body screaming with the exertion. "But I saw her fall."

"Indeed, Miss, but it's the house, it moves and shifts. A gable that wasn't there suddenly was, and your friend landed on that. Knocked the air out of her, it did. She'll be bruised for a good while and her attitude is none too improved, but she'll be all right."

"I need to see her," Lily said, shoving the blankets away.

Polly pushed her back. "What you need is rest. Cassandra will still be there when you wake."

The maid oozed her way out of the room. Through the window, Lily could see darkness had come again. The red moon hung ripe in the sky and painted the grounds blood red.

Sleep washed over her, and she fell into a deep void occasionally leavened with dreams. In the first, Lily saw Desdemona, dry wisps of her hair hanging from loose patches of her scalp. She clung to the bedroom wall, her head turned sideways like a dog hearing a far-off whistle. Lily reached for her, but her ancestor scuttled out of the bedroom.

In the second dream, Lily was riding in the Gardens. The perpetual gloom that covered everything had lifted. A brilliant yellow sun shone on the luminous green of Nightfall Gardens with a brightness that almost blinded her. Her white blond hair was loose around her shoulders, and the collar of her shirt was upturned. She rode a black horse with a white star on its forehead and was contented in a way denied her during the half year that she had been trapped behind the gates. Birds sang in the trees; bees, butterflies and hummingbirds fluttered about flowers and plants.

The perpetual chill was gone. It was hot enough that a sheen of sweat formed on her arms and legs. A figure stepped from the trees of the White Garden as she approached. He was taller than her, with a shock of black hair and full lips. His skin was the palest she'd ever seen. His eyes were such a pale blue that they almost had no color. He wore a frilled shirt and cravat with a black jacket and pants.

"I wondered if you would come this way," Villon said, mischievousness in his voice

"Ride with me," Lily said, patting her horse.

"I can't leave the Garden, you know that," he said. The expression on his face turned thunderous and dark. "I'm trapped until the world is no more or the box is destroyed once and for all. And when that happens I must die."

"Why?" Lily asked. She tugged on the horse's reins so that it would walk in place.

"As punishment for the things I did when I was alive," he said. "I once was human — so many years ago that I can barely recall what that means. My punishment is to carry the burdens of my evil and never be rid of them."

"But what of forgiveness," Lily asked.

"There can be none for what I did," he said sadly. "Forgiveness is for the living."

"And what exactly did you do that was so terrible?" Lily asked.

Villon stepped further from her into the shadows. "You'll never hear that story from my lips. For, if you were made aware of my sins, you would ride right by me as though I didn't exist. To be ignored by you in such a fashion would be my true death."

"And why do you fear me ignoring you?" Lily asked coyly.

"My lady knows why," Villon said.

"You can live on so little?" Lily asked.

"If I could sup from your lips, I would," he said. "The time for lovers' games has long passed." Villon stepped into the sunlight, and his skin shriveled and burned, parchment set to flame. His body exploded as if whale oil, dumped from a lantern, had been lit. Fire engulfed him, licking hungrily at his clothes. His eyeballs melted and dripped from their sockets. "The black castle," he croaked as his throat burned. "Trust not the Smiling Ladies." His body fell to the ground, little more than a smoldering skeleton. The sun blotted out overhead and dark clouds came from the west, stealing the sunshine and bringing perpetual dusk back to Nightfall Gardens. Rain lashed down and thunder crashed with such intensity that the ground shook and it felt as if the sky were being torn apart. Her horse reared on its hind legs and took off down the path, as trees crashed to the ground around her. The sky split open, and a spinning black funnel dropped from above; the whirlwind threatened to suck up everything in its path. The house lay ahead. As she watched, the tornado passed over Nightfall Manor, ripping the roof from it and swallowing it. A terrible rending of wood and stone filled the air as the house was torn from its moorings and came flying through the air to crush her.

Lily awoke with a start. The blankets were on the floor. She was drenched in sweat. One hand was shielding her face in a vain attempt to keep the house from crushing her.

"Bad dream?" Cassandra asked. The green girl was at the door. "I could hear you yelling across the way."

"I dreamed the house fell on me," Lily said, rubbing her hands over her face. She poured a glass of water from the carafe on the nightstand.

"How do you feel?" Lily asked. "I thought —."

" — the same as me," Cassandra said, "that I was falling to my doom, but the house saved me for whatever reason. I'm glad it did though."

"Me too," Lily said. Tears seeped from her eyes. "I —."

"Don't get sentimental on me," Cassandra said. "If there's one thing I can't abide, it's that. Besides, I thought you were finished as well. Polly told me what you did to Mugwump. If you keep that up, I might have to rethink my opinion of you."

"I did nothing. You were the one that faced him, how did you — what did you — do to him?" Lily sputtered.

Cassandra sat by the fire, her shoulders slumping. The confidence she normally displayed was gone. She tucked her face down and kicked the rug on the floor. "I'm not a person who opens their heart easily, especially on this, but we've fought together and almost died together and sometimes it feels like it *would* be better to share this rather than keep it locked up inside of me. You must promise one thing."

"Name it," Lily said.

"You can never tell your brother," Cassandra said. "I want your word on that. Should you ever go back on it, I'll give you a fat eye, no matter how beautiful you are."

"I promise," Lily said smiling and placed her hand over her heart.

The green girl didn't speak for a long time. She sat in the glow of the fire and stared at the floor. When she finally spoke, her voice was choked with emotion.

"My mother died when I was only a babe. I remember little of her. My father tells me she was a beautiful woman with a fine singing voice, but I have to take his word for it. She died shortly after I was born," Cassandra said. She wrung her hands and her body trembled. "I've always been this — this way. My skin — I thought it was normal for the longest time. My father never told me how it marked me. I knew I was different from other people, but I thought my mother was green and that there were others like me in the world. It wasn't until I grew older and I overheard some dusk riders making fun of me, saying that I was born in a cabbage patch, calling me sprout, asking if I liked vegetables, that I realized I wasn't normal at all. But there was something else that marked me, something that has tainted my life and means I can never leave Nightfall Gardens until the day my spirit leaves my body."

"What is it?" Lily asked.

Cassandra's voice cracked as she tried to say the words, words Lily knew she had never told another living person. "My touch is death." She grew quiet.

"What do you mean?" Lily asked.

"Any living being, animal or human, that I touch dies within minutes. Only supernatural beings can survive my touch. My mother was poisoned by the Angel Trumpet root when I was in her womb. I survived, but it made me a monster. I can never know human touch. My father can never stroke my cheek. I can never have a pet other than Osbold. I can't shake hands, touch friends, or have a boyfriend. To do so would put their lives in danger and that's something I will never do."

Her story was worse than Lily had imagined. Yet, surely there must be some hope.

"How did you first learn about this?" Lily asked.

"It was not long after my mother died when an old dog wandered in when the gates were open. He was blind in one eye and missing his tail. He used to sleep in our barn and follow my father wherever he went. One day, when I was old enough to walk, he came close and I grabbed him the way children do. Only, when I touched him, he stumbled and fell dead. I saw the light of life fade from his eyes. My father said the dog was old, that it was his time, but I knew the truth."

"What of your father? He must have touched you when you ate, when he hugged you; it seems impossible to have never happened," Lily thought of her own father, Thomas. Of how he slung her on his shoulders so she could look out over whatever town that they were living in. How lonely it must feel to never touch one's parent.

"It was only when I was older that I understood the precautions my father used to protect himself," Cassandra said wiping her eyes.

Mr. Hawthorne knew from the minute he saw Cassandra's skin that she had been poisoned. There were stories in the great history that the Hawthornes kept, stories of relatives who grew poisonous to the touch once they made contact with Angel Trumpet. He wore long shirts and gloves when she was a baby. When she grew older, he was careful never to leave any of his skin exposed. On her eighth birthday, he told her the truth of what was wrong.

"There were other incidents," Cassandra said. "You'd be surprised how hard it is not to have contact with the living even in this desolate place."

At four Cassandra had found a starling with a broken wing hopping in circles. She tried to mend it, but the bird's chest heaved a final sigh in her hands. Likewise, the speckled trout she caught in an icy stream in the woods, dancing on her fishing line until her fingers gripped it. Then, the spark of life fled. Frogs croaked their last when she laid hands on them. Grasshoppers, dragonflies, and the fireflies that lit the mist — all of those became shells after contact with her.

The barn where they kept their animals was where she learned her final lesson. One of their sheep gave birth to a baby lamb that was no more than a cotton puff with black hooves. The little sheep was so adorable that Cassandra couldn't help herself. She forgot and wrapped her arms around it, thinking that this time things would be different. The lamb took a handful of faltering steps and fell lifeless.

"I wouldn't get out of bed for a week," the green girl said. "I felt so horrible about what my selfishness had done. I determined then that I would never touch another living thing. I've found that to be harder than I thought, but I've done the best I can and there have only been a few missteps."

Cassandra finished her story and stretched her back. "And now you know why my best friend is a gargoyle." She laughed bitterly.

"I'm sorry," Lily said. It sounded horribly isolating. *'It would drive me mad,'* she thought.

"For what? You didn't do anything, and the last thing I need is pity," Cassandra said.

"I meant no offense. It's a lot for one person to carry on their shoulders," Lily said.

"As is the burden you bear," Cassandra said. "It's the way I am. I must constantly be alert around other people."

"It doesn't seem very relaxing," Lily said.

The green girl laughed. "I'll give you that; it's not relaxing. But I have something now that I didn't have before."

"What's that?"

"A confidante. Now you know my tale and must keep it to yourself," she said.

"I know what else I must do as well," Lily said. She pulled a velvet rope by her bed that triggered a bell in the servants' quarters. Minutes later, Ursula arrived with the pot of tea. The mood in the room slumped the moment the glumpog entered the room. The strange little woman waggled her unibrow. "Yes, my lady, anything else I can do? I know some absolutely terrifying bedtime stories, or we could sit around and talk about what happens when we die, if you like."

"That won't be necessary," Lily said. "But, I'd like you to do me a favor."

"Does it involve dissecting anything or delivering tragic news?" Ursula said.

"No," Lily said.

"Pity that," Ursula said. "What shall I do?"

"I need you to get my friend's gargoyle Osbold and have him brought here," Lily said.

"Nothing from the Gardens allowed in, Miss, you can ask Polly on that if you'd like," Ursula said.

"Aren't you from the Gardens?" Lily asked.

Ursula grew pensive. "True, Miss, true. But me, Polly and Ozy, we're reformed. No more evil for us."

"Talk with Polly and tell her that Cassandra's pet will come to play with us. Tell her I command the house to give him safe passage."

Ursula bowed. "As you wish. Sure you wouldn't like one truly fright-filled story that'll keep you awake at night?"

"That will be all," Lily said.

The glumpog bowed again and left the room. Once she was gone, the mood lifted and her friend smiled. "You didn't have to do that," Cassandra said.

"It was long overdue," Lily said. "Besides, he can help us explore the house. There's not much time left until my fourteenth birthday, and I want to be sure I'm prepared if I have to enter the Shadow Garden."

Lily and Cassandra waited in the main foyer until the front door opened and Ursula and Mr. Hawthorne entered, followed by the little gargoyle. Osbold rushed into the room and flew figure eights in the air. He was barely larger than a small dog with skin the color of stone, nubs of horns on his head and a curved beak. He flew to the ceiling before landing on Cassandra's shoulder, where he started picking at her hair.

"There he is. Miss Polly's not going to be happy having that thing in here," Ursula said smiling at the thought of unhappiness.

When the glumpog was gone, Mr. Hawthorne rushed to his daughter. "I heard all about what happened," he said. "I can't protect the house fast enough anymore. Sometimes, I think we should head north, where there are no gardens and no cursed heat."

Lily felt goosebumps on her arms. It was decidedly chilly in Nightfall Gardens, but going on about the heat was one of the gardener's favorite topics. Suddenly, a memory returned of looking out from the crow's nest and seeing Mr. Hawthorne talking with a woman in the Shadow Garden. What had he been doing? Who was he talking with? Those were questions she decided to mull over later.

"I can't wait until that brother of yours gets back," Mr. Hawthorne said. "He has a natural green thumb, whether he knows it or not. No word on him I suppose?"

"None so far," Lily said. *'Though I do need to talk with Skuld and see what he's heard.'*

"You'll be home in time for dinner tomorrow?" Mr. Hawthorne asked Cassandra. "And you'll be careful not to get in any more trouble?"

"No more trouble than I would get in out there," Cassandra said.

"Aye, I guess that's the best I can hope for," Mr. Hawthorne said. "I've got a whole row of witch vine to replace and only a few hours to do so. I should get to work or it'll never get done."

Mr. Hawthorne left, and the three of them went into the dining room for lunch. Lily's chest ached where Mugwump had crushed down on her and her throat was sore, but other than that she was surprised at how well she'd weathered the assassination attempt. *'I was lucky'* she thought. *'I have to be better prepared for the next time.'*

Ozy limped through the kitchen doors, balancing a silver tray containing lunch. He moved at such a glacial speed that they were ravenous by the time he reached the table.

"It's so nice to see you up and about, Miss," the mummy said, a cloud of dust wheezing from his mouth. "The kitchen has prepared something special for today. I do hope you'll enjoy."

The lunch was the best Lily had tasted since she arrived in Nightfall Gardens. There was a fresh summer salad with sliced strawberries and spinach drizzled with homemade salad dressing. The second course was an earthy-tasting soup made from basil and herbs grown in the gardens and was followed by an entrée of roasted chicken full of spices that she had never tasted before. The girls were so stuffed that they could barely eat the tarts with thick whipped cream for dessert. When they finished, Lily was afraid that they were going to have to wheel her out of the room. The world didn't seem as terrible on a full belly.

Rain pattering against the glass in the entry made her drowsy. If she closed her eyes, Lily could almost imagine this was her country estate and she was on vacation. Nightfall Gardens was not a place to let that illusion linger. The dining room stretched and groaned and dishes clattered. A pink chandelier shook as the room changed shape in front of their eyes. A bell clanged in the house with a deep, lustrous ringing so loud the girls plugged their ears and Osbold squawked and raced circles above them.

When the ringing stopped, Ozy shook his head. Dirty bandages spilled from his shirt collar. His neck was so desiccated that one good yank would it pull his head from his shoulders.

"What's wrong?" Lily asked once the ringing had diminished to a lingering vibration.

"The house, Miss. It's not healthy. In all my years here, I've never seen it behave so erratically," he said.

'The end is coming,' Lily thought. *'It may not be today or even weeks from now, but I can feel the house falling apart. And when it does, what will protect me?'*

With that thought souring her stomach, Lily set off for the library along with Cassandra and Osbold. Books spilled from every shelf: ancient tomes, Blackwood diaries, magazines and newspapers from the outside world, even a collection of account ledgers from Priortage. Osbold flew up to one of the upper shelves and began grooming.

"What are we looking for?" Cassandra asked, picking up a dusty volume with illustrations of the various bird species of Nightfall Gardens.

"Anything about the Smiling Ladies," Lily said. "Or that might help us find out more about what happened to the Blackwood women locked in the vaults."

Lily thought of Silas as she perused book after book. He would have loved this room. *'Where is he right now?'* she thought.

They searched the library until late in the afternoon, reading everything that they could find about the Smiling Ladies. What Abigail had written in her diary was right. Wherever there was a natural disaster, a plague or other calamity, the three skeletal women with their elongated necks and rictus faces seemed to be at the heart of it, always moving in the dark. Then, just as human forces would align against them, the three would disappear, leaving only sorrow and death in their wake. Cassandra found a reference to the Smiling Ladies in a weathered book called "Fables of the Bloodletting," a volume so old some pages were illegible. "They come only at night, and their kiss is eternal," she read out loud. The green girl looked up at her friend. "I can't make out any more. The words are too faded."

Dusk was turning to evening when the three left the library and made their way to the room where Lily practiced her swordplay. She was surprised to find Skuld and Arfast waiting when she entered. Her teacher sat in the chair nearest the fire and scratched the stump of his arm. Arfast juggled knives in the air while balancing a cup of cider on one of his boots. The knives disappeared up his sleeve, and he kicked the cup to his hand without spilling a drop.

"Skuld — I didn't think you were coming until tomorrow," Lily said, flustered.

"How could you expect me to stay away after I heard what happened?" the one armed man replied. He turned to Cassandra. "What I want to know is why in blue blazes you fought something as venomous as Mugwump on your own? That's a dusk rider's job."

"There were none here," Lily said with iciness. "Would you have rather let him slice our throats?"

Skuld banged his good hand on his knee. "I don't like this. From now on there'll always be at a rider within earshot of you."

"There are barely enough of you to take care of the Gardens," Lily said. "I'm as safe in the house as anywhere."

"She has a point there," Arfast said grinning.

"Stay out of this, laughing boy," Skuld spat. "You'd knock on the gates of hell with a smile on your face."

"What other way is there?" Arfast said. He plopped down on a sofa and put his hands behind his head.

"My command is full of drunks and wastrels, there's so much activity we can barely maintain the Gardens, and on top of that I must deal with his constant japes. Heavens help us all," Skuld said.

"But not for long," Arfast said raising one of his

fingers. A blue flame danced on its end.

"Aye, we'll get to that. For now, I'm putting a rider outside your door while you sleep at night," Skuld said. "If anyone wants to harm you, they'll have to go through them first."

"I've done well enough on my own," Lily said. "Why do you think I've had you train me?" The thought of having one of the men who lived in the bunkhouse shadow her every movement troubled her. *'This house is not the only thing with secrets.'*

"Must everything be an argument?" Skuld said. "There'll be a rider with you every second of the day, and I'll hear no more. Farragut is already here —."

"Farragut —" Lily thought of the hideous man who had been about to kill the nestler in the Gardens.

"I know your views on him but he is one of our best fighters," Skuld said. "He likes this no better than you. I promise you."

"What does Polly say?"

"She is concerned with your safety and troubled by how weak the Manor grows."

Lily held her tongue, but told herself the rider wouldn't be long in the house.

"There are other concerns as well," Skuld said. "More creatures have escaped from the Gardens, including a Jinkinki. It almost killed one of my men. Tore off his ear and ate it. Would have done worse, but one of the other riders heard him crying for help and drove the creature away. The Jinkinki ran into the mist as if he was tracking something. Now we have a flesh eater on the loose."

The name Jinkinki set off an alarm in Lily's head. Where had she heard that before?

"Silas!" she blurted. "He told me about the Jinkinki. How the beast tried to kill him in the White Garden and how he barely escaped. You were there," Lily said to Arfast.

The trickster sat up, and though the grin was on his face, there was hardness in his eyes.

"Aye, my lady. I saw that abomination, and, once a Jinkinki sets its sights on its prey, it won't quit until either it or the person is dead. They are obsessive, odious creatures who live in crypts and dine on the meat of the dead. They fixate on slights done to them and can appear in dreams. It doesn't bode well that such a fiend is headed in the direction of your brother."

"What are you going to do?" Cassandra asked. Her friend was tough as leather, but the green girl had a crush on her brother.

"Arfast is going after him," Skuld said. The one armed man paced the room. "He's also going to find out what's taking the others so long. We've heard no word from your uncle since they set out. I'm beginning to grow troubled. The last time, only your uncle survived what they found in the north. I fear it was a mistake for them to go off without better protection. The trickster will track the Jinkinki and slip into Priortage to see if he can find out what happened."

"I set out at first light," Arfast said. "If either of you would like to give a kiss to the brave warrior, my lips would not disapprove."

Skuld groaned. "I've got something you can kiss, but it's not my lips. Some hard traveling will wipe that smirk from your face."

"Just Arfast alone?" Cassandra said. Worried lines formed on her forehead. "What if the others need help? Shouldn't you send more riders?"

Skuld rubbed his tired eyes. "And where, pray suggest, should we get these other riders? I can ill afford to send Arfast, let alone anyone else. The riders work long days with little sleep and this is the lowest our numbers have been in years. No, it must be him and no one else. But don't worry; we'll make sure he brings the boy back safe. We'll let nothing happen to your beau."

"He's not my beau!" said Cassandra, cheeks flushing.

"Aye, and that's not why you've turned the red of the moon. It's for some other reason," Skuld grunted with laughter.

Lily watched Cassandra's hands clench and decided to interject before her friend blasted the rider with an obscenity. "We know you are doing everything you can, Skuld. My uncle is lucky he has someone so brave and cunning to watch over the men while he's gone."

Arfast tapped himself on the ear as if he were trying to clear water. "Did you say brave and cunning? You are talking about Skuld, right? Some people mistake his bravery for stupidity and his cunning for arrogance."

The one-armed man shot his friend a withering glance. "I do no more than any rider, to protect the Gardens and the outside world, as little as they may deserve us." He stood. "Time for us to leave, boy. Farragut is waiting downstairs."

Farragut was waiting in the entry. The passing days hadn't made him any more attractive. He was coated in filth from head to toe. Dirt smudged his cheeks and a sore oozed on his upper lip. His tunic was crusted with dried mud and wine stains. The only thing that appeared cared-for was his sword. The blade reflected light, and its edge was sharp enough to neatly split a hair. He scowled when he saw Lily and Cassandra.

"You didn't tell me Sprout and her flying rat were going to be here with the Blackwood girl. I've better things to do than watch these two play teacups," he said.

Skuld's good hand itched for his sword but he stopped himself. "You'll watch them and shut that rancid pit you call a mouth," he said.

Farragut scratched his neck. "I don't like this house. It makes me nervous. I'd rather sleep in a pigpen."

"It looks like you have been," Arfast said.

"One day you'll go too far, trickster," Farragut said. "On that day, I'll be there to laugh."

"As long as you brush your teeth first," Arfast said. "Sweet peppermint should do. Your breath makes a slaughterhouse smell fresh by comparison."

Lily rolled her eyes. Why was it that men felt the need to challenge each other so?

The two walked to the door. "I'll be back to check on you in the morning, Farragut," said Skuld. "I'd best find you standing guard and not curled up on the floor sleeping."

"If anything tries to harm these two, it will either be dead or never make such a mistake again," the rider said.

Arfast pulled his hood over his head and gave a shaggy grin. "About that farewell kiss …," he said, looking at Lily.

"I'm sure Farragut would be willing to give you one," she said.

The trickster chuckled. "Aye, and it would be a kiss that I would never be able to wash from my mouth."

Farragut growled. "I'm warning you —."

The two bowed to leave. Lily stopped them as they stepped out into the solid darkness of the night. "Be safe, Arfast. And when you find my brother, tell him that we are waiting on his safe return." She stood on her toes and kissed him lightly on the cheek.

"Yes, my lady," Arfast said, bowing gallantly.

The two girls and Osbold retired to Lily's room, where they spent the next few hours talking about Mugwump and the mural they had seen in the hall and what that could mean. They roasted chestnuts over the fire and drank lemon water. The gargoyle slumbered on Lily's bed, curled up like a house cat with his head tucked under his wings.

Occasionally, they heard Farragut cough in the hall. Lily looked out once to see if he wanted some chestnuts and saw him whetting his blade with a pumice stone.

Cassandra yawned as the hour grew late. "It's time for me to tuck in for the night," she said. Osbold snored softly on the bed. "I'll leave him here for you. He'll be good company."

"Are you sure?" Lily asked. She didn't want to appear eager even though the thought of sharing her bed with the gargoyle was attractive to her.

"Of course. Osbold is good company, as are you," Cassandra said.

Now it was Lily's turn to blush. "Thank you. It helps to have a friend like you."

"I've never had a friend before and now I have a best friend," Cassandra said. "Look at me growing sentimental. Anyway, I must sleep now. You will take care of Osbold, won't you?"

"As best I can," Lily said.

Cassandra smiled. "Off to bed then."

"See you in the morning," said Lily.

"See you," Cassandra said.

If she'd thought about it then, Lily would have realized her friend was plotting something. It wasn't until the next morning, when she and Osbold crept to Cassandra's room only to find an empty bed, that she realized her friend was gone. A letter lay on the blankets, written in the green girl's huge scrawling lettering.

Dear Lily,

I couldn't tell you last night because I didn't want you to try and talk me out of it (and I knew you would), but I'm going with Arfast to find Silas. If he won't have me, I'll go on my own. I have a feeling something horrible has happened and having lived my life in Nightfall Gardens, I've learned to trust my instincts. When I return with your brother, I don't want you to tease me or make jokes about how I like him. It makes me angry and, besides, what if I do? Please watch over Osbold and make sure he gets out twice a day to hunt. He really likes mice. Tell my father that I love him and I hope he understands. Watch out for yourself Lily, you're my best friend, and the only one who knows my secrets.

Your friend, Cassandra.

Lily read the letter twice and marched out to where Farragut sat, eyes half closed. He saw Lily coming and snapped to attention.

"Did you see Cassandra this morning?" she asked.

"Sprout? Aye, she left before first light to help her father with the planting," he said.

Lily cut loose with one of the many curse words Skuld had taught her.

"That's not proper language for a lady … or a sailor," Farragut said.

Lily disregarded him and hurried downstairs with the gargoyle on her shoulder and Farragut right behind. She found Polly suctioned to one of the walls, feather dusting an oil painting of a ship on a storm-tossed sea.

"I need you to get Mr. Hawthorne," she said.

The maid noted the concern in her voice. She oozed down the wall. "What is it, Miss? What's happening now? I don't know if your old servant can take any more."

Lily told her about Cassandra.

"Oh dear, oh my. I'll have him sent for right away," Polly said.

Mr. Hawthorne turned up not long after that. His bushy hair looked as though it could use a good combing, and a red bandanna was tied around his neck. The top button of his white shirt was undone, and he wore the same checkered vest as always.

"I can tell something's wrong by your face," he said. "Just don't tell me it has anything to do with my Cassie."

Lily didn't say a word but instead handed him the letter. Mr. Hawthorne collapsed into a chair and began crying as he read his daughter's words. Tears streaked his seamed face. He pulled a kerchief from his pocket and honked. "She's bull-headed, like her mother," the gardener said. "Her first word was 'no' and she's pretty much done what she wanted her whole life. I could never deny her anything. I've carried a heavy guilt at the life I've given her in Nightfall Gardens. She should have been able to play with other girls her age and not had to fear for her life. But what kind of life could she have outside of here? People would mock her and others would accuse her of being a witch. I did the best I could."

Lily touched the man on the shoulder. "I know you have, and more importantly, so does your daughter. Maybe we could still catch her."

"How? She's had a half-day head start. It's hard to find anything in the mist. I'm afraid we'd do nothing but stumble in circles and leave the house undefended. Someone has to maintain the barriers."

"Perhaps it would be okay for a day," she said.

"No, it wouldn't," said Mr. Hawthorne. He rubbed the tears from his eyes. "Cassie's independence cuts two ways. If anyone can survive out there and bring your brother back it will be her. And if I did catch her, how would I drag her back? She'd hate me for trying."

The gardener stood. "Thanks for telling me about this, but I must get back to work. The evening will be coming too soon as usual."

Lily watched him walk stoop-shouldered from the room and then she was alone with Osbold and Farragut.

The next few weeks passed in Nightfall Gardens without further upsets. No news came from Cassandra or her brother, and the hours and days melded into one another with Lily spending her mornings in the library and her afternoons training with Skuld. The one-armed man was a taskmaster who, when he could no longer get past her defenses, cheated by flinging salt into her eyes and smacking her so hard on the arm that it went completely numb. Some days Lily was so tired that she could barely get undressed before she fell into a deep, dreamless sleep. Osbold was her constant companion. The little gargoyle sat on top of a chair in the dining room and ate bits of meat she tossed him. Twice a day she let him out to hunt in the Gardens, but he always returned right before dark. At night, the gargoyle would pick at her hair and curl up around her head on the pillow. Farragut was a presence at the edge of her vision and she did the best she could to ignore him. She couldn't ignore his smell, however, and she ordered Skuld to make him bathe and wash his clothing. When he was finished, the rider shone, though his flesh was lumpy and pale. According to Polly, his leftover bathwater had been the color of squid ink. He might be clean now, but his disposition was as nasty as ever, and Lily talked with him as little as possible.

One morning she awoke to discover that it was her fourteenth birthday; the day had snuck up on her as some birthdays do. She examined herself in the mirror. How much had she changed since she had been brought to this place? She slipped into the blue dress she had worn here and found it fit loosely at the waist and was a full inch short. Could she have grown that much? Her white blond hair hung to the bottom of her shoulder blades. *'As much as I've grown on the outside, I'm no longer the same on the inside either.'* She thought of her old self; clueless, vain and selfish — and she shuddered with disgust.

As Lily came down the stairs for breakfast, she saw Polly standing at the open door, and the smile fell from her face. The maid was clutching a black envelope in her hands. Polly looked up and her voice trembled. "Someone knocked at the door, Miss. It's a letter addressed to you."

Lily descended the rest of the stairs as if someone else controlled her body. "Who sent it?"

"I don't — no one was here when I opened the door," Polly said.

She took the envelope from the maid's hand and, for a moment, she felt the envelope slither like a snake. Lily opened it, knowing already what it would say. Hadn't she read Abigail's diary? She read the first sentence and dropped the letter to the floor and walked in a daze to the dining room.

When Lily was gone, Polly picked up the letter, reading:

"The Smiling Ladies request the appearance of Lily Blackwood in the Shadow Gardens to celebrate her fourteenth birthday, one week from today."

13
JONQUIL AND THE GOBLIN TUNNELS

The fire edged low in the hearth, and the shadows seemed to draw closer as if they too wanted to hear his uncle's story. Silas pulled his cloak tight about him as Jonquil slipped into the memories of his youth. As if he still pictured them perfectly, Jonquil related his battles of long ago.

We found the dusk rider, early one morning while we were on a ride. His throat had been slit and the blood drained many hours before. I bent to examine the ground and saw the three-pronged footprint leading into the mist that meant only one thing — a goblin had escaped from the Gardens.

Thomas was queasy on his saddle behind me. "Is that Bill Bones?" he asked.

"Aye, what's left of him," I said. Old Bones, as we

called him, had been a rider as long as I could remember. He was a squat man with reddish-gray hair and a mashed nose that'd been broken when he was thrown from a horse. His sword lay in the grass next to him. I could smell the stink of loosened bowels."

This time your father didn't hold back. He leaned over his saddle and vomited. When he was finished, he wiped his mouth. "I'm sorry,' he said. "I've never —."

"No matter," I told him. "A man sees many things and more in the Gardens."

We rode back to the bunkhouse and gathered some men to help us bury Old Bones. We riders come from the dirt, and that's where we return. There's no firelight for us like you have for the Blackwood women or gray blocks of stone to mark our passing like people have beyond the gates. A dusk rider gets a hole in the ground and some hard earth tamped down over him, and that's the end. Once Old Bones was buried and wine drunk in his honor, I packed a bedroll and tied it to my horse. The red moon looked like blood had been dumped over it, and the night was too still for my tastes — that usually meant trouble.

As I finished packing, I found your father watching me from the porch. Thomas was all elbows and knees then, taller than me, but half the width. He was pale, with that same nest of hair as you and thick lips. He shifted on the porch from one foot to another.

"Well, what do you want?" I asked. "Either spit it out or quit standing there like you're going to water the nearest tree."

"I want to go with you," he said."

"Fat chance," said I. "Deiva would have me in a sling if I took her favorite son where I'm going. No, your place is at the house. I'm surprised she even let you ride with me today."

"She didn't know," Thomas said. "I told Polly I wasn't feeling well and slipped out."

"Aren't you brave?" I said, chuckling at the image of our mother's puckered expression when she found out her youngest son had disobeyed her. "But that's neither here nor there. Your place is inside the house."

"My place is with the riders. You think I don't know that? Blackwood boys are sent to the Gardens when they turn nine. It's written in those moth-eaten books in the library, and father drummed it into my head before he disappeared. You know what I say is true."

I brooded over that in the blood-red light, for Thomas was right. I remembered being awakened on my ninth birthday, Father standing over me in his wolf cloak, a grim look in his eyes. He flipped the mattress I was sleeping on and sent me tumbling to the floor. "Get up, boy and gather your belongings, for its time you learned of the cold truth of what fate has in store for you." I moved too slowly, and he slapped me hard enough to clear any cobwebs that remained in my head. I barely had time to put on my boots and pack my clothing before he dragged me out of Nightfall Manor and across the dew-soaked ground to the bunkhouse. We stopped on that very porch where my brother now stood. "Pack away your childhood and forget any foolish dreams you might have," he said. "The riders are your family now."

I could tell you of how I cried myself to sleep that

night or of the long days to come, but time is precious and only a fool wastes what little they have. I learned the way of the riders and the Gardens. I was taught in the ways of honor and duty by men like Piper Pete Sweetgrass, Eliot Hawk and daring George Rector, who everyone called Iron Jaw — men without honor, until they sloughed off their old lives at the gates and found a cause greater than themselves. They were my family more than the Blackwoods, whose name hung over me like the sword of Damocles. I broke bread and learned to fight with those men, while the house became a stranger to me, brooding over the landscape. I was only allowed inside by invitation, and those times were rare, like on my birthday or at solstice time. Deiva had always seemed as remote to me as the mountains that loomed beyond the gates, and Thomas was no more than a wailing babe when I was exiled. My father was a rider, and sometimes I wondered if that would bring us closer, but nothing could be further from the truth. He went out of his way to prove that I would be given no special treatment. I woke before first light to stoke the fire and bring in water and slept only after the last rider collapsed into his bed with exhaustion. He spent his nights at the Manor, only to come back fresh the next morning, ready to lead the riders on patrol and make sure the grounds were secure. He acknowledged me with little more than a steely-eyed gaze and occasional nugget of news.

"Your brother is as tall as a ripple tree; it won't be long before he joins you," he said. But he didn't reckon that Deiva would refuse to loosen her grip on her other

son. Thomas was the youngest, and her baby. She wouldn't consign him to a life of toil or herself to a life of loneliness. On Thomas's ninth birthday, I waited for him to be brought to the bunkhouse, but he never came. Instead, father rode up, out of breath and shaking with rage. "Centuries of tradition tossed, and for what?" he spat. "Thomas isn't strong enough … he'll catch his death of cold … his heart won't be able to stand the things that he sees …he's too sensitive," all said in tones mocking my mother. "Doesn't she understand hardness is what keeps this place from crumbling to dust?" My mother was mistress of Nightfall Gardens, though, and her word was his command. My brother wasn't to join us; his life would lead down a different path than the dusk riders.

Did it make me jealous? Aye, why should I lie? No one had stood up for me. No one was there to take my hand or wipe the tears from my eyes on my first nights at the bunkhouse, when the boy inside me smothered that foolish toy called childhood. No one was there to feed me soup when I was ill or pat my back after the first time I stood down a Shade from the White Garden.

I swallowed that bitter pill and threw myself into my work. Years passed. I saw little of Thomas, and when I did it was as though we were strangers who used to know one another. The words didn't come easy at first, but once we started, the ease of our kinship returned. It never occurred to me that he might suffer as much inside the Manor, with no companionship other than our mother, as I was outside. More years passed, and the wolves were growing stronger and more brazen. They *brought down a rider and his horse and were even seen sniffing about the house. Their leader was a great white brute with scars that mottled one side of his face. One red night, Father chased him into the mist and never returned. A rider's life is a momentary flicker in the mist. It's nothing for one of us to have our life stripped bare. That doesn't mean our lives aren't dear to us. We cling to that spark as fiercely as any on the other side of the gates, but we're always aware of the high stakes in the Gardens. The riders searched for days afterwards, but we never found him. He must have accomplished what he set out to do though, for the wolves disappeared— at least until recently.*

Father's death was the final straw for our mother. I was the one who delivered the news. "Liar! He'll be home for dinner," she said. "The table is set for his return — see." And indeed, the table was set for his return and would remain that way until the food was nothing but fetid remains of mold and maggots. She wouldn't have the rooms changed from how they were when my father was there, as though he would come back at any second. "Get out of my sight," she told me. "You're not a Blackwood. Where's my Thomas? Get my son?" You know the rest of that tale. Your grandmother sat by the window watching for a ghost to return, until the gilirot took her looks and her mind.

Thomas was of age now, a teen, and our mother and the house could no longer keep him from what waited for him in the Gardens. He watched me with the dark brown eyes he'd inherited from our father."

"'We'd best be going if we're to leave," I said. "The

*hours of light are precious few once we're in the mist.
We need warn the villagers of the threat coming their
way."*

*The villagers were already well aware of the threat
the goblin posed, as we discovered when we reached
Priortage two days later. It was a slow journey, made
slower by the saddle sores that inflamed your father's
backside, which meant we had to walk for long stretches
at a time. We talked little, but by the time we reached the
village, the distance between us had begun to shrink.
Your father was eager to prove his mettle — how eager, I
was too learn shortly thereafter.*

*Priortage was cloaked in a fog so thick that it felt as if
we were in a waking dream as we rode down the main
street. The shops that normally bustled were closed, and
the taverns, which were the heart of the village, were
empty. The only person we saw was a red-haired
washerwoman with her daughter carrying bundles of
clothing on their shoulders. The woman grabbed her
daughter, and they disappeared into the mist before we
could ask any questions.*

"'Where is everyone?" Thomas asked.

*"The goblin," I said. He had come straight for the
village, and something terrible had happened. Guilt
gnawed at me. We should have ridden faster. I had
dawdled to spend more time with my brother, and now
there was the blood on my hands.*

*We stopped at the jail and the Blix, the besotted old
jailer, told us what had happened.*

*"Saw it same as I see you 'fore me," the pop-eyed
lawman said. "Jumped out of the woods and snatched*

Fyodor's daughter away, before disappearing back into the dark. It was an ugly bugger, with gray skin and pointed ears and scythes instead of fingers. It had ridges down its back like a big lizard and his eyes were pure gold and full of malice."

The men of the village were still out searching for the missing child and the goblin, to no avail, Blix told us. The father of the missing, Fyodor, was a prominent businessman. He was offering a hefty reward for anyone who could rescue his daughter, Moira.

"My mother was kidnapped by a goblin?" Silas asked in disbelief.

The cabin fell quiet in those final minutes before the first strained light of dawn. A log burst and split in the fireplace. Trainer had a thin blanket pulled up to his neck, and the door to Mirabelle's room was closed. His uncle didn't answer for a long moment. "Aye, it was the first time either of us were to lay eyes on the beauty of Priortage as she was called then, but that wasn't to happen for a while, and it almost cost your Father and I our lives." Jonquil stirred the memories of his past and then continued his story.

We had the full tale of what happened when we arrived at your grandparent's home, that fortress of living wood on the outskirts of the village. One of his guards hustled us in to meet him. Fyodor was busy at work when we entered. He was writing on a scroll, his nose inches from the parchment. His quill scratched at paper. A bottle of ink was opened nearby. He looked up as he finished a sentence. Your grandfather was in the last bloom of his youth then. The lines around his face hadn't formed a permanent scowl. His hair was still black. There was a flush to his cheeks. The only indication he was under stress was the bags under his eyes that bespoke a sleepless night.

"So I suppose you've come about the reward," he said, pushing back from his desk.

"We've come about the goblin," I said, not liking his attitude. "And we'll save your daughter if we can. But first, we need know what really happened."

"I've told Moira a thousand times never to dawdle after dark when she visits friends," Fyodor said, picking up a pair of petrified hydra eggs and clacking them nervously in his hands. "This town is full of reprobates and leeches, and no man can see my daughter without falling under her spell. As you gentlemen know, there are things waiting with claws in the night. Moira is headstrong, though. 'You worry too much,' she's said on many occasions. Well, I ask you, did I worry enough? Because right now, my daughter is dead, captive or something far worse."

For a moment I thought he would cry, but Fyodor choked back his tears and told us the tale. Moira was walking through the village from her friend's house when the goblin leapt in front of her in full view of the townspeople. Before anyone could draw breath, the fiend whisked her into the darkness of the forest. Some villagers gave chase, but lost them in the woods. And that brought us to where we were now, sitting in front of him.

"Gentlemen, I can make you rich if you bring my eldest daughter back unscathed," Fyodor said. "I could find you a place in Priortage, and you could put away your cloaks and enjoy a less dangerous life than the one being a dusk rider offer."

"That's a kind offer, but I'm afraid we're wedded to where we come from," Thomas said.

"Why?" Fyodor demanded. "I've known many riders in my time, and their lives are nasty, brutish affairs. Many retire here if they live long enough."

"We're Blackwoods," I said, standing to go. You could have scrapped your grandfather's jaw off the floor. I've seen that avarice in many men's eyes when they look at the manor house and imagine the riches inside."

"'Bl — Blackwoods. Pardon me. I didn't know," Fyodor said, straightening his shirt and running his hands through his hair.

"Why should it matter? Come on, Thomas. If your daughter is alive we'll bring her back to you," I said as we left.

"What was that all about?" Thomas asked when we were mounted on our horses.

"Our name," I replied. "Half the people here despise us for the curse we brought upon the world, and the other half wants our wealth. That man saw coin and power when he heard who we are."

It wasn't long before we couldn't ride any further through the trees on our horses. We stopped at a cottage and paid the hermit who lived there to watch our animals until we returned. We humped the packs on our backs for another two hours before we made camp for the night.

"How will we find this beast?" Thomas said as we enjoyed a roast squirrel over a spit.

"What do you know of goblins?" I asked, taking a bit of the greasy meat.

Thomas rubbed his chin. "Not enough. Mother tried to keep such things from me. She said it would spoil my digestion and ruin my nerves to know what lurked in the Gardens."

"She was right about that. Better to have a ruined stomach though than to be caught unaware and not know how to defend yourself."

I wiped my fingers on my jerkin and washed down my meal with a skin of wine. I looked up hoping to see stars, those pinpricks of light that people on the other side of the gates take for granted, but all I saw was the smoke from the fire merging with fog. Anything could have been waiting in the darkness beyond the fire.

"The old books are full of tales of goblins," I started. "Their memory lingers beyond the gates even now. They are one of the most ancient races. In stories, they are thieving, conniving monsters with bulbous bellies that stand no taller than your knee. Reality couldn't be further from the truth. Goblins are hive-minded and reptilian, which makes them dangerous. Their needs are few: feast and fear. Anything beyond that is past their limited understanding."

"Should be easy to catch it then," Thomas said. He wasn't used to drinking wine and his face was flushed and his words were slurred."

"Him," I said. "This goblin is male, and just because he doesn't think the same way we do, doesn't mean he isn't crafty. If you make the mistake of underestimating our foe, it could get us both killed."

"You said that it was simple-minded," Thomas said. The wine was making him defensive. His Blackwood bluster was coming to the surface.

"I didn't say simple-minded," I replied. "I said hive-minded. Goblins burrow tunnels and build nests underground where they store their food. In some cases, hundreds of intricate tunnels that intersect. The oldest stories tell of these tunnels and the nests of goblins that had to be burned from the inside. These stories also tell of the people who were found inside. Fresh food, strung up by tree roots, raving with insanity at what the creatures had done to them. They tell of darker things as well — people missing fingers, toes, legs, eyes, and ears. The goblins ate them, piece by piece, keeping them alive as long as possible, a constant food supply at their command. This is the foe we face, and that's why we should put the wineskin away. We'll need all of our wits about us when day comes."

"The girl Moira —," Thomas paused.

"Might still be alive. Goblins have a single focus. First, he'll want to build a nest and then secure a consistent food supply. It might be that this creature will leave her unharmed until he has more than one person in his pantry. But thinking on that now though, won't bring sleep and we need be refreshed for what we face tomorrow," I told him.

There was little sleep that night though. Every snap

of a branch or rooting of an animal brought me to my feet with sword in hand. The next morning, your father was green in the face and his head pounded from the wine he'd drunk.

We trekked through the woods most of that day, feeling our way through the mist and stopping occasionally when we came upon a goblin track in the soil.

"It's heading into the lowlands," I said. "Easier to burrow in the soil there."

"What happens when we find him?" Thomas asked as the day waned.

"We'll know soon enough," I said, going down on one knee to examine the most recent footprint. I didn't tell him that I questioned whether the two of us would be able to kill the monster if it snuck up on us in the dark. Goblin flesh is hard as iron and they fight mindlessly until no more life is in them. Pain means nothing to such monsters.

I thought we were going to have to pitch camp for the night again when we finally found his lair. Have you ever seen a goblin lair, lad? They burrow tunnels with unholy speed, and in a matter of hours create a maze of passages that lead nowhere, or in on each other, or straight into darkness, where anyone foolish enough to go meets a quick death."

We saw the mounds of earth before we reached the tunnel entrance. Heaps of fresh earth piled as tall as a man and as long as several carriages hitched together. There were four mounds spread before us in the lowland. Who knew if there were others we couldn't see.

"He's been busy," I said, drawing my blunderbuss.

"He — it's impossible. He couldn't have dug so quickly," Thomas said. He peered unbelieving at the mounds."

"You wouldn't say that if you'd spent time in the Gardens," I said.

"What?"

"Doubt the impossible," I told him. "Spend enough time in the Gardens and any notions about what is impossible fly out the window. Only fools doubt what's before their eyes."

Thomas didn't say anything, but I could see fear in his eyes. It was one thing to hear about the terrors outside of the house and another to confront them face to face.

"What do we do now?" he asked, licking his lips.

I nodded at the tunnels. "We go down there, before darkness falls," I said.

"'Down — down there?" he stammered, and I wondered if he was rethinking his decision to come on this adventure.

"Relax," I told him. "One of us must stay here in case the goblin should surface."

Thomas calmed himself and said, "I can shimmy down that hole easier than you."

"Aye, you could," I told him. "But it's what I've been trained to do. There'd be greater risk to the girl as well if you were the first down there."

Your father nodded. "But if I hear anything—."

" — You'll stay right here until I return," I finished."

*I crouched next to the opening of the closest mound:
A hole, barely large enough for a grown man to fit
through. The walls were ridged with clay. Earthworms
wriggled in the soft earth. I fished a candle from my pack
and struck a flint; the flame sputtered before catching
hold.*

"You're going now?" he said, incredulous.

*"No time like the present," I said. I put a hand on his
shoulder. "Don't follow after, no matter what you hear.
Remember, you're a Blackwood. Our family has been
tested in ways that has put steel in our spine."*

"Jonquil, I —," Thomas said.

*"If the goblin should surface," I said, cutting him off,
"aim for his neck. That's his weak point. Stay out of
reach of his claws, they are sharp enough to slit your
belly and spill your entrails."*

*On that grisly sentiment, I clamped a dagger into my
teeth and slithered into the tunnel with the candle in
front of me. The inside of the tunnel was more cramped
than I had expected. Its walls hemmed me in on all sides,
and earth crumbled around me as my shoulders rubbed
against them. At any moment, I expected to come to a
place where the walls were too narrow or the ceiling to
collapse, but neither happened, so I continued inching
my way along. The candle illuminated the tunnel
around me, but blinded me to what lay ahead. I would
rather have that, though than the goblin crawling
toward me in the darkness and to not be able to see him.
Worms, stones and albino roots were exposed in the soil.
Sweat dripped into my eyes. The further I went, the
warmer it became.*

Up ahead, another tunnel met the one I was in. I wriggled to a stop and looked both ways, but the tunnel only led into more darkness. I continued along my path. I tried to swallow but my throat was parched and now I had a new fear: that the goblin would crawl up on me from behind. Thrice, I thought I heard something scrabbling after me, only to find nothing when I looked back.

I continued past more tunnels. The soil grew wetter and the walls leaked water. How far I went I do not know. Eventually, the tunnel widened, and I came to a chamber of sandy pebbles that gouged my hands and knees. The room was large enough to stand in and big enough to hold a feasting table. I held the candle up to see where I was. Tree roots hung like tentacles overhead, the roots were twisted and wider than my leg. Hundreds of roots curled down from the roof of the chamber, and that was where I found the girl.

She was strung up amongst the roots. Her wrists, waist and ankles fastened to them.. Fiery red hair hung down in her face, and she wore a green dress that was torn and coated with mud. She looked to be no more than sixteen and she was the most beautiful woman I'd ever seen.

I held the candle aloft but the room was empty. The goblin was off sleeping or else on the surface. I felt my stomach twist in knots at the thought of my brother alone above. There was no time for sentimental thoughts though. I had to get the girl down.

As I hacked at the roots, she stirred. Her green eyes blinked and then registered who I was and she smiled the most blessed smile I've ever seen. A spate of freckles dotted her cheeks.

"Is this a dream?" she asked.

"If it is, it's one we're both having," I told her."

I cut her down and took her in my arms, setting her against the far wall in case the goblin returned. I rubbed her wrists and ankles, trying to help restore the circulation.

"I'm Moira," she said as the feeling came back to her.

"Jonquil," I replied.

"You're a dusk rider, aren't you? My father told me about you," she said. "He said you were a bunch of damned men that were looking for salvation."

I laughed. "He's not far off the mark. Now we need to get back to the surface so my brother —."

The wall exploded behind us as the goblin sprang into the chamber. Earth rained down as he spun to face me. He was even more hideous to behold than I thought he would be. His mottled gray skin was grimed with clay and encrusted with white barnacles of age. His face was long and the chin curved up all the way to his nose. The goblin's eyes looked like honeycombs. He tilted his pointed head from side to side and hissed.

I cursed myself for letting my guard down, and jumped up to meet him. The goblin was on me and I tried to drive my dagger into his exposed throat. His hands were strong enough to crush stone. He squeezed so hard on my sword hand, I thought it would be little more than dust when he was finished. Round we danced in a circle. My dagger slashed at his throat and threw sparks from his hide instead. His hideous mouth was

ALLEN HOUSTON

inches from my face. I could see his yellow fangs and black tongue. He bit at my shoulder with his mouth, and his teeth crunched my bone and flesh. I bit my tongue to keep from screaming. The goblin tore savagely at my flesh as we twisted in our death struggle. I thought he would never loosen his grip, but all of a sudden, he let go and spun to where Moira stood. She was behind him with a rock clutched in her tiny fist. She must have struck him because he screeched with rage and cleared the space between them in a bound. I determined then and there I was in love with the red-haired girl and I'd let the goblin pick my bones clean before anything happened to her.

"'Here you go," I said, with my knife in hand. 'You don't want her, you want me."

The goblin looked from Moira to me and back, before deciding I was the bigger threat. He came at me again, but this time I was ready. I slammed his arm away and gouged at his throat with my knife. It pierced his skin, and a putrid substance gassed from the opening. The goblin drove me into the wall, where he raked at me with his claws. One of them slashed my face all the way to the bone. That's how I got this scar you see on my cheek, lad. Blood blinded me and warmed my face. I kicked his stomach, but I might as well have kicked armor. The goblin bit my shoulder again, feasting on my flesh. The strength fled my body. I was most sorry for what would happen to the girl, not for my own sad exit from life. The moment I resigned myself to my fate was when I was saved. The goblin's head jerked away and life rushed back to me. There before me was a sight I never thought to see.

Thomas stood over the body of the goblin with a knife in his hand. Moira watched from across the room.

"How —?" I tried to speak but the word burned in my throat.

"I — I followed you," Thomas said. I had never been so happy to see my brother before and was never so happy to see him again. He clutched a dagger whose blade was covered in green blood. The beast lay dead at his feet.

Moira looked from my brother to me and then back. If I had been a smarter man I would have realized that this was the moment she chose Thomas over me.

"And who might you be?" she asked Thomas.

I saw my brother's face go red from his neck to his shaggy hairline.

"Thomas," he said.

"Well, Thomas, would you help a lady tend that wicked wound on your brother's face and find her way back to the outside world?"

They cleaned my wound the best they could, and we crawled back through the tunnels. The hair prickled on my neck at the thought that the goblin might come back to life and grasp my ankle, pulling me back to finish the job he had started. Nothing happened, though. Thomas lent me a hand and dragged me out into the night. Never had the stink of the marshes smelled so sweet. Moira grinned at us covered in mud.

"You two do know how to introduce yourselves," she laughed."

We camped near the remains of the goblin tunnels

that night. In the morning, we set off for Priortage. I could bore you with the story of how on our return, your grandfather pledged Moira's hand to me as the eldest Blackwood. Of how I was lovesick enough to think she might be happy with me. And of how she told me shortly before our wedding day that she was in love with your father — my brother. I could tell you of the hurt I carry inside, a scar as wicked as the one on my face. But day is coming, lad, and tales of heartbreak are best served with cold ale or hot wine. It's a lesson I hope you never have to learn.

Jonquil finished as the last embers of the fire died. Dirty daylight was peeking through cracks in the cabin walls. Silas sat before his uncle entranced. *'Every one has secrets, and this is one my parents probably never thought I'd hear,'* he thought. Silas felt sorry for his uncle, but he knew his parents loved each other and he was a product of that love. *'People get hurt in love sometimes. It hasn't happened to me yet, but that doesn't mean that it won't.'*

Trainer stirred on the floor. The door to Mirabelle's room opened. His cousin came out stretching her arms.

"What are you two talking about?" she asked, placing a hand over her mouth to stifle a yawn.

"Coffee," Trainer said. "Hot and black, and lots of it. That's what I need right now." He got up and stoked the fire.

Jonquil limped to the door. He opened it and took a breath of cool air. "We were trading stories of the past and things that were never meant to be."

Mirabelle looked at Silas confused. He shrugged his shoulders at her.

The day passed in a blur. By afternoon, the four were growing restless.

"If your Gran doesn't come soon, we must leave," Jonquil said. "It's no longer safe here."

"She'll come," Mirabelle said though there was more doubt in her voice than there had been the day before.

"Keep telling yourself that," Trainer said. The rider set off down the hill to see if he could spot anyone approaching.

The clouds thickened in the sky. A fresh wall of mist blew in, making it impossible to see past the bushes near the front of the cabin. The fog was so thick, Silas wondered if Trainer would be able to find his way back to them.

"Don't worry," Jonquil said. "Dan's not the type to look for trouble if it needn't be. He'll return."

Daylight was but a memory when the dusk rider finally appeared, leading a gray horse.

"Gran's horse," Mirabelle gasped running to the animal. "Where did you find him?"

"Wandering the trail," Trainer said.

"Did you see — did you find — ?" Mirabelle stammered for words.

"I saw no signs of a struggle, if that's what you mean," the sour man said.

Jonquil placed a comforting hand on Mirabelle's

shoulders. "We know nothing as of yet. Don't let your mind range with fear. Remember what the Daughters taught you."

Mirabelle nodded, wiping tears from her eyes. "I — we have to go and search for her."

"Go back into that?" Trainer snapped. "Are you mad? I barely found my way back here. I told you — I told all of you — that we should leave but no one listened." He stomped past them into the cabin. "I'm done with good deeds for the day. I'll go out in the morning, but not before then."

"He's right," Jonquil said. "It would be madness to walk into this. Looks like we'll be here another night. We'll set out at first light and look for your Gran."

"And if we don't find her?" Mirabelle asked.

"Then we head to Nightfall Gardens," Jonquil said.

"Silas?" Mirabelle was inches from her cousin, and still the mist made her look ghostly.

"I — ," Silas wanted to comfort her and tell her that he would go with her as soon as the fog lightened and that she was his grandmother as well as hers. But he never got the chance to say any of that, for out of the swirling mist came the most unholy roar he'd ever heard in his life. The sound was louder and wilder than that of any wolf, bear or other natural beast. It was the sound of some extinct creature come back to life, of a new species from the most remote corner of the world. The bellow came from far off in the hills to the north and echoed through the valley, the full-throated sound of a creature on the hunt. The skin prickled on his arms. Mirabelle's hand slid into his, and as the sound died, leaving only silence, he felt her shaking.

"Get inside," Jonquil said, pointing his walking stick at them. "Now!"

"What was that?" Silas asked, as Mirabelle dug her fingernails into his palm.

His uncle looked at him, and Silas saw terror in his eyes.

"Eldritch," said Jonquil.

14
GRIM READING OF THE CARDS

'I could die of happiness,' Lily thought as she let herself drift to the bottom of the indoor pool that was fed by a natural hot spring. *'I'm sure it would be much more pleasant than what the Smiling Ladies have in store for me.'* The pool was marked on Abigail's map, but Lily only stumbled across it while walking in a daze after receiving the black envelope.

'In two days, my life may end,' she reminded herself.

Her feet touched the tiled pool bottom, and a hand grasped her ankle. Startled, she opened her eyes and looked down to see the gray faces of what appeared to be three long-dead children circling her. She pushed off the floor and swam the length of the pool. Her long legs kicked under the water, and she saw the spirit of one of the children racing her. He was younger than her, no more than eight or nine, with black hair, pale skin and circles under his eyes. He smiled and she saw the gap of his missing front tooth. *'They can't hurt me, they are only ghosts.'* She felt no ill will coming from the children, only curiosity, and the longing to have life back once again.

"Sad things they are, Miss," Polly had told her when she first discovered the pool. "Orphans the Blackwoods took in. No one knows what happened. Their bodies were found floating lifeless in the pool. There's some that say the oldest drowned the other two, and their spirits came and took his life before he could get away. Others say they were poisoned. It was before my time, Miss. You're the first person to use the pool in many years."

'I won't let them drive me away,' Lily thought, popping to the surface and gasping for air. The spring water piping into the pool was hot enough to warm her bones and untie the knots in her neck. For the first time since she'd come to this place she felt truly warm, and she wasn't going to let the spirits take that from her.

Lily swam for the next hour with the ghosts of the dead children racing alongside her: a young girl and two boys dressed in old-fashioned bathing suits. Lily wore an ill-fitting bathing suit that she had found in her grandmother's belongings. When she was finished, she toweled off and dried her hair by the poolside. She could see the spirits of the children watching from beneath the surface. "I'll see you tomorrow," she told them, before setting off to her room.

Once inside, Lily changed into riding pants, a sapphire-colored shirt, scuffed boots and a silk-lined cloak. She finished by strapping on a dagger, which was a gift from Skuld, and lighting a candle. *'I must be quick. I only have a few hours until Polly comes searching.'* She pressed the hidden spot that opened the passage in the wall. The wall groaned open, exposing cobwebs and darkness. A draft made her candle flame flicker.

Lily's journey through the passage was fraught with distractions. Voices whispered to her from adjacent rooms. Eyes seemed to follow her, but when she turned nothing was there. She stepped into a spiderweb and was reminded of the chittering spider as big as a kitten that she fought the first time she discovered this passage. Far beneath her, banging and clanging sounds came deep from within the house. Lily stopped. She thought she heard a growling voice call "Work hard and faster," but it was so faint she wasn't sure if it was real or imagined. Down she went until she came to the gate that led out behind the Shadow Garden. The gate was rusted, but when Lily pushed, it opened as if on new hinges. *'It knows I'm a Blackwood,'* thought Lily.

There was no time to admire the scenery once she was above ground. If the dusk riders saw her, they would send her back to Nightfall Manor, and if she stumbled upon a creature from the Gardens, it might mean the end of her life. She drew the cloak about her and hurried into the mist. The woods were deep and foreboding in the afternoon light, but, she had explored this route with Cassandra before and she knew the way.

Soon, a cottage appeared before her in the forest. The cottage had a straw roof that sagged with age. Smoke puffed merrily from the chimney, and the surroundings were free of fog, as if some invisible barrier circled the property. A pair of crows watched from the rooftop as she approached.

"Well, well, if it isn't the lady of the manor. I wondered when you'd be coming along," Raga said after answering Lily's rap on the door.

"How did you know I was coming?" Lily asked, following the old witch into the cottage.

"Oh, you Blackwoods always do," Raga said cryptically. "Now, how can I help you, dearie? Do you want me to read your future? Mother Raga can mix a potion that will make you forget your woes or one that will ease your journey from this life if you wish. Before any of that though, there is a price to pay."

Lily took a chair across from Raga in front of the fire. She glanced into the flames and thought she saw the orange outlines of tiny beings composed entirely of fire, watching from atop one of the logs. On the mantle, the stuffed head of a monkey stared back at her with glass eyes. She shifted on the seat and tried to not show surprise when she looked at

Raga.

Cassandra had warned her that the witch didn't like it when people stared at what she'd done to herself. "Her head's on backwards," the green girl had explained the last time they visited. "Raga botched a transmigration spell and hasn't been able to change it back since."

The old witch's face peered at Lily over her shoulder blades, while the front of Raga's body warmed its hands at the fire. Raga's greasy hair looked like it hadn't been washed for as long as Lily had been alive. One of her eyes swam behind a milky caul, and long black whiskers dangled down from her chin. A jagged yellow tooth jutted up from her bottom lip and her wrinkled face looked as if it had been beaten against a rock every one of her hundred-plus years. For all that, though, Raga used her powers for good, or at least that was what Cassandra told her.

"Pretty, aren't I?" Raga said, catching Lily staring.

Lily blushed. "I wasn't trying to — ."

"It's all right, lass," Raga said, chuckling. "I was once a fair maid, but time has played me like an accordion full of pleasant and sour notes."

Lily remembered the story of how Raga had been driven to Nightfall Gardens. Once, she lived in a mountain village where she taught herself how to use the plants of the woods to make healing poultices and other white magic. One day a boy fell out of a tree and broke his leg. Raga mended him using magic and afterwards the frightened villagers drove her away, after almost killing her. Cassandra said that the witch had lived here in these woods for more than a century.

"Before we get started, what did you bring Raga?" the witch asked.

Lily dug in her cloak and took out a sack filled with chocolate-covered dates.

The old woman's mouth drooled with hunger, and the spittle rolled down into the long whiskers of her chin. A leathery tongue popped out and licked her lips.

"You know what to do next, yes you do," Raga said. The old witch had trouble feeding herself since her head was on backward. She also had a notorious sweet tooth. Lily plucked one of the dates from the bag and popped it into Raga's mouth.

"Mmmm, dat's good," the old witch said, around a mouthful of fruit.

Lily fed the rest of the bag to her, doing her best to ignore the grunting, smacking and the feeling of the old witch sucking on her fingers. When she was finished, Raga leaned back and sighed. "My stomach's going to pay for that later on, but, at my age, every sweet you eat might be your last. Now clear a space on the table for me. There's some reading cards on the mantle, best get those as well."

Lily pushed aside the skeleton of a cat, a jar filled with eyeballs and a cage with a black sheet thrown over it. She heard something rustling inside. Then she got a stack of begrimed cards from the mantle. She turned one over and found herself staring at an illustration of a family that was being devoured by wolves.

"Not so quickly," Raga said. "We have to do this properly. You don't want to receive someone else's future by accident."

The witch turned around so the back of her head and front of her body was facing Lily. Her hands searched blindly on the table, until they found the deck of cards Lily had placed there and she began shuffling them with a deft hand. Lily wondered how Raga could tell what she was doing, but the old witch shuffled the cards back and forth so rapidly that they were a blur.

"Put your hand on them and think of your life," Raga said when she was finished. Lily placed her hand on the cards and made a silent wish that everything would turn out all right.

After a few seconds, Raga pulled the cards away and shuffled them once more.

"Pick a card," the witch said, when she'd finished.

'This is foolish,' Lily thought, but she tapped one of the cards and pulled it from the deck.

Raga flipped the card over and it showed a knight in a suit of shining armor carrying a lance onto a battlefield strewn with dead bodies. The visor of his helmet hid his face. The banner on his horse was black, with a red broken heart. None of those things were what caught Lily's attention. What made her gasp were the black grotesqueries with demonic faces that clung like parasites to his arms and back. One of the creatures tore at the knight's throat, but he rode on, seemingly oblivious.

"Who — who is this?" Lily asked. There was something oddly familiar about the person, something that she couldn't pin down.

"Raga didn't tell you that you would like your future," the witch said. All Lily could see was Raga's lank hair and the bald spot on the back of her head. "It's your Love, the tormented twisted soul you give your heart to. He is consumed by the evils that rend his flesh and threaten to kill the last part of him that is good."

'No,' Lily thought. *'She's wrong. It's only trickery'*

As if to prove this thought, Lily snatched not one, but two cards from the deck. The first showed a crumbling gray castle in a landscape that looked alien and barren. Nothing could be seen in any direction as far you looked. The walls were breaking apart with age, and bats flew out of the empty windows into the night sky.

"This represents the house where you live. All buildings must crumble and fall with time, but something is rotting this one from within its core," Raga said. "Until you find out what that is, the house will grow weaker until it collapses."

The old witch pinned the third card to the table. The illustration showed a woodcutter and his wife standing by a cottage not unlike Raga's. The woodcutter was holding an ax in his hands, and his wife was dressed in the simple clothes of a peasant, with her hair wrapped in a bandana. Two children, a boy and girl, walked away from them into woods that were dark and deep.

"A child must grow and leave his family," Raga said. "The terror for all parents is not knowing what lies along the paths their children take."

Lily thought of her parents, trapped on the other side of the gates, and how frightened they must have been feeling for these many months. She reached out and chose another card from the deck.

Raga flipped the card over and she jabbed it with her finger. "Death looms for you or someone that you love," the old witch said. Her head shook as she spoke, but since her face was hidden Lily couldn't gauge her reaction. "You know this already; what you don't know is how to change your fate."

The card on the table in front of Lily showed the inside of an abattoir, where the bodies of cows, pigs, sheep and what looked suspiciously like a young boy and girl, hung from hooks. They were being carried along by a conveyor belt toward a boiling vat. Workers in bloodied smocks wielded carving knifes and were hacking away at a wide-eyed steer that bled out on the floor.

"Look closely at the faces," said Raga.

Lily spotted them immediately. The Smiling Ladies lurked at the periphery, sketches in the shadows, watching the bloodletting.

"The Smiling Ladies," Lily said.

"Some call them that," Raga said. "But they have older names, ones that were used before the written word, when people still painted on cave walls."

"What does it mean? How can they be in this picture?" Lily asked, sweating. The cabin was small and cramped, and the roaring fire was stifling. The stuffed head of the monkey seemed to watch from over the mantle. She saw movement in one of the corners as a black cat slunk from beneath a chair and across the dirt floor.

"They've always been here. They are the minions of the darkness that threatens to consume this world. But where there is darkness, there is also light," Raga said. "It is in that light that you will find a way to defeat them."

"I — I have to go to the Shadow Garden," Lily said, blurting out the story of the black envelope and her fourteenth birthday.

"Raga has seen many strange things here and many wonderful sights, but also more tragedy than any family should have to endure. She knows of this rite of passage, of what awaited Abigail and the other Blackwood women who never returned from the Shadow Garden. You must protect yourself; you must keep your wits about you, no matter what they show you or what they offer. They can do you no harm while you are their guest. They will try and turn you into an instrument of

241

your own destruction. If you keep your mind clear and your heart pure, you will come away stronger than ever. One slip, however, one taste of the temptation they offer, and you will end up in one of the stone crypts under Nightfall Manor, restless for all eternity with the others of your family."

Lily thought of the scuttling creatures, buried in the tombs under the house, and shuddered.

The next card that Lily picked showed a closed door, to which a woman pressed her ear as if straining to listen to what was taking place inside.

"Secrets and answers," Raga said. "What Abigail sought and didn't find, what you are searching for, all will be revealed if you search in the right place."

"Pandora's Box," Lily said. "Abigail believed that it was buried on the grounds of Nightfall Gardens. She believed that it held the answer to breaking the curse of our family."

"It holds other things as well," said Raga. "It holds great evils, those that are still trapped inside. It also contains the key to capturing all of the evils that sprang forth when Pandora opened the box and of finishing this place."

The sixth card showed a man locked inside a dungeon. The prisoner looked to have been there a long time. His beard grew to his knees and he wore tatters of clothing. He was chained to the wall. A skeleton hung in shackles next to him. Light penetrated through bars on the door. The prisoner looked longingly toward those shafts of light.

"The curse that binds you," Raga explained.

"Pandora's Box," Lily said.

"Pandora's folly is more like it," Raga said. "Yet, she is no better or worse than any of us. The same temptation that ensnared her could have trapped anyone."

"What does is it mean?"

"What do any of the cards mean? They are guideposts. They are match strikes to illuminate the darkness. There is also truth in them."

"What sort of truth?" asked Lily. She was growing tired of Raga's puzzles. Why couldn't anyone in Nightfall Gardens say what they meant without speaking in code?

The old witch must have read her mind. "As curses are made, they can also be broken. The answer to the age-old curse that has plagued the Blackwood family lies buried beneath the ground in one of the gardens."

'I knew it,' Lily thought. *'Pandora's Box is real, and once I find it…'* What would she do then? How could she draw everything back inside without releasing those evils that were still trapped inside?

"Where is it? What do I do with the box once it's in my possession?" Lily asked.

Raga cackled. "If I knew that, Nightfall Gardens would have been dust many years ago. This place clouds my vision. Be glad that it does, for if I could find it, so could the creatures of the Gardens."

A wolf howled in the woods, and Raga went straight as a rod. "The white beast is drawing his pack. Some wickedness is bound to be done. They are calling to each other. You must leave before darkness falls on these woods."

Raga turned over the last card that Lily chose. The illustration was of three paths leading into deep woods, with a traveler standing in the foreground, unsure of which one to take.

"A sacrifice and a choice," the old witch crowed. "You must give away that which you hold most dear and you must choose between that which is light and that which is dark."

"I've already made my choice," Lily said angrily. "I'm here, aren't I? They've already taken my parents and my dreams of Paris and the stage. What more do they want? I've chosen the light. How much more must I do to prove that? I've fought the creatures of the Gardens and barely escaped being killed. My brother may be dead. I have but one friend. Death waits at every turn for me. I've done all of that for the light; so that those monsters won't destroy the world."

Raga turned around then, so Lily could see her face. The old witch's dead eye swam blue behind the film of her caul. Her other eye penetrated Lily as if she were looking at her naked.

"Hmmm. I wonder if you have," Raga muttered.

"Unless you have anything more to tell me, I have to get back," Lily said. Her voice was shaking. *'I thought I had learned to control my emotions but I haven't.'*

"No, Raga's said all she's going to today," she

said. The old witch stood and thumped her cane on the ground, walking backwards to the door. "I have some honey dram that would give you dreamless sleep if that would help."

Lily shook her head. She needed all of her wits to prepare for the Shadow Garden.

"Futures can change," Raga called as Lily left. "Hearts aren't set in stone."

Farragut was hammering on her door when Lily slipped back into her bedroom. She draped a blanket over her shoulders and opened the door, rubbing her eyes as if she'd just awoken.

"What do *you* want?" she asked.

"Did I wake your highness from her beauty sleep?" Farragut asked. "You must have the most comfortable bed in the world, as much time as you spend in your room. Don't worry about me out here on my hard chair. I have my whetting stone and the voices from the other rooms to keep me company."

The last few days hadn't gone well for the dusk rider. Voices constantly whispered to him from the rooms along the hall and kept him from having a moment's rest. He had awoken once to see a boy with a purple velvet jacket and knee-high pants with a satchel of books thrown over his shoulder at the end of the hall. Only when he looked more closely, did Farragut see the blood and gore running down the boy's face.

"Saw him same as I saw you," Farragut had said. "Popped into one of the rooms, and the door slammed after him."

He looked even worse than normal, if such a thing were possible. Almost overnight his hair had turned gray and there were dark circles under his eyes that never went away. His right eye twitched from nervous exhaustion, and his grouchiness had been exacerbated.

"Skuld wants to see you," said Farragut. "He's waiting for you now."

The one-armed dusk rider was standing in front of the windows that looked onto the Gardens when Lily entered the practice room. He was rubbing the nub of his arm as if it pained him.

"So you leave tomorrow?" Skuld asked.

"I have to," Lily said. "I go to the Shadow Garden tomorrow eve."

"And there's nothing I can do to talk you out of it? Mayhap I could go with you?"

"I don't think the Smiling Ladies would think well of that. Besides, their letter of invitation doesn't apply to you. They can't hurt me while I'm their guest, but I'm certain that they would be all too happy to rid themselves of the commander of the dusk riders."

Skuld grunted as if he'd thought of that already. "I don't like this one bit."

"That makes two of us," Lily said.

"You're but a girl —," he began.

"I'm Lily Blackwood, last of the female Blackwoods, and I'm made of stronger stuff than you think," Lily said. "You've taught me well. Now

I must stand on my own. Something tells me that it won't be how well I fight that determines whether I return of sound mind or not."

"We could ride in there as a group and —."

" — die," Lily finished the sentence for him. "Who would protect the Gardens then? No one. You must trust me."

Skuld didn't look as if he were convinced. "As you wish," he said.

"Good. Then there's one last thing I need to do tomorrow morning…"

Lily didn't sleep that night. She tossed and turned, considering what the upcoming day would bring. She had never been so scared in her life, even when the emissaries from the Gardens tried to kill her. At one point, she hopped out of bed and paced frantically from one side of the bedroom to the other. *'This is all a dream, this must be a dream,'* she thought. All the bravery that she'd shown in front of Skuld was gone. Alone in her room, she was a terrified fourteen-year-old girl trying not to go crazy with panic. Just when Lily managed to calm herself, Farragut shouted from the hall. "Would you shut the bloody hell up," he yelled to the voices that were coming from the other rooms. Weary, she watched the miserable gray light of what might be her last dawn come through her bedroom window.

After her morning tea, Lily found Skuld and two horses waiting for her outside of the house. The air was heavy with drizzle, and the temporary commander of the dusk riders looked like a drowned rat. His wolf cloak was pulled over him to keep his head dry, but the fur was soaked and matted. Rain beaded on his weathered face like tears. He stared mournfully up at the pregnant rain clouds that blanketed the sky.

"It's going to be a corker today," he said. "Almost as if Prometheus himself is weeping at your folly."

"You don't approve of what I'm about to do?" she asked.

"There are not enough minutes in the day for all the things I disapprove of," Skuld said. "But no, I don't think it wise to place your trust in one that lives in the Gardens. Everything from their mouths is a lie."

"And yet Villon warned me that someone was going to make an attempt on my life. He saved my life when the emissaries from the Gardens tried to kill me," Lily said.

"All for his own purpose, I'm sure. Never doubt that," Skuld said.

"Be that as it may, I have nowhere else to turn," Lily said. "Now lead me to the White Garden."

Skuld handed her the reins of her horse, and they took off down the hill. Thunder crashed overhead and echoed for seconds afterwards. Lily saw purple lightning buried within the black clouds. The horse's hooves dug into the soft soil and left prints that filled with water. To her right, Lily glimpsed the Shadow Garden with its dazzling red rose bushes and white trees that were drained of life. The sky was always darker over the Shadow Garden, as if any sun would burn the heart out of the creatures that lived there. *'I go there tonight,'* she thought, looking away. *'But will I come back as I am now or like one of those pitiful creatures beneath the house?'*

At the bottom of the hill, they rode alongside the White Garden. Everything grew lush and green inside the garden of death. *'It looks like a perfect spot for a picnic or an afternoon nap,'* Lily thought, but she knew what happened to any living thing that strayed onto its verdant pathways. They would never be heard from again.

They neared the spot where Farragut had captured the nestler. Lily slowed her horse and dropped to the ground.

"Remember what I said: Don't leave the path," Skuld said. He loosened the leather on his sword in case he needed to draw it quickly.

The rain was coming down in a sheet now. The damp autumn feel to the air that always pervaded Nightfall Gardens chilled her to the bone. Lily's hair was plastered to her cheeks, and her clothes clung to her skin. She wiped the rain from her eyes and looked into the White Garden.

"Francois," she called. Her voice sounded loud in the emptiness. The gardens seemed abandoned, as if everything were seeking shelter elsewhere. "Francois!" Lily said again, louder. The only sound in return was the tin-sheet rustling of more thunder overhead.

"He's not here. Let's go. I told you this was pointless," Skuld said.

Lily peered into the White Garden again, but all she could see were the verdant trees and grass and some blue crocuses. Red and white tulips grew along a path. *'I was foolish to think that he would be here.'*

"Ma cherie." The words were a mere whisper on the wind.

She stopped and looked where the voice had come from. What remained of Francois was lashed to a tree. Only a tattered carcass was left of the boy who had protected her. This grimy, emaciated creature before her looked nothing like the beautiful, haunted emissary that had saved her life. The skin was peeled from his body, leaving only raw, exposed flesh with soulful blue eyes peering out at her. He was naked, tied to the tree with strips of thorn branches that rent his flesh. Francois's face was a horror of bruises and gashes, and what remained of his black hair was shorn to the scalp.

"Francois?" Lily gasped, stepping closer to the edge of the path.

"Oui," he said. His head lolled on his chest. "I mean, yes."

"Wh — what happened?"

"The old ones discovered that I had helped you," he said. "The wolves told them."

"How?" Lily whispered.

"The wolves, a Shade, I do not know," he murmured. "They punished me."

"Your skin —," she faltered.

"Pretty, no?" he laughed. "They stripped me of my flesh and hung me here as a warning."

"To whom?" Lily was horrified and repulsed by the figure in front of her. None of this would have happened if he hadn't helped her. It was all her fault.

"To you …as a warning that if the Shadow Garden doesn't get you, the old ones will come for you. They are gathering strength now. This — this place won't hold them much longer," he wheezed.

Lily stopped at the edge of the path where the trail met the grass. Francois was only a dozen feet away, in amongst the trees, a figure that barely looked human anymore. The rain wept from the sky, but couldn't wash the gore of his exposed flesh away.

"I have to get you out of there," she said.

"No!" Francois cried. He raised his head to look at her with anguished eyes. How much strength it took for him to do that, she didn't know. "They are waiting for you to do some such foolish thing. There are Shades in the trees and others hiding in the depths that await your first step off the path."

Lily saw only the trees swaying with the wind and rain, but knew that meant less than nothing. *'Who knows what is hiding there?'* Shades could change shapes, become anyone or anything. For all she knew, this was a Shade in front of her. Yet somehow, she knew that it wasn't though. No, this was Francois, what was left of him. She was as certain of that as she was of anything.

"He's right," Skuld said behind her. The dusk rider had been watching the exchange.

"What can we do? We can't leave him?" she said.

"You must," said Francois. "Go and know that what I did, I would do gladly again."

The bloody lump that was now Francois tried to move, but the thorns tore new wounds in him.

"Francois —," she started.

"Go and don't look back," he said. "Wear your necklace tonight, the one that your grandmother gave you, that belonged to Pandora. It will help protect you. Ignore all you see in the Shadow Garden, ma cherie. The Smiling Ladies will play on your human weakness. You must be who you are, the last mistress of Nightfall Manor. Anything less and they will own your soul, the same as the others you saw, the same as the others they feed from. Now go, please."

Lily felt tears well in her eyes, but he was right. She was the last female Blackwood and there was nothing that she could do to stop what was happening to him. Lily had never felt so helpless. She climbed back on her horse and readied to leave.

"I'll be back for you," she said.

"If you are wise, you will forget me," said Villon. His face cracking in a gash of a smile.

They rode away. Lily looked back when they were almost out of sight and gasped in horror. Shades, more than she ever knew existed, were dropping from the trees and floating up from beneath the earth. The black creatures were no more substantial than shadows, but they surrounded what remained of Villon and she had to look away.

"That was brave but stupid," Skuld said. He spit from atop his horse. "I still trust nothing that comes from the Gardens."

Lily said nothing the rest of the way. When they were back at the house, she dismounted and said goodbye to Skuld. "I'll see you on the morrow."

The one-armed dusk rider looked skeptical. She could see the doubt hovering behind his features. "On the morrow then," he finally said and rode away.

Lily spent the rest of the day preparing for the night to come. She warmed her bones in the hot pool and raced against the spirits of the dead children. She intentionally let the youngest one beat her. The spirit of the little girl made a silent cry of victory. Afterwards, Lily had a steaming bowl of potato soup and a pot of tea in the dining room. If Ozy knew what was to happen he didn't let on. She passed Ursula on the way to her room for a nap. "Terrible day, innit. Just absolutely horrible with rain. Nothing more beautiful, I say."

"Another bloomin' nap?" Farragut complained, as he took up his chair in the hall once again. "You sleep more than a bear in winter."

Lily stopped in the doorway and smiled. "Thank you."

"For what?" he griped.

"For watching over me. For helping to protect me," she said.

Farragut's chest sagged. "Well, it 'tweren't nothing. Couldn't have anything happening to you, could we?"

Lily fell into a dreamless sleep and stayed that way throughout the afternoon. She woke to Polly standing over her with a candle in her hand. The flame flickered shapes on the walls.

"Time to go, my lady," Polly squelched.

"I thought it would be," Lily said. She changed into a black dress that had belonged to her grandmother, pinned her white blond hair back and put on the amethyst necklace. When she was finished, Lily walked through the door and then looked back at the room where she had spent the last seven months. "Goodbye," she said.

A carriage, black as midnight, waited outside for her. It was drawn by four skeletal horses that pawed and pranced on the gravel. A figure wearing a top hat and trench coat with the collar upturned to hide his features sat with a lash on the buckboard. All Lily could see where open pits where his eyes should be. The door to the carriage swung open under its own power.

Polly took her hands. "Be careful, Miss. So much depends on you. I promised your Gran that I'd take care of you, I did."

"You have," Lily said, looking into the gigantic grub's white eyes. "Now I have to stand on my own."

Tears of pus streamed down Polly's face. "You'd better come back to me, you will."

Lily touched the maid's cheek. Her hand sank into its mucus-like flesh. "I will," Lily promised, but she was certain of nothing, only that she had to get into the carriage.

Lily looked back at the house. Nightfall Manor seemed to pulse in front of her eyes. She climbed into the carriage. A panel slid back and the trench coated figure's face appeared.

"Next stop, the Shadow Garden," his death rattle of a voice intoned.

The carriage pulled away from the house, leaving Polly watching until it finally rolled out of sight.

15

AN UNNATURAL MIST

The witch came for Silas first. One moment Eldritch's nightmarish roar was echoing across the fog-shrouded valley like some prehistoric beast dragging itself from the mire, and the next Bemisch's foul presence was settling over him. *"So this is where you've been. Cozy. Your grandmother took longer to break than I would have thought. They always break though. Yes, they do."* The voice that whispered in his head was so malignant and full of spite that Silas felt physically ill. He swallowed hard to keep from vomiting.

"Are you all right?" Mirabelle asked. His cousin was still gripping his hand. A look of concern etched her face.

"Fine," Silas said, barely able to get the word out. *"Oh, she's a tender morsel she is. I'm going to enjoy bending her to my will. Such sweet meat will go insane before too long, I think."*

"Nuh — No," Silas stammered, trying to regain control of himself. *"Don't fight me, boy. I can give you anything that you want. All you have to do is open your mind and let Bemisch in for a while."*

Silas took out his dagger. The witch's voice grew excited. *"That's right, that's right. Kiss your cousin with the blade. Drive it into your uncle's back. What kind of man is he anyway? He brought you and your sister here. None of this would be happening if it weren't for him. Do it now!"*

He closed his eyes and gouged his palm with the blade. Fiery pain shot through him and he heard the witch scream as her presence fled from him.

"Silas?" Mirabelle jerked away in shock. "What have you done?"

"Lad?" Jonquil gripped him by the shoulders and squeezed. His uncle stared into his eyes with a penetrating gaze.

"The witch," Silas gulped. His mouth was dry as cotton. His knees shook and he felt faint.

"We need to bandage that," Mirabelle said. "He scored himself something fierce."

"We need to get out of here," Trainer said. The rider's face twitched with fear.

"And go where?" Jonquil said. "Night is here. The fog is thick as sleep. We'd be lost before we made it off the mountain. We've waited too long."

"So what do you recommend?" Trainer asked. He tied the horse to a hitch.

"Barricade the cabin and wait out the night. Mr. Hawthorne's protective barrier should still have some power," Jonquil said.

The four of them went about preparing for the night as best that they could. Jonquil and Trainer made sure the windows were locked and blockaded the door. Silas and Mirabelle brought in as much wood as they could carry and stoked the fire so high that soon they were all sweating through their clothes. Mirabelle cleaned and bandaged Silas's wound and they sat near the hearth together while the dusk riders huddled with each other across the room.

"You heard the witch?" Mirabelle asked. The beatific look on her face was gone.

"In my head," Silas said. He was trembling. "She says awful things. Haven't you heard her before?"

"Oh yes," his cousin replied frowning. "It used to be almost every night. She came to me in my bed."

"And what did she say to you? What did she want you to do?"

Mirabelle shuddered. "Terrible things best not said. What she really wanted was to choke the spirit inside of me. She offered me everything that I've vowed to abstain from as a Daughter. The price was too steep though. It would have killed the person that I am and left nothing more than a vessel for her use."

"How did you — how do you resist?" Silas

asked.

"Think of something that you care about deeply, focus on that when the witch comes and you can push her away," said Mirabelle.

The weight of everything that was taking place fell on them. A heavy silence blanketed the room. The only sound was the crackling of the logs in the fire.

"Best try and sleep," Jonquil said finally. "We go nowhere until dawn. If anything comes we will all know soon enough."

Silas thought sleep would be well nigh impossible. The witch, Eldritch, and who knew what else, were waiting for them.

Mirabelle yawned and stretched. "I believe I'll meditate and seek guidance."

"You do that," Trainer said spitefully. "If you get any advice on how we are supposed to deal with those things out there, let us know."

Another hour passed, heavy with the expectation of what was to come. Silas lay on the mat, turned so he could watch the fire. He passed into a state between wakefulness and sleep where dreams are sometimes the most vivid.

He found himself in front of the crumbling remains of a temple, one that had been dedicated to the old gods. This place must have been magnificent in its day, but looked as though it had been abandoned for centuries. A figure dressed in white came out of the dark opening of the temple. As she came closer, he saw that it was Mirabelle.

She was dressed in a white gown that revealed one of her shoulders. She wore hammered gold bracelets on her wrists.

"Mirabelle?" he asked.

She smiled when she saw her cousin. "You must go. You don't belong here,"

"Go where?" he asked. Before she could answer, another figure came from the temple; this one was dressed in black. He would have known her white blond hair anywhere. Lily was pale as death and as sorrowful looking. Her solemn face stared at him.

"You said you could help me," Lily said. "But you couldn't, nobody could."

"No," Silas shook his head. "I tried, I'm trying right now — I," he got no further before both Mirabelle and his sister burst into flame in front of him.

"Go now, before it's too late," Lily said. "Hide as far away as you can before the Gardens fall permanently."

Silas reached out to his cousin and sister and then felt a boot planted in his side and he was awake. Jonquil was standing over him. The dusk rider had a finger raised to his lips as if to say, "Be quiet." His uncle pointed toward the front of the cabin. Trainer was peering between the cracks at something outside. Silas rose and pulled the dagger from his belt. In the next room, he heard Mirabelle moaning in her sleep.

"Wake your cousin," Jonquil whispered. "They're here."

Heart hammering in his chest, Silas crept to his cousin's room. Mirabelle had kicked her sheet loose and was thrashing in her sleep as if she was being tormented. Silas shook her gently until her eyes opened. There was a wild look in them.

"Silas, I had the worst dream," she whispered. "You were there and —." Mirabelle stopped when she saw the worried look on his face. "What's wrong? You look pale as a ghost."

"They've come," he said. "We have to defend ourselves."

Mirabelle was up an instant later. They made their way into the living room where both dusk riders were looking at something that was taking place outside the cabin.

"What is it?" Silas asked.

Trainer stepped out of the way and gestured at the opening. Silas pressed his eye against the slit. At first he saw only the fog that was thicker than it had been a few hours before. Nothing moved in the plumes of smoky mist that lapped at the outside of the cabin. Just when he was about to give up, a figure ran across the porch, low and loping, and leapt back into the whiteness. Silas caught a glimpse of something bent and twisted with a squashed face that glared with hatred from under a cowl — and then it was gone.

"Is that thing — a person?" Silas asked, looking at Jonquil.

"A Bakhtak," Jonquil said. "They feed on the nightmares they create. They enter a human's mind as they sleep and plant a thousand horrors there. Soon, the victim is unable to tell the difference between the waking and dreaming world. Did either of you have particularly vivid nightmares tonight?"

Silas and Mirabelle exchanged a glance. Jonquil raised his eyebrow. "I see," he said. "We have seen other beings in the mist as well."

"Our old friend is there," Trainer said to Silas. "We should have gutted it when we had the chance."

"What?"

"The creature from the cell next to us," Trainer said. "The bat horror that drained the blood from that guard."

"It's a Sigbin," Jonquil said. "They kill their victims by wrapping their wings around them and devouring their flesh and blood."

"There are villagers here, as well. Traitors that are so far under the spell of the witch that they would kill for her. Right now, they're wiping away the protective circle we placed around the cabin," Trainer said.

"Grandmother?" Mirabelle said.

"We haven't seen her, lass," Jonquil said, packing his blunderbuss. He crammed gunpowder into the barrel with a ramrod.

"Eldritch?" Silas asked, as he looked through the crack into the impenetrable night. The fog swirled about the cabin. Not for the first time, he felt as if they were the last people in the universe.

"Who knows?" Jonquil said. "The mist is unnaturally thick. Right now, our goal is to survive this night. Dawn will weaken Bemisch's magic." Jonquil finished loading his weapon and cocked the hammer. Trainer pulled his cloak down so that his face disappeared within the wolf's head. The eyes gleamed malignant yellow in the firelight. He drew his sword. The edge looked cruel and sharp.

"We're going to send our friends a message," Jonquil said to Silas and Mirabelle. "When I say so, fling the door open, and then close it when I give the command."

Mirabelle placed a hand on Jonquil's shoulder. "I feel bloodlust coming from you two. If you walked in the light that binds us you would realize that the death of any living thing, even those from the Gardens is wrong. For the sake of your souls I implore you to keep the door closed."

"And what?" Trainer asked angrily. "Wait for them to slaughter us. What do you think they've done to your Gran, taken her for a summer vacation? I'll slice their throats before they do ours and sleep like a babe when I'm finished."

Jonquil bared his teeth. "I don't relish this more than any you do, but what do you think they are doing out there? They are wiping away the protective spell. They are getting ready to attack us, if we don't attack them first."

"Silas?" Mirabelle turned expectantly to her cousin.

He shook his head. "No, they are coming to kill

us. We have to protect ourselves."

Mirabelle gave them a sad nod. "I will meditate for you. I will ask the light that binds us all to intervene." She went off to her room.

"And you'll get the same answer that you do every time. Nothing," Trainer snorted.

"Open the door, lad," Jonquil said. He hugged his blunderbuss close.

Silas swallowed hard. His throat felt dry, and there was a tremor to his hand. He yanked the door open, and a chill blast of air swept into the cabin. The fire sputtered for a moment before springing back to life. Custard-thick fog rolled into the cabin. Jonquil stepped through the door, his blunderbuss out, as a shrieking Bakhtak charged out of the mist. The creature was four feet tall and wrapped in monk's robes sashed with hemp. The scratchy woolen cowl framed his nightmarish features. The creature's nose was a mashed fig and its face was squat and lopsided with suppurating knobs ridging its forehead. Jonquil held his gun at waist level and pulled the trigger. *Kaboom!* The explosion rocked the silence. The Bakhtak's features exploded in a cloud of smoke, and it was blown off the porch. One of its boots was left standing on the porch. No sooner had Jonquil pulled the trigger than a villager leapt to the doorway with his sword drawn. Dan Trainer brought his blade down and with a single swipe slashed the man's chest, sending a spray of blood across the cabin floor. The man looked down at his bloody front and screamed with the realization that he was about to die. Jonquil drove the butt of his rifle into his face, and Silas heard bone crunch. The villager staggered backward into the yard. Suddenly, two wolves appeared out of the mist and dragged him into the darkness. It was a long time before the man stopped screaming.

"Shut the door!" Jonquil yelled. Silas swung the door closed just as something black as night flew toward the cabin. He threw the latch as the monster crashed against the door, wood splintering with the pressure.

Jonquil's face and cloak were splattered with blood. But beneath the blood, his face was bleached white. He reloaded his weapon. *'My uncle's not well,'* Silas thought. *'He should be recovering, not fighting another battle.'*

"That should give them pause," Jonquil said. "But they will come again, there is no doubt of that."

"Did you see the way I cut through his wrist?" Trainer laughed. The dusk rider wiped the gore from his blade.

"He was bewitched, Dan, not a being from the Gardens," Jonquil said. "We should show more respect for human life."

"As he should," Trainer said. "I only did what I needed to keep us safe."

"How does laughing at the poor soul's death do that?" Jonquil asked. "He was under the spell of the witch, the same as any of us could be."

Before the dusk rider could respond, something crashed against the door again, and it shuddered in its frame. Trainer looked through the cracks in the wall. As he placed his face against it, a sword blade came from the other side. If it had been one inch to the left, it would have taken his eye out, but instead it sliced loose a flap of skin from his cheek. Trainer screamed and stumbled away. Outside, something laughed evilly and footsteps pounded away across the boards of the porch.

"My face," Trainer moaned. He pressed a strip of bloodied cloth across the wound. "You see?" Trainer said to Jonquil. "They would kill us without compunction."

An instant later, the attack began anew. At the same time as the Sigbin crashed against the door, the trapdoor leading to the cellar banged against its latch. Silas saw a hand with black fingernails trying to unlatch the lock. He slid across the floor and drove his dagger into the creature's hand, whose color resembled mold on a tombstone. The trapdoor slammed shut. Underground, he heard the monster bellow in pain.

"A ghoul," yelled his uncle. Together, they flipped the heavy wooden table and covered the trapdoor with it. In the next room, Mirabelle was praying loudly enough to be heard above the sounds of the attack. "Protect us from that evil which seeks to do us harm …"

"Shut her up! Shut the little wench's mouth," Bemisch shouted in his Silas's mind. He squeezed

his throbbing palm, and the witch was gone again.

"It won't hold much longer," Trainer said. He was pressed against the door as the Sigbin slammed against it once again.

"Fire," Jonquil said to Silas. "It's the only thing that can hurt a Sigbin. Fetch me a burning log, and be careful of your fingers."

The blaze they had built earlier was still roaring. Silas felt the heat biting his skin as he knelt and drew out a log that was lit on one end.

"Good lad," Jonquil said, taking it. He handed the blunderbuss to Silas. "Pull the trigger at anything that comes in after the Sigbin. Dan, let's welcome our guest."

Trainer nodded through gritted teeth. The bandage wrapped around his jaw was soaked with blood. *'He looks mad,'* Silas thought.

The dusk rider threw open the splintered door as the Sigbin came flying in from the mist. The "V" of a bat face with oval eyes and fangs so thin they looked like would break off in whatever they bit, was followed by a long black shadow of a body and wings lined with bulging veins.

No nightmare Silas ever conjured was as terrifying as what happened next. The Sigbin swooped through the doorway at Jonquil, who was holding the torch in his hands.

"Come on, come and get —" his uncle struck the bat creature with the flaming log and they tumbled across the floor.

"Boy, pull your head out," Trainer said

excitedly. "More are coming."

Figures appeared out of the mist. Silas saw the hunched figure of another Bakhtak peering from under its monk's cowl. A handful of mist people drew closer, with the same red hair and green eyes as his mother, except that theirs pulsed green and black. The ghoul was further back, half a head taller than anyone else and wearing a death shroud. Its face was little more than a skull, with wisps of hair curling from the top and teeth jutting from what remained of its gums. The red eyes of wolves glowed like stars on all sides. The witch was out there as well, hiding somewhere.

'And what of Eldritch,' Silas thought. *'Where is he right now?'*

Silas pulled the trigger of the blunderbuss as the Bakhtak put its feet on the steps. The force of the gun was more powerful than he expected. The weapon kicked his shoulder and Silas was knocked backward by the backlash. The roar of the gun deafened him momentarily, but he saw that his shot had missed the Bakhtak. His uncle was struggling for his life with the Sigbin and Trainer was clashing swords with a villager trying to fight his way into the cabin. Other creatures pushed in behind him.

'We've lost,' Silas thought. It was the most dismal feeling of his young life. There was no way they could fight off everything that was out there. Trainer kicked the villager away and plunged his sword into the Bakhtak as the ghoul grasped at

Silas with his lifeless hands.

'No, it can't end like this,' Silas thought. He yanked the dagger from its sheath, preparing to plunge into the fray. He hadn't taken two steps when a brilliant flash of white light exploded in the doorway, leaving behind an after-image like crashing lightning. White radiance covered everything, and in that light he could see the essence of every being. The ghoul's spirit was total blackness, devoid of light. Trainer's spirit looked ill and unhealthy, with writhing shadowy tendrils consuming the white bits of what he used to be. Silas caught a glimpse of one of the village men as well, and he could perceive the corruption that dominated the poor man's soul. Then, the flash of white light began to fade and the witch's army fled into the night. Trainer collapsed against the doorway, his eyes glazed as if he were drugged, saliva frothing at the corners of his mouth.

Silas turned and saw Mirabelle standing at the point from which the light came. Her palms were extended outward and her robes were open to reveal the tunic beneath. There was a strained expression on her face.

"What did you do?" Silas asked.

"Merely showed them their true natures," she replied.

He was about to ask about what he had seen when he heard a crash by the fireplace. In the midst of the battle, he'd forgotten about his uncle and the Sigbin. Jonquil was on top of the creature, pinning its wings with his knees and plunging its head into the fire. The Sigbin shrieked an unholy howl and bucked his uncle off as its head lit up like a matchstick. The shrieking horror took off flying out the door as its body burst into flame. It flapped away into the mist, a comet momentarily illuminating the gloom until it was swallowed by the fog.

"They've gone for now," Jonquil said, dragging himself shakily to his feet. "Hand me my walking stick, lad, and bar the door. We had luck, and your cousin on our side this time."

Mirabelle blushed, her face the same shade as her hair. "It was only a little of the Daughter magic," she said, looking at the floor, embarrassed.

"That saved our lives," his uncle added.

The fog already seemed less thick, Silas thought as he slid the bolt on the door. No traces of battle remained, and the night seemed dead calm. *'It's a trick. They are waiting for us to let down our guard. They'll be back,'* Silas thought.

He was wrong on that, though. The night passed as all nights must. Mirabelle made a poultice that she smeared on Trainer's wound, before bandaging it again. The dusk rider woke briefly, his eyes fluttering, and he glared with loathing at the girl. "You turned me inside out witch. You treated me no better than those creatures of the night. You made me see things no man should see."

Mirabelle touched his face, and the rider recoiled. "I only revealed who you are."

"That wasn't me!" Trainer shouted as he tried to sit up, but collapsed in exhaustion on the floor. His eyes fluttered and he fell back to sleep.

As Jonquil watched for the intruders to return, Mirabelle and Silas talked by the fire.

"I didn't know you could do that," Silas said.

"I know only a little of the Daughter's magic, but what they call 'true seeing' is one of the first things that they teach a novice. It's simple but powerful magic that reveals a person's true nature. The degradation of the spirit is awful to behold, and when revealed it can tear a person's mind asunder."

"The creeping tendrils that I saw in Trainer —," Silas was unsure how to describe what he'd seen.

"Every lie, every sin, every foul or petty thought preys on a person's mind. It grows and spreads like a cancer that consumes the soul. I've seen village men far worse than your dusk rider," she said. Mirabelle looked intently at Trainer, who shivered in his sleep on the mat. "I've told you before that there is something troubled about that one."

The two huddled near the fire with a blanket over them and closed their eyes. Before long, Silas heard his cousin's breathing become slower and deeper as she fell asleep with her head on his shoulder. Sleep didn't come for him or Jonquil, not after the attack. His uncle watched through the crack with a loaded blunderbuss on his lap, while Silas thought of his sister and of what had happened to his grandmother. Hours passed.

When it seemed the night would never end, Jonquil finally spoke. "Wake up. It's time to leave this place." Mirabelle stirred and smiled at Silas sleepily. "No bad dreams this time," she said. Trainer was silent as he packed his meager belongings.

The mists had scattered, and a muddy sky peeked through the treetops when Jonquil opened the cabin door. He held his rifle before him, scanning the area while Trainer followed with his sword drawn. Blood was splattered across the porch. The picked-over carcasses of the villager and a Bakhtak were left by the trail.

The shadows of the woods seemed to watch as they weighed their next move. Trainer went to check the lean-to where their grandmother's gray horse was tied but came back not long after, shaking his head. "Gone," he said.

"There's only one thing to do," Jonquil said, as he slung the blunderbuss over his shoulder. "Set out on foot. We'll have to stay off the roads and we come closer to Priortage than I care for, but it's the only way to get to Nightfall Gardens from here. We'll need all of the dusk riders to fight this foul perversion that threatens the mist people."

"What of our grandmother?" Mirabelle asked.

"I'm sorry, but she'll have to wait," Jonquil said. "The fate of everyone hangs in the balance right now."

His cousin nodded her head as if she understood, but Silas saw tears in her eyes.

They set off from the cabin with Jonquil in the lead, hobbling on his walking stick. Trainer came after, his face wrapped as if he had the worst toothache in the world, and Silas and Mirabelle were last. Silas took one last look at the cabin before it was swallowed in the fog.

'It'll take us days to make it to Nightfall Gardens at the pace we are going now,' Silas thought after they been on the road for several hours. They came down out of the hills into the lush river valley. There were oaks and walnut trees and white maples mixed amongst the pines. A cardinal flapped in front of them before taking off into the woods.

It was just before noon that they came across the body strung from a tree. Silas turned away in horror as Jonquil approached the figure and poked it with his staff. The man's head was bent at an odd angle, his eyes were wide, and his mouth was open as if about to scream. There was a gaping wound in his chest were something had ripped out his heart.

"Another villager," he said. "Who knows why Bemisch did this?"

More long hours of walking followed. By late afternoon, they had come close enough to the village that Jonquil thought it would be wise if they took to the woods.

The dusk riders went off to have a talk while Silas and Mirabelle sat on a fallen tree and rubbed their sore feet.

"How far is the village from here?" Silas asked

while they waited.

"We could be there shortly after dark if we kept going," Mirabelle said. "The witch will have patrols out, and the wolves will be looking for us."

"We must find someplace safe to spend the night," he said.

Mirabelle furrowed her brow. "I know a place that we could go," she said hesitantly.

"Where?" Silas asked.

"The other Daughters would protect us," she said.

"I don't think we should put anyone else in danger," Silas said. He thought of the villager tied to the tree and of the witch's wrath.

"We may not have a choice," Jonquil said. He and Trainer had appeared from the trees. They had heard their conversation. "There is nowhere else we can turn."

Mirabelle nodded. "They would take us in and cast the protection of their white magic over us."

"Not that again," Trainer said in disgust.

"They could hide us from the witch's presence and the others that seek us. Even Eldritch wouldn't be able to find us," she said.

"How far away is the cloister where they live?" Jonquil asked.

"Closer than the village," Mirabelle said.

"Then we'd best set off now," said Jonquil. "I don't like the way the shadows lengthen in the trees."

Mirabelle led them through woods that were so

thick that Trainer had to hack their way through limbs and vines, until they finally came out along a gurgling creek. They followed the creek north as it grew dark in the woods. Frogs croaked along the banks and insects buzzed, sure signs that the red moon would ride high before long, Silas thought.

Ahead, the creek broadened into a pond and plumes of black smoke rose above the trees.

"That's funny," Mirabelle said. "It's too early for them to have such a fire going."

On the wind, Silas caught a whiff of ash. Black flakes floated on the air as they came to the edge of the woods. Mirabelle gasped when they came in sight of the cottage where the Daughters lived. All that remained was a charred shell. Scorched beams jutted where the structure had collapsed. Smoke curled up from the skeleton of the building and coals glowed inside the cellar of the house.

"The Daughters!" Mirabelle screamed. She broke from the group and ran toward the fire. "They — they aren't here. But why would someone do this?"

Mirabelle sobbed with her hands over her eyes.

Silas put his hand on Mirabelle's shoulder and she jerked away. "Don't," she said. "I need to be alone." His cousin ran into a grove of cherry trees, stumbling blindly with tears.

"Well, what do we do now?" Trainer asked. "Night will be here soon and we are as helpless as a hog in a slaughterhouse."

The long walk and the battle of the night before

had drained Jonquil of energy. His face was as pale as a corpse's and he looked more exhausted than ever, Silas thought.

"They are cutting off any escape we have," Jonquil said. "We're as good as dead if we stay out in the open when they are at full power."

"You have friends in the village," Trainer said. "Can't you talk with them?"

"None will take us in," Jonquil said. "Not with everything that's happening."

Silas tuned them out and went into the cherry grove seeking his cousin. He found Mirabelle sitting under one of the trees, her legs pulled up to her chin and eyes red.

"It's my fault," she said. "The Daughters warned me to stay out of the affairs of the village, but I couldn't sit idle when I saw what was happening."

"Don't blame yourself," Silas said. "They are probably locked up in jail. That means they can be saved."

"Do you think so?" Mirabelle asked hopefully. She stood and wiped the dirt off her dress.

"I know so," Silas said.

"Thank you," Mirabelle said, giving him a light kiss on the cheek. Something moved in the corner of his eye and he heard laughter.

"You've been busy, I see," said Arfast, coming out of the woods.

"Arfast!" Silas said shocked. "What are you doing here?"

A grin split the trickster's face. "Don't stop on my account."

"Or mine," a familiar voice said, and Cassandra stepped out from behind a trees. A scowl was carved on her features and a storm of anger crossed her face.

"Cassandra," Silas said uncomfortably. He stepped away from his cousin. "How did you get here?"

"Horses," she said. "Which I'm going to tend to now. We didn't mean to break up your party. Some of us were worried about you — in vain it appears."

"Who are these people?" Mirabelle asked.

"Fr — friends," Silas said. Why did he feel like he'd been caught doing something wrong?

"Friends, is it?" Cassandra glared. "Well this friend is going to set up camp before night falls. Have fun with *your new friend*."

"Wait," Silas said, but it was too late. Cassandra was powering through the trees as if she'd mow down anything that got in her way.

"Why is she so angry?" Silas asked.

"Isn't it apparent?" Arfast said, laughing. "I'd have off after her, lad. You're squirming worse than a worm on a hook."

"We can't stay here. Mirabelle will explain everything. Take him to Jonquil," he asked his cousin.

"I'm sorry if I did something to upset her," Mirabelle said.

Silas shook his head. "She'll be fine. I just need to speak to her."

He found Cassandra banging pans and storming around the camp as if she were daring someone to get in her way.

"Cassandra," he said quietly. Her green eyes jerked up and blazed fire at him.

"Didn't I just tell you that I didn't want to see you?" she said.

"I know, I just didn't want you to think —," Silas started.

"Think what," the green girl barked. "What I saw with my own eyes."

"Its not — she's my cousin," Silas whined.

"You must really love your cousin then," Cassandra snorted. "Besides why do you care what I think?"

"Because —," Silas tried to find the words. Why did he care exactly? On her best days, Cassandra was downright rude to him. But there was something about her. Hadn't he always known that? He looked at her and soaked her in for the first time. Cassandra's yellow green hair hung halfway down her back, and her face was oval-shaped with full lips. Her skin was the color of a jasmine vase, beautiful and flawless.

"I —," he faltered trying to find the words. "You know that I—," his throat was suddenly dry. "I think you're — you're…,"

"Spit it out!," the green girl roared.

"I — you're pretty," he finally stammered and

then just as quickly wished he could take the words back.

"I'm — *what*?" she bellowed and balled up her fists as if she were going to smack him in the nose. "You're insufferable," she spat.

Silas took a step towards her. "So are you," he sighed.

"Clueless," she said as Silas took three more steps toward her.

"I am," he said, closing the distance between them. He was close enough now that he could smell the fresh scent of her breath. He reached out for her and, trembling, she jerked away.

"What are you trying to do? Stop playing," she said. "You — you're just…"

He reached for her again, and Cassandra danced away like grease hitting a hot pan. "Don't," she said, and any tenderness was replaced by the familiar cast-iron hardness of the gardener's daughter. "I — I can't," she mumbled.

"But why? I — you, we like each other," he said. "You came to save me."

"I came to make sure my best friend's brother didn't get himself killed traipsing around like an idiot in the fog. Now, go … go back. I have things to do," she said.

Silas opened his mouth to say something. *'I don't understand this. She's not telling me the truth. I can see it in her face,'* he thought. But he said nothing. Instead he went back to fetch the others.

It was only when he was out of sight that that

Cassandra's iron resolve failed her and she began weeping bitter green tears.

16
THE BLACK CASTLE

'The Shadow Garden is a land of darkness,' Lily
thought as the carriage rattled along a rocky road
that headed into saw-toothed mountains. Nightfall
Gardens was no longer visible. She looked back
when they crossed the dividing line between the
house and the Garden, but all Lily could see were
the strange white trees that grew here and red
rosebushes that were almost painful in their
brightness. A road that she had never spied from
her window opened ahead, and the carriage
clattered onto it and drove deeper into the interior.

Lily took a deep breath the way Skuld had
taught her, to calm her nerves. The carriage
windows were open, and she leaned out for a
better view. Tin lanterns swung from hooks on the
carriage to illuminate the way. Their pale and
yellow light flickered across the rushing landscape.

Bats swooped in and out of the light, little more than shadows. The red moon was dimmer here and the sky was darker. *'The creatures here are of the night,'* Lily thought. And as if that were their cue, a group of loping figures appeared beside the carriage. The lantern light shone on one of their faces. Lily saw bristling fur and the elongated snout of a wolf. A butcher's row of teeth filled its mouth. There were easily half a dozen of them keeping pace with the carriage. The driver growled something indecipherable, and the wolves turned away into the night.

Mountains appeared, though how that could be was beyond Lily's comprehension. She had ridden around the Shadow Garden with Arfast and Skuld in less time than it took to have a proper lunch, yet inside the landscape stretched into an immense dreamscape.

Lily saw horrendous things as the carriage whipped through the night, things that would have destroyed the sanity of anyone who wasn't the final female of the Blackwood line. Grotesque owl and raven creatures, dressed in powdered wigs and courtier clothing, drank from golden chalices at a moonlight garden party, and severed human heads, mouths frozen in screams of pure terror, lined the table where they ate. Further along, a storm of winged suckered beings enveloped the carriage for seconds like a school of fish swimming in the ocean. One of the creatures attached itself to the carriage like a barnacle. It was translucent and no more than the width of her hand, but its underside was covered in suckers lined with little teeth. Smoke rose from the wood where it attached itself. Once the storm passed, the driver stopped the carriage and pried the creature loose and stomped it to mash on the ground. Then, the carriage was off again, passing through barren farmland of scorched earth where the only thing that grew was purple rotting fruit that burst with that reeked of something long dead. Patchwork scarecrows guarded the fields. Suddenly, one of them reached up and snagged a bat from the air with its straw hand, crushing it as Lily watched.

Lily took another deep breath and tried to banish the horrors of the Shadow Garden from her mind. *'I've seen the worst that they have to offer, and I can handle it. I have to.'* What other option was there? She fingered the amethyst necklace that belonged to Pandora and thought of Villon, wondering what kind of torment he was going through.

The ground was now covered in dirty snow, and the temperature dropped until Lily's breath plumed. Her skin goose-pimpled, and she wrapped herself tighter in the sable coat she'd worn. The carriage passed through the remains of a city that looked as if it had been abandoned for centuries. Gloomy imperial palaces and grand houses crumbling to ruin abutted alleys of shanties. Dark, spectral figures moved along the streets and among the ruins. Malevolent eyes watched from the shadows as the carriage passed.

They were in the mountains then, climbing into frost-covered hills. A family of trolls crossed in the distance across the plateau with the backdrop of the ruby moon. There were four great hairy beasts with jutting bottom jaws, naked as the day they were born and walking in a line. The tallest would have had a hard time standing straight up straight in the entry of Nightfall Manor. One had a large deer that was kicking and rearing with its great antlered head slung over his shoulder as if it were no more than a babe.

A castle appeared on the horizon; its great spires and towers of lichen-covered stone clawed up from the landscape. The castle's walls were formidable and stretched the length of its massive roof, which looked to Lily like the lid on top of a sarcophagus. *'I've seen this before, in the mural painted on the wall when Cassandra and I ran from Mugwump,'* she thought. The number 23, the same number etched in Pandora's tomb, had been written on one of the towers. But what did that mean? She looked down at her hands. Her knuckles had turned white from squeezing the amethyst necklace.

A moat filled with brackish water surrounded the castle. As they neared, a great oaken drawbridge lowered from one of the walls. The carriage slowed as it approached. The castle was almost as big as Nightfall Manor, but where that house shifted and expanded with life, this place felt dead and withered, its stone impassive. Before she could draw anymore conclusions, the carriage rattled over the drawbridge and traveled under an arched entrance into a massive courtyard that was surrounded by covered walkways that led to different parts of the castle. As she watched, the silent figures of two young men stumbled along one of the arcades as if trying to find their way. At the sound of the carriage, one of them turned and Lily gasped. His eyes were sewn shut.

The carriage drew to a halt and the door creaked open. Lily stepped into the Shadow Garden for the first time. Cold stone met her feet. The driver bowed while holding the door of the carriage, his face obscured by his top hat and collar. The skeletal horses pawed the earth. Movement caught Lily's eye, and she glanced up to see the figure of a woman in white crawling along one of the tower walls.

"Beautiful, isn't she?" a silky voice purred. One of the Smiling Ladies stepped from the shadows of a walkway and gestured toward the woman on the wall. "You'll see many more like her once we are inside," the Smiling Lady said. "Perhaps you may even recognize some of them."

With a reed like neck and milky white face marred with red blotches on her cheeks, the Smiling Lady towered over Lily. She had the same strange rictus grin frozen on her face as Esmeret, the sister Lily met when the emissaries of the gardens came to Nightfall Manor. Lily pretended she didn't see the thick fangs that her grimace revealed. She was wearing a violet dress with lace along the wrists that showed off long hands and glossy fingernails filed to points.

She snapped her fingers and a grotesquerie slid from the shadows. Painful-looking quills burst from every surface of the being's skin. Large, golden eyes stared at her. The creature whimpered in misery when the lady spoke.

"He will take any belongings that you have," she said.

"I don't plan on staying that long," Lily said. *'Breathe,'* she thought. *'Remember what Skuld taught you.'*

"If you only knew how many times I've heard that before," the Smiling Lady said tinkling with laughter. "Come along then, the others are waiting to meet you."

The Smiling Lady turned and whisked into the darkness. Lily followed after her. The barbed creature whined in pain as it followed along behind.

"I'm Vallia," the Smiling Lady said as they entered the castle. A blast of freezing wind came from deep inside, tousling Lily's hair and running invisible fingers down her spine. She ground her teeth to keep them from chattering. Torches hung on the walls at far enough distances that they gave off only the minimal light required for a person to see, as if what lived here couldn't bear the presence of light. More than once, Lily's feet snagged on uneven bricks because she couldn't see the floor of the dim corridor.

"My sister told me how you hurt her with that necklace you wear," Vallia said, laughing at her sister's misery. "It was the first time in centuries Esmeret felt anything but selfish hunger. I'm afraid you've made her very angry."

"She shouldn't have broken the truce then," Lily said defiantly.

"Oh, I'm afraid she doesn't see it that way," Vallia said. "No, you've made an enemy of my sister; though, she was wrong about some things."

Vallia stopped in the hall, her strange smile stretched from ear to ear. "She said you were smart, but there have been smarter Blackwood women who have left this place with their minds in tatters. And she said you were beautiful, but there have been more beautiful Blackwood women. Look up Alexandria Blackwood specifically, if you live to search your records. She was so beautiful that she made the creatures of the Garden recoil in horror when she arrived, but no person would have found her so when she left us. Keep that in mind, child."

"I'm not afraid," Lily said. *'Take a deep breath, remember Skuld's lessons. They want you to lose your calm.'*

"Ah, but you should be," Vallia said. The torchlight flickered off her face and elongated her grin until it looked ready to split her face in two. "Enough of this dance. The others are waiting. My sisters will be furious if they don't get their chance to tear you to pieces."

Lily stumbled blindly through the dark after her. The weeping quilled creature sniffled and sobbed along behind her. "Oh, the mistress won't be pleased, she won't be pleased at all," the being whimpered. They crossed a corridor that led into more darkness. Lily looked down it and saw three pale women beneath the torchlight, bloodless and beautiful, watching them pass. The women bared their fangs and hissed at Lily, before retreating into the dark.

'Is everything in this place cursed?' Lily wondered. She felt numb and exhausted as if she could fall asleep on her feet.

She heard voices ahead and cruel laughter. The end of the corridor was filled with unnatural light, and soon they came to a huge banquet room. She stood in the center of a great hall surrounded by three long black oak tables gnarled with age. At each table sat the evil beings that Prometheus had bound to the Shadow Garden. Three thrones made of yellow barbed thorns were the focus of the room. The other Smiling Ladies sat on two of the thrones, grins frozen on their faces as if set with mortar. Esmeret rubbed a withered hand that was charred and black. The darkness extended to her wrist. *'That's the hand she touched the necklace,'* Lily thought. *'But why should it do that?'* The last Smiling Lady wore her hair in braids that fell over her breasts and made her look younger than her sisters. Chained to Esmeret's throne with a thick iron ring were the remains of a girl who was missing her bottom jaw and whose skin was peeled away in leathered strips. The girl's eyes were empty sockets, and wisps of brittle hair clung to her scalp. She was trying to gnaw a bone, but, without a bottom jaw, the best she could do was to scrape it against her upper teeth.

"Desdemona," Lily cried in disbelief. Conversation died. She felt all eyes focused on her. The twisted creature glanced up at her sharply and then fell back to the bone.

"Our pet has come home," Esmeret said, patting Desdemona on the head. "All the Blackwood women that fail the test would come back to us if they weren't bound beneath Nightfall Manor in their tombs. That's something they didn't tell you, did they?"

"My grandmother didn't know," Lily said, trying to steel her trembling legs. The other beings in the room snorted raucous laughter.

"But your great-aunt Abigail knew. She sacrificed herself so her sister could live. She thought she could outwit us, but few Blackwoods survive a night in our castle," Esmeret gloated. She stroked her ruined hand with renewed vigor as if that would bring it back to life.

"Oh sister, there will be plenty of time for our boring games later. Introduce me," the third Smiling Lady said. She giggled like a girl of seven.

"Where are my manners," Vallia said. She swept her hand out over the gathering, "Morta, our distinguished guests, allow me to introduce Lily

Blackwood, the last of the female Blackwoods."

The room erupted with a hideous roar. The beasts in the room hammered the tables and dishes clattered. A werewolf, flexing its muscles, howled so ferociously that the walls trembled with the noise. Lily examined the occupants of the room for the first time. Hate-filled faces stared back at her, faces that longed to rip her head from her body, faces that weren't even remotely human. There were the hag-ridden countenances of witches and the flat-nosed faces of ogres and trolls. There were the deathless expressions of goblins and amphibian eyes and gills of some green-skinned swamp beasts that she had never seen before. There were sprites that buzzed with firefly lights and a being with the head and body of a bee that was the size of a man but that rubbed its thick ichor-laden limbs together. She saw men with eyeless faces that raised their hands in the air while a dozen eyes blinked from their palms. There were stonelike gargoyles with beaked faces and batwings that squatted on tables devouring raw meat. There were warlocks with bloodstained beards and a white wolf the size of a man with a scared face that chewed ravenously at a bone. A murder of giant crows roosted at one of the tables and cawed in shrill anger. At another, a man who was covered in pox scars smiled with blackened teeth as he chatted with a woman dressed in a stately gown and a tiara resplendent with goose-egg-sized diamonds whose neck was split all the way across by a jagged gash. Lily saw foul-spirited genies, a woman dressed in blue who wept tears of blood and a being that seemed more shadow than substance, who wore a cloak pulled down to hide its features. There were mountain beasts covered in thick fur so pungent that Lily could smell them across the cavernous hall. There were little people as well, gnomes and elves, that watched her slyly as if plotting exactly how they would cut out her heart. A red-scaled dragon was curled in the back of the room, eyes glowing and smoke pluming from its nose. Movement caught her eye, and Lily saw something slither under one of the tables. The great head of a nestler turned to look at her and feel the air with its suckers, then turned away. There were many other things as well but she couldn't process any more. She felt isolated, exposed and on display in the center of the room. The mistress of Nightfall Manor was replaced by a fourteen-year-old girl who longed to run back home, where she could bury her head under the covers and pretend none of this had ever happened.

Vallia must have read her mind, as the grin spread even wider on her face. "Where are our manners, sisters? Lily Blackwood must take an honored place at the table. She is surely tired after such a long journey and seeks refreshment."

"Oh let her sit next to me, please let her sit next to me," Morta said. The Smiling Lady patted the throne next to where she sat. Lily saw the razor sharp thorns tearing through Morta's hands, yet no blood came from her.

"I'm afraid that wouldn't leave much left for the rest of us," Vallia said. "No, we have saved her a place at the table with some of our most distinguished guests."

Holding her head high, Lily was led to the center table by Vallia. *'I will be home this time tomorrow. I only need survive until the morning. Play their silly games for tonight but be watchful,"* she thought, *"for I have no friends here.'*

"A historic moment, quite historic, indeed," said a soft dulcimer voice to Lily's right. She looked before she could stop herself, and the creature locked eyes with her. He was old, older than Ozy, older than time. His face was a network of wrinkles, bumps and ridges that dripped like oatmeal batter and folded in on itself. Tufts of white hair sprouted from his misshapen ears that were no more than nub holes growing in his skull. His lips were perpetually pursed, and his gums worked like a cow chewing cud. He was dressed in a scratchy monk's habit and a stitched bag hung around his neck.

"Quite historic, wouldn't you agree? The last female Blackwood is sitting among us, the fate of so many riding on someone so young," the being said. "It has all the makings of an epic, that is if humans still write such things."

"You won't bore her with your stories of the days before humans, will you?" Vallia interjected. "You know what a frightful bore those stories are."

"Yes, a frightful bore," the being glared at her. "The time when we ruled the world and weren't chained to this accursed place. I will have to find a much more *riveting* story that passes your approval."

"See that you do," Vallia said. "Or my sisters and I will have your innards picked clean by the birds."

The Smiling Lady bowed to Lily and left without a look back. The quilled creature followed after her whimpering with each step that it took.

"…dares to talk to me that way," the ancient being muttered. "I've wrought more devastation than they're even capable of contemplating."

"The Judge is a pitiful old fool, but none the less dangerous for that," a woman on Lily's other side whispered in a voice that was devoid of emotion. She was striking in an unearthly way. Blond and black hair fell on either side of her oval face. Her skin was leeched of color, like the women Lily saw in the corridor. Lilacs were woven in a crown around her head. There was something familiar about her, something Lily knew she had seen before, but she was so overwhelmed by everything taking place that the answer danced out of reach.

"Judge?" Lily said.

"Oh yes, he tips and weighs the scales and almost always rules with a guilty verdict. How many humans have fallen prey to what he offers, only to discover later that the price is death? He is the one that will judge the competition between you and the Smiling Ladies."

"Competition?"

The woman's lips stretched back, and Lily saw fangs that were as wide as paring knives hidden under her gums.

"They've told you nothing of the horrors that the night ahead holds, have they? Perhaps that is for the best, so that before you die, you won't be driven mad with fear."

'I know this woman, but from where?' Lily thought. An image flashed in her mind of lightning crashing. Lily was looking down from the crow's nest, and Mr. Hawthorne was talking with a woman in the Shadow Garden. *'It's her. She's the one he was speaking with. But why was the groundskeeper talking with one such as this?'* Lily looked at the woman again. She had seen those features many times before. This time the answer came to her, but it couldn't be.

"Cassandra?" Lily asked.

The woman's expressionless face watched Lily. There was no humanity there, only the avarice that all the creatures of the Gardens had.

"You're much smarter than your brother," the woman finally replied. "I told him I would rip open your throats and bleed both of you dry, but he still didn't understand who I was."

"You're — her — mother," Lily said, puzzling it out in her mind. "But she said —."

" — that I was killed by an Angel Trumpet plant? She only mimics what her father told her.

Lies heaped on lies."

"What — what happened?"

"My husband's cowardice made me what I am and ruined our daughter so that she carries death in every touch of her hands."

"Now, Belinda, that's not quite right," the Judge said, leaning in from Lily's other side. He was picking at the food on his plate, and Lily saw with a start that it was a heap of maggots.

"Mind yourself, Judge, I'm not on trial," Belinda said.

"We are all on trial from the moment we come into existence," the Judge said. "I only hasten the invariable conclusion. Why not try a novel approach and tell the child the truth?" With that, the Judge raised the plate to his mouth and noisily slurped down its contents.

Cassandra's mother stared at Lily with dead eyes. "Why not, indeed? The Smiling Ladies gave me my true birth, before that I was weak, prone to let emotions cloud my vision. I lived in fear and was married to a simpering fool more interested in the plants of the Gardens than our love. I was drawn to Nightfall Gardens, the same as the others that walk through the gates. I was attracted to this place, to its danger, to something larger than the little life I'd lived in a mountain village up to that time. You could even have said that Horatio Hawthorne was an attractive man then, bound and determined to protect the world. It was heroic, meaningful, for one of such limited vision as mine.

So we married under the poplar trees before Lady Deiva and the dusk riders and the mist people. Little did I know that the Smiling Ladies watched from the Shadow Garden and marked me as one of their own."

A fight broke out just then on the other side of the room between a warlock and a shape shifter. There was yelling and the crashing of chairs. Lily saw the wizened, bloodstained warlock crush the throat of a being that shifted effortlessly from a Smiling Lady to manticore, to a mermaid, to an ogre, to a hissing lizard man and then to the warlock himself. The room was riveted by the spectacle. The Smiling Ladies sat on their thrones with grins ratcheted to their ears. Esmeret patted Desdemona on the head. Unholy voices echoed off of the walls of the castle, gibbering with excitement. A gargoyle flung a plateful of raw meat at the fighters, splattering them with offal. The excitement was overshadowed by an oppressive feeling of foulness that weighed everything down like a physical presence. Lily looked to see if there was a glumpog draining the mood, but apparently they weren't of high enough standing to join the banquet. The sheer multitude of creatures that shouldn't exist anywhere except in storybooks wore on her nerves. Lily felt her sanity walking on the edge of the unknown, and, if she were to experience much more, she might never come back. To her right, the Judge opened the pouch around his neck and hungrily fingered a pair of gold scales that shone with age.

The shape shifter changed to a squid creature with tentacles dangling from his mouth. He hammered at the warlock, but made the mistake of stepping on the paw of the massive white wolf that was gnawing the bone. When he accidentally stumbled over the animal, the wolf snapped at his legs. The shape shifter howled, giving the warlock enough time to shove his opponent away. He raised his ancient hands, muttered an incantation, and the shape shifter dropped lifeless as a sack of barley to the floor. The room howled its approval. The Judge smiled. "Justice is served," he said.

More wolves dragged the body away as the tables were reset. A jester in cap and bells with a demonic face took to the floor for entertainment and began juggling human skulls. The dinner continued as though nothing had happened. A familiar face in a maid's uniform squelched across the room, offering more wine and a dish of simmered bones in a black sauce. Lily felt as if the air had been sucked out of her.

"Polly!" she blurted.

"Oh, very naughty, Miss. Very naughty, tee hee," the grub tittered.

Only when she stopped in front of her could Lily see that it wasn't her housekeeper. The creature was more corpulent. Her maid's uniform strained against her grub flesh. Lily could see where the fabric cut into the gelatinous skin. While the maid had the same bald head and white eyes, there was something malignant in her features.

"Blood pudding, Miss?" the being said. Even her voice sounded different than Polly's.

"No," Lily said, shaking her head at the food. "You're not Polly at all."

"No Miss, tee hee, but if you survive tonight, tell that traitorous sister of mine that Justine can't wait to pour a dram of salt on her and watch her writhe in torment. You just tell her that, Miss."

'Polly has a sister?' Lily thought. This world grew stranger and stranger.

Dinner resumed, and the creatures of the Shadow Garden fell to the food with renewed vigor, as if the killing had made them famished. Belinda and the Judge slurped greedily at their blood pudding. Lily waited until Cassandra's mother paused and asked her to continue her story.

"You said that you were marked on your wedding day?" Lily asked, trying to prod the woman.

Belinda looked at her with lifeless eyes. "Yes, but for no other reason than that the creatures of the Gardens can't abide happiness. And I had it — that petty, paltry emotion that humans want so desperately and that lasts for such a short time. Horatio and I made our cottage a home. I helped him work the Gardens planting to protect the house. The threat of danger lurked always, beings calling to us, trying to entice us from the path, but we ignored the voices and were sure in our arrogance that no harm would befall either of us."

The happiest moment came on the day that Belinda gave birth to Cassandra, though if any memory of that feeling lingered in her, Lily couldn't perceive it. She spoke with complete detachment, as if she were sharing someone else's story and not her own.

"Raga, curse her name, was the one who delivered our beautiful baby. She made a draught of dream tea for me to ease the baby's passage into this world. Not long after, I pushed for the last time and heard the first cry of my daughter gasping air. She was pink and beautiful and cried for her mother's breast. I named her Cassandra after an aunt who I had loved."

"Pink?" Lily said. "But what of Angel Trumpet? And of you being lured into the Shadow Garden?"

"A lie, all of it, to ease poor Horatio's mind. Cassie was born as normal as anyone outside of the gates. What happened to her came later, after — after I had been reborn by the Smiling Ladies," Belinda said.

The last day of her old life had ended with her, Horatio and Cassandra, little more than two at the time, fortifying the plantings of Dragon's Breath around the Manor.

"It was a small life, but it seemed like everything at the time," Belinda said. "Little was I aware that I would never partake of that pleasure again."

The sky darkened as the three made their way past the Shadow Garden. The red moon prepared to creep over the horizon, and they hurried to be safely home.

"I was carrying Cassie in my arms, singing a mountain lullaby that my aunt taught me. Horatio was lugging the spell toolbox that he carried everywhere with him. Neither of us was paying attention or we would have recognized what happened next for what it was: a trap."

Horatio was the one to spot their downfall. A madrigal flower bloomed effervescent off the path in the Shadow Garden, under the drooping arms of a willow tree that stirred in the evening breeze. The flower chimed with music when the wind caressed its petals.

"The blind fool," Belinda said. "Do you know what a madrigal flower is?"

Lily shook her head. The Judge leaned in from her other side. "Fool's gold, a magic plant that doesn't exist. The Fountain of Youth and the Holy Grail all rolled into one," he chuckled malevolently. His polished scales had disappeared into the bag, though he stroked the cloth as if he were uncomfortable with it out of sight.

"New flowers come and go in the Gardens every day. Species push through the soil and two days later are gone forever. Some, such as the agave, only flower every century, while others have even longer cycles. The madrigal flower was the holiest of holies to the Hawthorne family. It had been written about once in the dim reaches of his family's past, a vermilion-colored, flute-shaped flower that trilled music and vibrated with a sound like a finger running around the top of a wine glass."

"Why was it so important?" asked Lily.

"His relative wrote that the plant had healing properties. It could take ten years off a person's life and restore the beauty and vitality chipped away by time. The plant withered so quickly once it was taken from the ground, that all that was left was an obscure entry in the Hawthorne plant journal that was hundreds of years old. My husband searched many years, believing that if the madrigal really existed that it might be harnessed to restore youth and to do away with death," Belinda said.

"Wouldn't our brethren in the White Garden *love* that?" the Judge chuckled.

"This is the land of shadows, where the dark part of human imagination conjures up all that terrifies it the most," Belinda said. "My husband didn't see that, though. He saw another trophy for his collection, and he went about retrieving it."

Even during the day it would have been a dangerous task to stray from the path, but with night almost fallen it was infinitely more perilous.

"That gave my husband only short pause. He had grown up here and thought that he knew the ways of the Gardens. He was wrong. It only takes a second and one careless decision and they will achieve their retribution. I was so foolish in my youth that I didn't say more than 'be careful' before he ran to the willow tree where the madrigal bloomed in all of its beauty."

Horatio was kneeling to dig up the flower when three shapes drifted out of the gloom. "They appeared from nowhere as though made of the same dark that grew with the night. That was my first sight of the Smiling Ladies."

Her husband barely made a sound as he discovered he was surrounded. "Belinda, take Cassie and go," he said calmly, frozen in front of the flower.

"What could I do? He was my husband and my love burned bright. I think back on that and laugh. Of the thousand weaknesses humans are heir to, that is the most ruinous."

"So, gardener, you trespass on our land," Esmeret said. She was the tallest, cruelest and the oldest of the Smiling Ladies, though some say that they were born only moments apart.

"I — I'll just be leaving now," Horatio said rising to his feet. The madrigal plant disappeared; it had been nothing more than an illusion to draw him off the path.

"Oh you won't be leaving ever again, I'm afraid," said Vallia, the smartest of the three.

"I want to play, can I play with him?" Morta asked.

"Belinda, go now with my love and take our daughter," Horatio said. His voice trembled so badly that he could barely get the words from his mouth out.

"I didn't go. I couldn't go," Belinda told Lily. "And how glad I am that I didn't. The Smiling

Ladies offered me a choice; my husband's life for mine. A simple trade. They drew more pleasure out of hurting him than of taking his life. I kissed our sleeping daughter and laid her in the grass near the path. How you should have heard him wail and tear at his hair as he begged me to run away and take our daughter. I suppose I thought that he would save us somehow, pull something from his magic box and chase the Smiling Ladies away. That was a foolish wish. They threw him on the path and encircled me with their arms. It wasn't until their teeth found my neck that I screamed for him to save me. When I looked back for the last time, he was clutching our bawling daughter and calling my name. He never came for me though. He took our daughter and ran. He left me here to serve at the Smiling Ladies' leisure."

The story was ghastly, horrible beyond description. Lily couldn't help but wonder what Cassandra would think if she knew the tale.

"If — if she was born normal, how did she turn green?" Lily asked.

"The coward has been working ever since to make a serum that would protect people from the creatures of the Gardens, that would kill whatever evil laid its hands on them. He thought he had perfected the vaccine and tried it on Cassie. It turned her into what you know now, turned her skin green and made her fatal to human touch," Belinda's dead eyes stared at Lily.

"The scales will weigh harshly on that man," the

Judge said. "Of course, they will weigh heavily on all humans once we are free."

Lily could hardly believe what she'd heard. It was impossible that Mr. Hawthorne was to blame for what happened to her friend. Yet, the story had the ring of truth.

"But why was he talking with you? I saw you with him during the storm," Lily said.

"He seeks me out to beg forgiveness, but I never give him what he comes for. Now you'll hear no more of my tale. It will do you no good anyway. You won't see the sun rise," Belinda turned from Lily and brought the conversation to an end.

The entertainment commenced once dinner drew to a close. A jester somersaulted into the room, cap and bells tinkling. He was dressed in yellow and red motley so filthy that Lily could barely make out the colors. The jester landed with a mock bow in front of the Smiling Ladies. He was stunted and dwarfish, with a wide nose and bulging eyes that glistened in the light. Stubble rode his cheeks, and when he opened his mouth he displayed a mouthful of teeth filed to points. Morta clapped her hands in excitement. The great hall stirred as the jester spun, raising one finger as if feeling the air, and began to sing.

Oh, the mistress has come tonight to play
To Nightfall Manor she found her way
While in the Shadow Garden we prayed
Of her golden head bejeweling a spike
Of roaches eating her ice blue eyes

As she was being swarmed by flies
And her poor soul twisted and died!
The Blackwoods they were no more
It was the end of that load of bores
And the Gardens they opened wide
Followed by endless night
What a blessed sight!

The jester curtsied as though he were lifting an invisible skirt. The great hall echoed with laughter as the buffoon began to tumble for their amusement.

"You mustn't take it personally, my dear," the Judge said, cupping his mouth to her ear so she could hear him over the roar. "The scales are always changing balance. For too long they were on your side, but now they shift back to us."

'Breathe,' Lily thought. *'Push all of this away. It's not enough that they want to kill you; they also want to break you and scatter the ashes of your mind. They only have the power that you give them. They can't harm you; they can only force you to harm yourself.'*

But was that true? The emissaries from the Gardens weren't supposed to harm her when they came to Nightfall Manor, yet two of them had tried to kill her. They even sent an assassin after her. The Smiling Ladies could be toying with her the way that a cat does with a bird that has a broken wing. Could they do to her what they had done to Desdemona — drain her soul and keep her alive as a pet, a reminder of the family that had plagued them for thousands of years?

Lily focused on one of the candles on the other side of the room. She thought of her mother and father, and of her brother. There were only four months remaining until the gates reopened and Moira and Thomas would come to save them. Silas was surely alive somewhere among the mist. Cassandra would find him and bring him back. Lily thought of her bed at Nightfall Manor and how good it would feel to slip under the blankets. It would even be good to see Farragut with his dirty face and rough manners. That house of torment seemed a paradise compared to this land of nightmares that she inhabited now.

Lily heard the scrape of chairs and saw movement from the thrones. Esmeret and the other Smiling Ladies were standing. The jester had disappeared back to wherever he had come from. The night must surely be half over, Lily thought. Desdemona yanked restlessly on her chain. The other beings were silent. With a start she realized that she was the only one who wasn't standing. She came to her feet as Esmeret began speaking.

"Our *tradition* — what a moribund word, says that each generation a Blackwood woman must come before us in her fourteenth year. Thus it was written since Prometheus, damn his soul, and thus it is still written," Esmeret said. The room stirred uneasily at the name of the dead Titan. "They come before us in the last innocence of childhood. They come to us before the corruption of the world buries its roots in them. They come before us to

306

judge whether their hearts are pure and tradition will be upheld or they will be erased in dust as we all must be."

"Kill her!" An ogre called from one of the tables. The creature was a great stinking beast as wide as a two doorways with a squint-eyed gaze and potato-sized nose. He wore a suit of armor made from animal hooves, and a necklace of bones hung around his neck. Growls of assent filled the air. Someone pounded a table in agreement.

"If it were that easy, it would have been done long ago," Esmeret said, stepping down onto the floor. "The old magic still holds strong here. If anyone should care to make an attempt, go ahead and see what the results will be."

The room filled with a babble of noise. Esmeret and the other Smiling Ladies watched with plastic expressions of mirth as the creatures of the Shadow Garden tried to work up their courage.

"I'll do it," a voice called from the back of the room. "It can't be worse than enduring this hell for one second more. We were made to bend humans to our will, not be imprisoned here like stinking animals in a cage."

A man cloaked in darkness came from the shadows. He looked like every beggar that Lily had ever seen in the many cities her family had traveled through performing as the Amazing Blackwood family. *'We were on the run from this place and my father's family, but we couldn't run far enough,'* Lily thought. The beggar wore an outfit made of rags and leaned on a crutch made from a twisted oak limb. He was missing a leg, and a dirty strip of cloth covered his eyes. The man limped toward her as if he barely could walk.

As the beggar hobbled closer, she instinctively crouched in a fighting stance and slipped out of her shoes so she would be able to move more quickly. Someone cackled laughter, but Lily didn't care. The rest of the room disappeared as she focused on the hideous beggar that came toward her, though how he could see she had no idea.

"Know that you do this at your own peril, Urelias," Vallia said. She and Morta had joined their sister on the floor.

"Stuff your peril," Urelias said. "It's a girl whose naught more than skin, bones and a beating heart. "Your fear has made you blind, but Urelias isn't blind. He can still see." With that, the beggar reached up and removed the blindfold, and Lily gasped. His eyes swirled like the cosmos, like a fire that had been built and fueled for centuries, but never allowed to burn out until it burned with a glow hot enough to melt iron. There were no eyes, only bits of flame and gas that spilled forth toward her.

"Stare into my eyes, child, and your hard journey will be finished," Urelias said.

'No,' Lily thought. She blinked and glanced away. Breaking his gaze took all of her will. An invisible strand that felt as if it were connecting them snapped. She swept her leg outward, taking out his good leg. As Urelias lost his balance, he screamed and clawed at his eyes. His face was enveloped in a blaze of light that distorted his features and covered his body. The light blazed until he was nothing more than an outline of shimmering star-fire. Before he struck the floor, the light flared and he was gone. A great murmuring broke out in the hall. The beings of the Shadow Garden stirred with restlessness trying to make sense of what they had just seen.

"I warned him," Esmeret said. "The old magic is still strong. This girl is protected as long as she walks in the light and doesn't embrace the darkness. She has safe passage here."

"Why is she here then?" a witch cried. "I'd rather see her dead and be done with it."

"We all would," Vallia said, raising her hand to calm the riot that was threatened to erupt. "But the only way that happens is of her free will. Each Blackwood woman must make her own journey through the castle. At the end, they take the path of shadow and illusion or journey back to Nightfall Manor. Some chose the path home, but more chose the path that whispers lies to all of us. Either way this is done of her own accord."

"Are you ready to begin your journey to discover which you will chose?" Vallia asked.

"It's dark and dreary, and few come back the same as they were," Esmeret cautioned.

"Play, oh do play with us," Morta said.

Lily wondered if it hurt having to smile all of the

time, having to pretend that things were fine when they weren't, never able to show the true feelings of your heart. "I'm ready to finish this and go home," Lily said, hoping that they didn't hear the fear in her voice.

"Home is where the heart is, and it's such an easy thing to misplace," Vallia quipped. She clapped her hands, and Polly's sister came slithering across the floor holding a candle. "This is for you, Miss. To help you find the way ... or better yet, to lose it."

Lily took the candle in her hands. The creatures of the great hall were watching her with avarice and hatred. The Smiling Ladies were watching as well.

"What do I do now?" Lily asked, looking at the object that had been given to her.

"Do?" Vallia said. "A simple task, really. You make your way out of the castle before dawn. If you do that, you go home, but if you should choose the path of the shadow, then you stay here with us for all eternity."

'I must keep my wits about me for whatever is to come,' Lily thought. Without another word, she chose a doorway and set off to discover the secrets of the castle.

17

RACE AGAINST THE RED MOON

Silas had never been so fearful of night's arrival.
The group plunged through the mist, trying to find
a safe haven before darkness fell. A fine patter of
rain fell, soaking through their cloaks and chilling
them to the marrow. The mist swirled like a living
creature, grasping with invisible fingers. Trainer
led the group, his ratty wolf cloak pulled down,
obscuring his face. Silas and Mirabelle came next,
followed by Cassandra, with Jonquil and Arfast
bringing up the rear, leading the horses.

As they walked, Silas looked back at Cassandra
to see if she was still angry with him. He got a
scowl in return for his effort. He supposed that was
better than the growl he received earlier, when he
tried talking with her.

"Is something wrong?" Mirabelle asked as she
struggled to keep up with him.

'How can I tell her when I don't know myself?' Here they were in a life-or-death situation, and Cassandra was more upset at him than worried about the fact that they were being pursued by a mind-destroying witch and an all-powerful deity who was as old as the earth. He laughed out loud.

His cousin arched an eyebrow. "You're a strange one Silas Blackwood."

"I'm sorry," he said, trying to stifle the laugh. "This whole situation ... it's crazier than anything my father dreamed up in the plays he wrote for us to perform."

"I'd like to meet him one day," Mirabelle said. "And your mother as well. It was brave what they did."

"Brave?" Silas asked.

"Leaving here. Running away from this place," she said.

"Why?" Silas asked. The rain began falling harder, drumming against the leaves on the trees. At least, the rain was driving the mist from around them. They could see further into the woods than they had been able to all day. The trees were thick, and the ground was covered in pine needles and vegetation. How long did they have before night came?

"Because if they had stayed here, all you would have known was that dreary house and the Gardens. This place steals joy. Your parents did their best to protect you and your sister for as long as they could," she said.

Silas had never thought of it that way. When he looked back on the wayward life that his family lived, all he remembered was how their father struggled to keep them afloat, as though he was not made for that world, while his mother, the rock of the family, remained silent and stoic. When he had first found out about Nightfall Gardens, he thought it had been cowardly that they ran from this place, but now he saw it differently. They had given up the only life that they knew in order to protect their daughter. How strange it must have been for them, those first days in the outside world. Silas had been conceived and born outside of the gates. He probably wouldn't even exist except for the fact that they had decided to leave this place.

"Have you ever been outside of the gates?" Silas asked as he watched Trainer disappear through the trees ahead.

"To the world outside? No, but I'd like to go someday. There are some in Priortage who are born and die without ever having seen the sun," she said.

Silas stopped in his tracks. It had never occurred to him that there were people who went their whole lives without seeing a clear blue sky. The warmth of the sun was such a delicious feeling. To be denied that was unimaginable.

Cassandra was suddenly on them, gesturing impatiently. "Move along, you're blocking the way."

"What about you? Have you never seen the

sun?" Silas asked.

"I don't give a whit for your sun," Cassandra said. "All I know is that right now night is approaching and you two are slowing us down."

"Your father never took you outside of the gates?" Silas asked, surprised.

"What business is it of yours what he did or didn't do? Now move out of my way." With that, Cassandra pushed past him and continued along the path.

"You have angered her?" Mirabelle asked, watching Cassandra follow where Trainer had led. "What's wrong?"

"She thinks that ... never mind," Silas said, flustered.

They stopped talking after that and continued walking in an awkward silence. Silas thought of Lily and wondered what she was doing at that moment. *'Thank goodness she's somewhere safer than here.'*

They walked for another hour, pushing through the woods. By then, it was apparent that night would catch them in the open unless something happened soon.

"Do you know this area?" Jonquil asked Mirabelle, shaking his head at the darkening sky overhead.

"We must be southwest of the village. I — I'm afraid I have little to offer in the way of advice," she said.

"Running like foxes being chased by dogs. I say

we build a fire and prepare to fight," Trainer said.

"Start a fire? How? The wood is soaked," Jonquil said. "I fear there is nothing for us to do but keep pushing ahead."

Arfast pulled up his sleeve and fire danced on the tip of a finger before being extinguished with a sizzle by the rain. "Well, so much for that," he said.

"Mayhap you could juggle them to death," Trainer scoffed with disdain.

In the last light of the day, they stopped to rest and Silas examined the group with him. His uncle Jonquil looked nothing like the person who had brought them to Nightfall Gardens only eight months ago. He was thinner and weaker. Only his blue eyes shone as brightly. They burned with the fire of life. Trainer fidgeted as though he wished he were anywhere else. Cassandra's yellow-green hair was plastered on her forehead, and she watched the woods as if waiting for something terrifying to arrive. Mirabelle clasped her hands and mouthed a prayer. The only one that didn't look beaten down was Arfast. The trickster stuck out his tongue out as if he were trying to catch a snowflake. "Might be raining?" he said with laugh.

Jonquil leaned on his walking stick and closed his eyes. When he had been silent for more than a minute, he suddenly opened his eyes and stared at Silas.

"Lad, do you still have the box Mr. Hawthorne gave you?" he asked.

"Yes," Silas said. He unrolled the blanket under

his arm to reveal the spellbox that the gardener gave them before they started on their journey.

"May I?" Jonquil asked. Silas handed the box to him. The dusk rider examined its contents and nodded as if he'd found exactly what he was looking for.

"There's trail killer in here," Jonquil said cracking a thin smile. "Bless your father for that," he said to Cassandra.

"What's that?" Silas asked.

"It hides the trail of whoever uses it so that they can't be followed," Cassandra said.

"Then why didn't we bleeding use it before?" Trainer asked irritably.

"A tracker who is following his prey and loses the trail is apt to keep searching until they find it again. Those who search hard and long enough will stumble on the trail eventually. We are dealing with supernatural beings. If they lost the trail cold, they would likely use magic to sniff out the new trail."

"What good does it do us then?" Silas asked.

"What if we gave them a trail to follow?" Jonquil suggested. "But the group went in a different direction."

"How exactly would that work?" Trainer asked.

"Someone would have to give them a false trail to follow" Jonquil said.

"Who would do —" Silas started, and then realized the answer. "No, you can't," he said, shaking his head.

"It's the only way lad," Jonquil said. "Each of you give me one of your belongings."

"But it's madness," Silas said.

"Only if it doesn't work," Jonquil said. "Now do it. There is little time."

Arfast spoke up then. "It should be me. I'm faster. I'll lead them on a merry chase and meet up with you later."

"No," Jonquil said. "You and Trainer must protect the children and get them to safety. There's no time for discussion."

Mirabelle took out a silk cloth from her bedroll. "May the light protect you," she said. Trainer and Cassandra were next. The dusk rider gave him the rag he used to wipe his sword and Cassandra passed him a tie from her green hair. Arfast gave one of the colorful balls that he used to juggle. Finally, Silas cut a piece of cloth from his shirt and handed it to his uncle. As Jonquil took it, they heard the baying of a pack of wolves from far off in the distance. Everyone froze as the sound echoed in the woods.

"They come," Jonquil said. "Go quickly, and I'll meet you back at Nightfall Gardens."

The dusk rider handled the purple flask to Cassandra. "Wait until I'm out of sight and pour this on the ground behind you as you go your way."

Jonquil shoved the items inside of his cloak and prepared to go. He pulled Silas aside and placed his hands on his nephew's shoulder. "We head into dangerous waters now. Follow the dusk riders and do what you must to stay safe."

Silas nodded. He couldn't help feeling this was a final leave-taking. He must have had a crestfallen look on his face, because his uncle smiled at him. "Cheer up, lad. Where there's life, there's hope. I'll see you at the Manor." With that, Jonquil hobbled into the woods. Silas watched his uncle until his figure disappeared in the trees.

"Let's go now," Trainer said. "Each minute we waste is one that they come closer." The dusk rider set off in the opposite direction with the group following after. Cassandra was last, pouring the smoking potion on the ground to mask their trail.

They plunged through the woods, the day long gone and the terrors of the night just beginning. Trainer and Arfast moved with deft swiftness through the trees that the others found difficult to follow. A screech owl cried out in the branches above them. A white-tailed bobcat moved like a ghost through the trees ahead of them. It was so dark that Silas could barely make out Mirabelle's cloak ahead of him and Cassandra was invisible in the light just a few steps behind him. *'How far will my uncle get before they find him?'* Silas wondered. *'And what will they do to him once they discover the trick we have played on them?'*

They moved swiftly through the woods with Trainer leading them as if he knew exactly where they were going.

How long they journeyed like that, Silas didn't

know. It felt as though hours passed in the woods, but it could have been far less. The rain finally dissipated. The temperature fell, and Silas shivered with the cold that clamped down on them. No one spoke. Once, Trainer stopped, unsure of which direction to go, and then he sniffed the air and turned right. The woods were thick, with tree trunks so big around that they had to squeeze between them, leaning on bark that was slimy and wet with rain. Exhaustion overtook them, and still they marched on. Trainer finally held his hand up, and they came to a halt in a clearing.

"Five minutes," he mouthed. "No more."

Arfast and Trainer stood vigil as the three children fell to the ground and rested their tired legs.

Mirabelle was the first to speak. "I've never seen Nightfall Manor. It will be interesting to see a house that I've heard so many tales about."

"If we make it that far," Cassandra said, finally speaking to them.

"You must show me around," Mirabelle said. "It's a tale that many villagers tell. But it's where you've spent your life. It must seem ordinary to you."

"The Gardens are many things, but never ordinary," Cassandra said.

Trainer gestured for them to get up and continue their journey.

Mirabelle reached out to touch Cassandra, and the green girl jerked away. "No one can touch me," she said angrily.

Silas's cousin smiled sadly, as if she understood. "That must be terribly lonely," she said. "But loneliness, like happiness, only lasts for a time."

"Don't preach at me with your religion," Cassandra said. "You know nothing of me."

"Oh, but Silas has told me so much about you. He can't stop talking about you," she whispered, smiling at the green girl.

"Silas — he's insufferable," Cassandra said.

"Men always are," Mirabelle said.

The journey became a mad scramble through the woods. Suddenly, the forest opened up and ahead lay farmland where spinach grew from the rich soil.

"That's odd," Mirabelle said as they skirted the field. "We're close to the village. I thought we'd be much farther away than this by now."

Somewhere in the night, wolves howled, but the sound seemed to come from miles away. The group froze as a blunderbuss fired, its boom echoing through the night. Once the gun blast had quieted, there came was the frantic sound of a wolf pack going wild and, in the midst of that, they heard a man cry out in pain.

"Jonquil!" Silas said, stepping in the direction of the sound. Arfast stopped the boy.

"No, Silas," he said. "Jonquil didn't give of himself to have us rush to the rescue. I know your uncle. He would be angry if we did anything but continue toward Nightfall Gardens."

Silas nodded as if he understood. His heart sank in his chest as the tragedy of the last few weeks overwhelmed him. "He's —."

"— dead, lad, and we're alive," said Trainer. "And, I intend to stay that way."

They left the field behind and continued into the woods, Trainer leading them with urgency as if he knew exactly where he was going. The red moon had shifted halfway across the sky in its nightly journey when a wolf howled ahead of them. That sound was followed by another howl to their right and another to the south and left of them.

'No, no, no,' Silas thought. *'They weren't supposed to be able to follow us.'*

"Faster," Trainer said. "This way." They were each running now, going as fast as they could through the trees, like animals who felt the breath of the hunter coming down on them. Silas and Arfast brought up the rear, while Mirabelle and Cassandra leaped like gazelles over tangled tree roots on the forest floor.

A trumpet blared in the woods, with the sound of wolves baying. The sound seemed barely beyond the next rise.

"This doesn't make sense," Arfast said, running next to Silas. "It's as though we are being herded."

No sooner had he said this than they stumbled from the woods into a clearing, where the mist hung low on the ground. The red moon cast a deathly crimson light here. Trainer threw up his arms to stop the group from proceeding. Across the clearing from them, something was emerging out of the woods. At first, Silas thought he must be hallucinating. The figure was twice the size of a man but whip-thin with antlers that twisted from his head and branched into points, sharp as thorns. A beard hung down to its waist, and something seemed to writhe inside of it. The creature looked at them with dead, white eyes. There was only one thing that it could be.

"Eldritch," Silas said, and his heart froze in his chest. The creature stepped toward them as if it had all the time in the world. Other figures moved out of the forest as well. Wolves came from the trees in every direction, as did village men wielding swords and spears. Dark things that had escaped from the Gardens came forth as well; they were little more than shadows. The final two figures to come from the woods were Silas's grandfather, dressed in the robes of the council, and a shape bent so low its face almost reached the ground. It was Bemisch — her head was twisted sideways and her gray hair hung down. partly covering her foul face.

'Thought you could escape boy, but there is no escape,' the witch Bemisch said. *'You will learn to serve your new master well and when the time comes you will kill your sister.'*

"No," Silas blurted out, loud enough that Cassandra and Arfast turned to look at him.

"Doesn't make any sense, it's as if they knew we were going to be here," Arfast said.

Trainer had drawn his sword and turned to look back at them. A look of perverse anger had overtaken his features.

"Dan, wait, it'll do no good to fight —," Arfast said, but before he could finish the sentence, the dusk rider stepped forward and in one fluid motion, plunged his sword into the person standing nearest to him. The sword tore through Mirabelle and came out her back. He gave his sword a final cruel turn, and Silas screamed in horror as blood gushed from her mouth.

"Si — Silas," she moaned as the light fled from her eyes.

"Curse you and your religion," Trainer said. He glared at the rest of the group with madness in his eyes. "Curse all of you. There is only one true god!"

Silas felt his legs grow weak as Trainer pushed the lifeless form of his cousin off his sword and she fell to the ground. *'It was him,'* Silas thought. *'He was the person that I saw talking with the wolf that night. I saw him on the mountain with a wolf as well. He was passing messages to them. He only killed the wolf because I saw him. He was leading us into a trap this whole time.'*

Arfast was on him then, his sword a whirl as he and Trainer battled. "Traitor," Arfast yelled, deflecting Trainer's blade. The figures on the other side of the field, watched impassively, until Eldritch raised one whip-like arm and spoke in a voice that was deep and ancient. He said one word — "Enough."

323

With that, the wolves and villagers moved in on the group. Silas fell back next to Cassandra. Arfast had Trainer on the ground and raised his sword to strike. Trainer had a mad look in his eyes. "Do it, you coward. Do it!" Something moved in the trees behind Silas, and he drew his dagger as he heard branches crack.

"Silas, I —" Cassandra was trying to speak, but he barely heard the words. He turned to look at her and the last thing he saw were her eyes shining with softness. Then an object struck him hard on the back of the head. As he lost consciousness, he heard the witch's voice in his head, *'At last you're mine,'* and then he plummeted into darkness.

18
THREE VISIONS OF LILY

Lily had barely crossed the threshold she had chosen when Polly's sister, Justine, stepped from the shadows. "Follow me, Miss or you'll never make it out alive," said Polly's sister.

Lily followed her along a passage that was darker than the inside of a crypt. The only light came from the candle she held. Melting wax slid down from the wick in rivulets burning her fingers, but Lily never once thought of dropping it to forgo the pain. Candlelight reflected a nimbus from the back of Justina's bald head, which glistened with ooze.

The great banquet hall was behind them now. The Smiling Ladies and the others were continuing their feast; their voices were little more than hateful whispers in the distance. *'They will make merry until I escape or am dead,'* Lily thought. She closed her eyes and tried to think of her mother and father, but the only image she could conjure was that of Villon strapped to the tree, his skin peeled from his body and eyes imploring her to save herself. She shook her head and continued. Why should she be thinking of him now?

"This is as far as I go, Miss. No reason to risk my life for you," Justine said. The passage emptied into a gigantic lightless room full of massive gray bricks. Three passages exited in different directions.

"Chose one, Miss, but wisely. Each one was made for you, but only one leads to your freedom. The others lead to… well, I think you know the answer to that one." Justine giggled and slithered back the way they came, adding as she departed. "And don't forget to tell my sister that I'll have her ever-grubbing eyes for what she did to me."

When she was gone, Lily held the candle high to examine the three passages. The candlelight seemed to stop at the entrances, allowing her no hint of what might await her beyond, should she step into any of the corridors. *'How am I supposed to know what to do? I was never any good at sorting out puzzles. I don't have the patience for them.'*

She paused, listening for any sounds coming from within. Lily held the candle out until it touched the darkness of one of the entrances. The flame was swallowed, leaving her in pitch blackness. She jerked the candle back. *'What should I do? Why isn't Silas here to help me?'* Minutes ticked by, and Lily was no closer to making her decision when she heard noises coming from behind her. The sound, was almost imperceptible, was the sound of slippers pattering on the stone floor. At first, she thought it might just be the sound of the great castle settling, but it grew louder as though someone were approaching.

'What is this on top of everything else?' Lily hoisted the candle back the way she came and saw flashes of white crawling along the ceiling toward her. It was the women in white that she had seen before. All of them young, pale, and drained of life, with no sign of humanity on their cruel faces. 'The Smiling Ladies has done the same thing to them that they did to Cassandra's mother.' The women came closer, moving silently, as if they were lighter than air. There was a hungry expression in their eyes. 'They can't harm me,' Lily thought. 'I'm protected.' Still, she had no wish to chance it. As they entered the chamber like a swarm Lily plunged into a random corridor and…

…all was darkness around her — a living, breathing consciousness that she stumbled in with no clear idea of where she was headed. The last of her candle flame, flickered, grew small and was no more. Fear gripped her like a vice. Were the women in white following her? She reached out, touching stone and grit. Using the wall as a guide, Lily hurried onward. A prick of light appeared at the end of a long corridor. She thought she was imagining the cone of light at first, but it grew brighter and slowly the walls took on color. The restoration of light made Lily hurry with anticipation. Soon she was running, holding the hem of her dress.

As she rushed toward the light, the corridor changed; castle stone turned to curtains, and the corridor morphed into a familiar scene of theater backdrops. She now found herself among painted canvases of sunrises, sitting rooms and other props. Ropes and pulleys hung from a catwalk overhead. Ornate gilded trim ran along the walls of the room. Actors in grand costumes with powdered wigs and faces rouged with makeup rushed past her. A stagehand with rolled-up shirtsleeves showed hairy arms as he smoked a cigar and pulled on a rope, sweeping the curtain closed. From behind the curtain, Lily heard thunderous applause and shouts of encore. *'I'm in a theater, but how did I —,'* Lily didn't have time to finish the thought, before an impeccably dressed gentleman sporting a pencil-thin mustache was standing in front of her.

"Oh, magnifique," he said. "What a performance. You brought the house to its feet. Listen to that audience. I've never heard the like of it in all my years of managing the Grand Guignol Theatre. Listen to them call for you."

Lily was puzzled. There was something that wasn't right about this. Just a minute ago she had been — where had she been? An image of women in white came to her, but was overridden by the calls of her name coming from beyond the curtain.

"Go," the man said. "You mustn't keep your audience waiting."

'I'm sick, that's all it is,' Lily thought. *'It's the biggest playhouse in Paris. I've worked so hard to get here that I'm suffering from exhaustion.'* The curtain swept open to reveal an audience giving her a standing ovation. It was the most beautiful theater that she'd ever seen. Marble statues lined the walls of the massive space. Gold banisters and classical carvings covered the balcony. A mural was painted on the ceiling that revealed gods watching from the heavens above. *'Mother and father would be so proud of me.'* Where were they and Silas? Something flitted through her mind and then was gone. Lily bowed to the audience, soaking in the adoration pouring from them. She did three bows before the curtain swept back and the audience was gone.

"The critics from all of the major newspapers were here tonight," the manager said, rubbing his hands greedily. "Everyone who is anyone will want a ticket."

Lily suddenly remembered the man's name: Bertrand, the stage manager of the Grand Guignol Theatre. She felt a flash of anger. "Well, if you want me to continue performing you'll need to increase how much I'm paid and give me exclusive billing," she said, stalking off in the direction of her dressing room.

"But we agreed to —," he started.

"Contracts are made to be broken, and without me how long do you think this place will continue to draw these crowds?" she sneered.

"The others —," he said, hustling alongside her.

"There are no others. There is only me. Those I perform opposite of are no consequence. Name one of them that is half the actor that I am," she said.

"I know, I know, but there are egos to consider," Bertrand said.

"The only ego you need to consider is mine," Lily said, turning on him. "Now leave me." With that, she slammed her dressing room door in his face.

Lily's assistant was waiting for her. She was a tall girl with a pretty face and dull eyes who Lily had brought with her from New Amsterdam — rescued her, really, to be honest about it. Cassandra was the daughter of a dullard named Horatio Hawthorne who owned a flower shop down the street from the Golden Bough. Lily shuddered thinking of that creaky firetrap that she had played on her way to Paris. She would never have met Cassandra if it hadn't been for Silas. How her poor brother had mooned over the flower shop owner's daughter. He was too shy to say anything, though, and when Lily had been plucked from the Golden Bough to perform at the biggest theater in New Amsterdam, she'd brought Cassandra with her. It was her one concession to the past. Was there a part of her that had done it to spite her brother? Where was her family again? Lily shook her head.

"Nonsense," Lily said out loud.

"Ma'am?" Cassandra said, withdrawing as if

she were afraid that Lily was going to strike her.

'Why?' Lily thought. *'She's my friend. Her skin isn't like mine, it's —.'* The thought slipped away from her. She took off her earrings. "Well don't just stand there. Help me out of this ridiculous costume."

"Yes, ma'am," Cassandra said with a bow. She unzipped Lily's dress.

Lily's eyes caught the half dozen bouquets of flowers that stood on the dressing table. "Who are these from? Anyone important?"

"The Grand Duke sent you another bouquet of red and white roses from his private garden," Cassandra said. "And a note declaring his undying love for you."

"The fool is three times my age," Lily said with a cruel laugh. "But he's also the richest man in Paris. What else?"

"The poet Raphael has penned another ode to you," Cassandra said.

"A poet's words come easy, while their money comes hard," Lily said. "Still, the masses snap up every line that he puts down."

"You've been invited to a ball at the home of the Commandant and his wife," Cassandra said.

Lily snickered. "Hopefully it will be livelier than the last. Still, tell them I will come. Everyone will be there."

"Yes, ma'am," Cassandra said.

Lily slipped into a dress to greet her fans. "I am dining at Le Riche un Pan after I greet the seals," she said. "Make sure they've saved a table for me."

The liveliness backstage was dying down as Lily left her dressing room. She noticed that the other stagehands and actors went out of their way to give her space. Many of them wouldn't even make eye contact. *'They fear me, as they should.'*

A stagehand opened the backdoor so that she could go out and greet her fans. A throng of them waited for her, pushing against the burly doorman who tried to hold them back. "One at a time. One at a time," he barked.

A family squeezed in first for Lily to sign their playbill. They had the bourgeois look of the Parisian middle class. The father wore white gloves, a top hat and pince-nez spectacles that threatened to fall off the end of his nose. He stayed in the background as his wife and daughter rushed toward her. The mother and daughter were doughy, with dimples deep enough to put a finger in and curls so tightly wound that they looked as if they would spring from their heads.

"Oh, the performance that you gave was simply —," the mother said.

"— amazing," the daughter finished.

"I'm grateful, I'm sure," Lily said, smiling as authentically as she could. *'This is my hardest performance of the night.'*

They shoved their playbill at her and Lily signed her name. Others swarmed toward her. The doorman had to blackjack a scowling one-armed man who tried to come too close. "This wasn't supposed to happen. All is lost," the man mumbled before staggering into the Parisian night with a bloody nose. *'Wait, I know him. That's — that's — who was that?'*

Lily signed more autographs and shook the hands of her admirers as if she didn't want to be anywhere else. *'This grows tedious,'* she thought.

The poet Raphael appeared looking half-mad, as if he hadn't slept in days. His long, foppish mop of hair was tucked behind his ears, and he wore a lightly tied cravat and a wine-stained jacket. *'This is how he tries to entice me?'* Lily thought, incredulously.

"My darling, did you receive the poem I wrote for you —'Ode to Lily on First Waking in the Morning?" Raphael pleaded. "I plucked the very chords of my soul for you."

"Then your soul played a sour tune," she said. "I've told you before to stop sending me your drivel."

Raphael flinched as if stung. "That poem is on half of the city's lips."

"It *must* be good then," she said sarcastically. "Because we all know what excellent taste the masses have."

"If I can't have you then I'll kill myself," Raphael said sobbing.

"I hear the Montmartre Bridge is a good place to jump from," she said with a spiteful laugh.

"You mock me," he said stunned.

"You repulse me," Lily retorted. She turned to

the doorman. "Please escort him away. There'll be no more autographs tonight."

As Lily went back through the stage door, she glanced once more at the adoring crowd. A man moved in the darkness at the back of the crowd. He wore a wolf-hide cloak and there was a wicked scar on one of his cheeks. Once again, she had a feeling that she knew this man, and then the door swung shut behind her and the thought was lost.

Paris glowed like a beautiful gem as Lily's carriage set off along cobbled streets. Houses new and old with peaked gables pressed close. The streets were choked with cafes, bakeries and bars. Gargoyles watched from the top of crumbling churches. Gas lamps flickered along the streets, adding an unearthly atmosphere to everything. *'This is where life is,'* Lily thought. She watched a butcher smoking a cigarette in his shop. Even the slabs of meat hanging over the counter seemed more brightly lit, more colorful than usual. The carriage passed over the River Seine, and Lily saw young lovers strolling hand in hand, while an old man played the accordion mournfully under a full moon. Off in the distance, the massive frame of the Eiffel Tower rose, its intricate metal latticework only half complete, a reminder of the grand future that awaited everyone at the turn of the century. *'This is everything I've ever wanted,'* Lily thought and then sighed. *'Then why does it feel wrong?'*

Le Riche lit up the night, teeming with the upper crust of the city. Wealthy old men with bushy mustaches and slicked back hair dressed in tuxedos, and their wives wore colorful dresses with tight-fitting corsets and ostrich-feather boas, smoking cigarettes in ornate holders. Inside the restaurant were the captains of industry who drove the fiscal engine of the city. When Lily entered, the room froze. She had made exactly the kind of entrance she wished for. The conversation stopped as a hundred pair of eyes turned and were transfixed, as a waiter led her to her usual private nook at the back of the restaurant.

"Simply outstanding, my dear," a patron and his wife said, as they stopped to pay their respects on their way out of the restaurant. Lily flashed her most radiant smile, while silently wishing that they would leave her alone. *'Sheep,'* she thought spitefully. By the time she finished dinner, several more admirers had stopped to say that they had seen her performance. Once, the waiter came over, looking apologetic. "From an admirer," he said, holding a bouquet of red gardenias. Lily looked where the waiter gestured and saw a handsome young man who didn't look much older than she, sitting in a corner on the other side of the room. Even from her nook at the back, Lily could make out the pallor of his face and the redness of his lips. He lifted a glass of wine and winked when he caught Lily looking. She glanced away in embarrassment. "Send them back," Lily said, angered that she'd been caught with her guard down.

"He said that you would say that," the waiter said apologetically. "He said that a gift once given can't be returned."

"Oh, he did, did he? Well, tell him there is a first time for everything and that he can eat these flowers for all I care." She gestured impatiently for the waiter to leave.

"As you wish," he said, bowing and backing away.

Yet, as she left the restaurant later, Lily wasn't entirely displeased to see the young man waiting in the darkness outside, smoking a cigarette and watching the denizens of the city pass around him as if he'd always been a part of this place.

"You should never return a gift given with good intention," he smiled, dropping the cigarette to the ground and tamping it with his boot.

"I've found that most gifts come with invisible strings," Lily said. "Now, if you'll excuse me, I have some place that I'd rather be."

He laughed. "Close by, I'm sure, for you can prefer no place more than Paris."

"Part of the beauty of this city is that it's big enough that you don't have to see the same person more than once," she said.

"Yes, but it's also small enough to be intimate," he said. "It's ever-changing though its heart remains the same." The youth turned from her and watched as a washerwoman and a pair of drunken workers passed.

Lily stopped outside of her carriage, intrigued.

Something about him bespoke his natural attachment to his place. She was rootless, a wanderer with no more sense of home than the wind. "How long have you lived here?"

"Since the old gods were new," he said with a laugh. And again, something tugged at her mind, a feeling that something wasn't right. *'I'm coming down with something.'*

"I must be on my way. Maybe I'll see you again," she said.

"Maybe, though I'm not as handsome as I once was," the young man said.

"What do you mean —," Lily started to ask, but when she looked back at him, for an instant she saw a face that was nothing more than flayed skin with blood weeping from the surface. She gasped and stumbled backward, but he stepped toward her and she saw that she was wrong. His skin was a flawless alabaster. His intense blue eyes stared at her. "There are worse things than not having a home, Lily Blackwood," he said.

"How do you know my name?" she asked.

He smiled and shrugged. "How could I not know your name?" he replied and started to walk away.

"What's your name?" Lily called.

He stopped and turned. "Villon, but you already know that," he said.

Lily puzzled over that on her ride home. Cassandra was taking care of her correspondence when she entered her apartment.

"Anything of interest?" Lily asked.

"Only the usual letters from adoring fans and one from your brother," Cassandra said. The gardener's daughter clutched the cream envelope as if it might take flight in her hands.

"What does he say?"

"I — I didn't open it," Cassandra stammered.

"Well do, and be quick about it. I'm tired," Lily said.

Cassandra ripped open the envelope and skimmed the note inside, her face turning white. "He says that they are the managers of a playhouse in St. Charles and that they plan on staying there for some time. The owner has offered to sell the theater to your father when he retires."

"St. Charles? Their aspirations grow bigger and bigger," Lily said laughing.

"Anything else?" Lily yawned.

Cassandra sat stunned for a moment before speaking. "Your brother, he's — he's met someone."

"Silas? How shocking. I never thought he'd pull his head out of a book. What does he say?"

"He says that she works at the orphanage there. She has red hair and is very beautiful and …" Cassandra trailed off as if she could read no more.

"And what?" Lily said, her impatience growing.

"And they are to be married in the summer. He'd like you to come back for the wedding," Cassandra said. Her lip trembled and tears shined in her eyes.

"Oh, don't be upset," said Lily. "You're better off without my fool of a brother. Why, think of all the wonderful things you've seen here in Paris."

Cassandra's shoulders slumped as if she were defeated. *'Why am I taking satisfaction out of this?'* Lily thought. *' She's my friend. We fought Mugwump together.'*

Lily froze. Mugwump? Who was that? Again, the feeling returned that something was not right. *'I have everything I ever wanted. Why am I not content?'* She looked out the window at the full moon. For one second it turned a dark bloody red, before returning to normal. There was no mistaking that moon. She had seen it many times before. It dominated her life at … where? The thought was tantalizingly close. *'This is not me. I am not this … this person. She is cruel. Even at my most vain, I was not this horrid.'*

The world shimmered. Her Parisian flat and weeping Cassandra were replaced with the castle of the Smiling Ladies. Shooting pains tore at her body. Needles gouged her flesh. She was back where the three chambers split in different directions. She felt something clamped on her wrists and her legs. Coming to, as if waking from a deep slumber, Lily looked down. One of the women in white had her mouth pressed against her wrist and was sucked her blood greedily from the punctures on her arm. More of the women in white had their mouths pressed against her skin searching for veins. Lily screamed as their fangs tore into her flesh and blood pumped like a spigot into the creatures' mouths. *'But they can't,'* she thought. And then, *'No, but what would have happened if I had stayed in that place, where my fondest dreams had come true?'*

Lily grabbed the amethyst necklace from her neck and pressed it against the head of a woman drinking from the other wrist. The moment that the stone touched her flesh the woman threw back her head and howled before fleeing. Lily slammed the stone down against another woman who was crouched to drink from one of her legs. Pandora's stone connected with a thud and the woman's head ignited in a blaze of flame and she too was gone. The other women hissed and clawed at Lily, but when she raised the necklace, they backed out of the chamber. Once they were gone, Lily examined her wounds in the tepid light to see how bad they were. She gasped in wonder as the puncture wounds closed up and healed before her eyes.

'Where do I go now?' Lily thought, but she knew the answer. There were two more chambers to explore. *'One of them must show me the way out of here.'*

Steeling herself, she picked another passage to enter. She plunged into the darkness and stumbled along until she was suddenly standing in her father's office in the Golden Bough. Signs of celebration were everywhere. Streamers hung from the ceiling, a bottle of champagne was almost empty on Thomas's desk, and the sound of a party came from outside. Her father sat behind the desk. He was dressed in his best suit that was worn to a shine on the elbows. His face was in his hands and he was sobbing.

"What's wrong?" Lily asked as she drew closer.

Thomas looked up and wiped his eyes dry, giving her a faltering smile. "I truly am sorry, Lily. I never — it wasn't supposed to happen this way."

"What — what wasn't supposed to happen?" Lily was confused. How had she gotten here? And where had she come from?

"It was the only way to keep from going broke, to ensure that you had a future," he said. "You understand that, don't you? If only you knew the sacrifices that your mother and I made to protect you."

"Father, what are you talking about?" Lily asked.

"How can you not know?" he asked perplexed. "You threatened to run away. You said that you hated your mother and me."

"Hate you? What are you — ."

The door to the office opened and the sound of "For He's a Jolly Good Fellow," came from the other side. Gideon Wassum, the loathsome owner of the Golden Bough, entered. His head looked like a gigantic walnut stuck on a bowling pin. His hair was parted down the middle and greased to his skull. His jelly cheeks quivered as he pulled a pinch of snuff from a box and snorted it up his nose, eyes flaring. "Oh there you are dear, I wondered where you'd gotten to. It's time for our dance."

"Dear?" Lily flinched as he reached out his nicotine-stained fingers to touch her face.

"We can't keep them waiting. They've come to see the blushing bride and her resplendent husband off on our honeymoon to Europe," he said.

"Bride?" Lily looked down and gasped. She was wearing a wedding dress that was festooned at the waist with a garland of lilies. A sheer white veil hung down over her eyes and she could feel the flowers that were pinned in her hair.

"As of thirty minutes ago," he said impatiently. "Now come, come. I want to show off my pretty dove."

It suddenly came crashing back to her. Wassum was going to kick them out of the Golden Bough. The Amazing Blackwoods were going to have to move on to the next town once again this time, destitute. "The only place we have left to go is the poorhouse," Thomas had told Moira as Silas and Lily listened from the other side of the grate outside the office. But, Lily had caught Wassum's eyes. He was a wealthy man, and the Golden Bough was only one of his many real estate holdings. Lily would never have to worry about money, and the Amazing Blackwoods would never have to worry about a place to perform again. To her parents' credit, they never considered the offer. It had only been as the date neared for them to vacate the place that Lily had gone to the grand home of the owner and told him that she had overheard everything that they'd said and that she would marry him if he would sign over the Golden Bough to her parents and make sure that they never struggled for money. And now, here she was on her wedding day, about to dance with a man whose touch she would gladly drink poison to avoid.

Lily shuddered as his sausage fingers closed around her hand as he guided her back to the stage, where her mother, brother and Wassum's guests had gathered. Silas looked almost as forlorn as she felt. He had told her a secret that morning before the service. He was running away to the mountains as soon as he could. "I've been having strange dreams lately," he said. "There's this house that lives and breathes like a living being, and there are these gardens and a girl, a green girl," he laughed at that. "Its hard to describe."

As Wassum guided her onstage to applause, Lily caught Moira's eye. Her mother was crying, and Lily didn't think that it was for joy. *'I am doing this for you,'* Lily thought. *'Because if I don't you will have to go back to Nightfall Gardens'.*

The room shifted around her, and Lily jerked away from Wassum's embrace. The stage disappeared before her eyes and she was once again back in the passage with the corridors that split in three directions. The women in white watched from the darkness behind her. *'My family would never ask that of me, nor would I sell myself in such a fashion,'* Lily thought. She was angry now — angry at the false images that had been paraded before her in the guise of reality. There was only one passage left, and without another look, she entered.

Far off, a point of light glowed in the corridor. It was the same drab light that lit Nightfall Gardens on any given day. She made for that sheen. Could it already be daybreak? The rainy-day radiance grew as she drew closer. She heard a cart rattling by and a bell ringing. A commanding voice called out in clipped New Amsterdam tones. "Bring out the afflicted. Give us your dead. Bring out the afflicted. Give us your dead." The bell rang loudly enough that it could be heard from blocks away.

A crowded street appeared before her, with fish markets and taverns and flophouses catering to sailors on shore leave. *'I know this place.'* Lily thought. *'It's Fishbone Lane in New Amsterdam.'* Fishbone Lane was a congested thoroughfare on the waterfront, where fishermen sold red snapper, giant tuna, swordfish, octopus, clams, oysters, sea bass, eels and every other sea creature imaginable. The street usually buzzed with flies and life and the fishy aroma of urchins netted from the brine. It was a street where burly fishermen sang sea chanteys as they tossed red, yellow and black-striped fish the size of a small child to their mates and unloaded warped dinghies that had trawled the ocean so long that they had turned a sodden brown. Sailors from many ports drank their fill of beer and whisky in saloons with name like the Whiskered Fish, Black-Eyed Dave's, and the Blue Pearl. Scantily clad women called to men from open doorways, while immigrants from the Far East crowded ten to a room in the firetrap-apartments over the shops. Colorful laundry hung on clotheslines over the street, full of flapping long johns, undershirts, women's garments and work pants. Peddlers pushed clanking carts full of tin cups and plates down the streets, hawking whatever wares they had to sell. From one block to the next, you might a dozen different languages.

Silas and Lily had come here once. Her brother had been goggle-eyed with all of the sights and sounds, but she couldn't wait to get away from the stink of poverty and the throngs of filthy people. *'No, that was the old me, that was —,'* but the thought was already fading from her mind. *'Why am I here again?'* As she walked into the narrow street, she was surprised by how much it had changed. Gone was the mad press of commoners and servants trying to find the best catch of the day. Gone were the sailors with their stocking caps, peacoats and arms bulging with muscles. The taverns, usually full to bursting, were almost empty. The fish markets were deserted. Only a few people moved on the streets, and those who did, hurried quickly and cast furtive looks at one another. *'What's wrong? This isn't — .'*

That bell rang again from just ahead, and a strange sight came toward her. A man, dressed all in black with a silver mask that swooped into a massive curved beak, was walking ahead of a cart with a cage on the back. The man was ringing a bell. "Give us your afflicted. Give us your dead," the man intoned with the solemnity of a priest.

"Buggers give me the creeps," a woman next to Lily said. Bent with age and carrying a freshly wrapped codfish, she watched suspiciously as the wagon approached. "Mayhap, 'tis necessary though, anything to stop the end of days."

Lily turned to ask what she meant, but the woman hurried into one of the buildings, the silver fish poking out of the end of the wrapping paper.

The cart drew nearer. A tavern keeper and two of his customers came out of a shop a few doors down. They were leading a man who was bound with ropes and foaming at the mouth. "Come on, move it," the tavern keeper said, tugging on the rope. In response, the bound man cackled manically and snapped at the tavern keeper. "Hold him tight!" the tavern keeper bawled to the other men. *'He's scared. He doesn't want that man anywhere near him. None of them do.'*

"They must have gotten into his room last night," one of the men said.

"Well, he's as good as dead now. We're only doing what we'd want done if it were us."

"Aye, but what do I tell his wife when I get back to Liverpool?" the man asked.

"It's dark times, indeed. Dark times everywhere," the tavern keeper muttered.

The cart rolled to a stop in front of them. The man in the silver mask gestured for the cage to be unlocked. Two men holding long poles with loops on the end came forward and tightened the nooses around the bound man's neck.

"Careful with him," the man in the silver mask commanded.

'They are taking him to be burned,' Lily suddenly realized, as if she had seen this many times before. *'Something has happened. Something has come back into the world and no one knows exactly what it is. It comes at night though, and in the day there are less of us than before.'* She looked at the basket she was carrying that was full of fresh oysters. *'I must hurry back before mother worries about what has happened to me.'*

As Lily hurried past the wagon, she looked inside and saw that it was full of men, women and children with the same crazed look in their eyes. One of the men lunged, trying to grab her through the bars. Very clearly, she saw bite marks on his neck.

"Go home, girl, and say your prayers, for night draws close again," the man in the silver mask called out to her.

Lily hurried through empty streets. Where had the sun gone? New Amsterdam was a northern town, but it was full summer and a chill still clung to the air. She passed boarded-up shops with signs like "Taken by the plague" or "Repent for your sins" scrawled on the shutters. Twice she saw a strange symbol painted in red on buildings. Before her father was taken, he had told her that it was a mark of the old gods. 'Eldritch,' he had said, whoever that was. Even Silas hadn't known. The way Thomas and Moira had exchanged a terrified look, she could tell that they knew very well what it meant.

One night, Lily heard her mother and father talking through the walls.

"Deiva must have died at last," Thomas said. "The Gardens must have fallen. Jonquil—."

"Hush," Moira said. "Jonquil stayed for what he believed was right and we left for the same reason."

"To protect our daughter, I know," Thomas said, and Lily heard the bed creak as if he was getting up. "But what if we made the wrong decision? What if we doomed her and everyone else in the world?"

"Nonsense. It's just the plague come again. This too will pass," Moira said.

But that had been before the night they had heard a man screaming for help outside of the Golden Bough. The man screamed for long minutes in agony, calling on the mercy of anyone nearby to save him, shrieking that something had attacked his family in the dark and that he was bleeding to death.

"Isn't anyone going to help him?" Thomas asked, and for the first time, Lily saw her Father's face flushed with anger.

"We — we can't," Moira said. "Remember what

the papers said."

"Yes, don't go out after dark. A man is dying though," he said. He left the bedroom where the family had gathered the last few days as the plague worsened. Thomas came back soon after with a sword that had been in the prop room. "I'm going out there," he said. "It's what a dusk rider would do."

'A dusk rider? What's that?' Lily wondered. "Be careful," she said.

Their father stopped at the door and smiled at Lily and Silas. "I will. When I get back I'll tell you of your mother and me as children."

Thomas never came back, though. He went outside and the screaming soon stopped, but it was followed by a malicious laughter and the sound of a blade clinking on cobblestones. Silas and Lily wanted to rush out to help their father, but Moira held them back. "It's the last thing that he'd want," Moira said, lips trembling.

At the first light of dawn, Lily and Silas rushed outside, but all they found was the sword lying on the street. Their father was gone.

The sun was setting as Lily sighted the Golden Bough. A sign on the door read "All performances canceled until further notice." She entered the dingy lobby with her basket of food and found Silas double-checking the locks on everything. Her brother was more pensive since their father had disappeared. His heart had hardened and his gentleness was gone.

"I was beginning to grow worried," he said. "What's happening outside?"

Lily told him of the deserted streets and the affliction cart as they made their way to the kitchen.

"It grows worse and worse," he said.

"Come now. Mother says the plague will burn itself out as it always does," Lily said.

"It's no more a plague than these oysters you carry," Silas said. "There are things out there. Things that didn't used to be here. And they took our father."

"Hush," Lily said and the word came out too loudly in the darkened theater. "Don't talk of such things. It's a sickness. Nothing more."

'None of this is supposed to exist,' Lily thought. *"It's all an —."*

Moira appeared as they entered the kitchen. The oven was burning and she was making fresh bread.

"No more of that talk, Silas. You're scaring your sister," their mother said tiredly. Moira had aged a decade in the week since Thomas disappeared. Her ginger hair was streaked with gray, and for the first time, Lily noticed crow's feet around her eyes.

'This has shaken her to her foundation.' Lily set the basket down and gave her mother a long hug. Her mother hugged her back. "Thank you, child."

"If you want to ignore this, you can, but I won't," Silas said. He stalked off to make sure that everything was locked for the night.

"Don't worry about him," Moira said when Silas

was gone. "Your brother feels that he must take the place of your father in protecting us."

Lily began to unload the basket of oysters and place them on ice.

"There's something I need discuss with you," Moira said as they worked.

"What is it?" Lily asked.

"I — I'm afraid that we can't stay here much longer. The city is about to fall. More people are disappearing or turning to strange worship. I fear that before too long no place here will be safe. There is a place where we may be safe though."

"Where's that?"

"It's a place like no other. If any of it is still left," she said.

'She means Nightfall Gardens,' Lily thought, but the idea scurried away before she could pin it down.

"We will discuss it later tonight, the three of us," Moira said.

The last light of the day leeched from the sky, leaving behind a moonless night. Lily watched from an upstairs window as passersby hurried home, rushing as if the devil were on their heels.

They ate dinner in the kitchen by candlelight. The great theater creaked with the wind. Otherwise, all was silent. The normal sounds of the city — the rattle of carts, horses clopping by on cobblestones, people calling out their wares, music drifting from saloons — all of that was gone.

When the food was finished and the plates

cleared, Moira drew them close and said, "I want to tell you of the place where your father and I come from." Silas and Lily exchanged a glance with each other. They had heard the story about the orphanage where their parents had grown up many times.

A door slammed with a bang somewhere in the house. All three of them jumped.

"What was that?" Lily asked.

"I checked all of the doors," Silas said. Shuffling footsteps came from the darkness down the hall, from the direction of the theater.

"Who's there?" Moira called.

"The prop room," Silas exclaimed, jumping to his feet. A trapdoor in that room led into secret tunnels that ran down to the sewers. He and Lily used to hide there and listen through the heating grates when they wanted to hear what their parents were talking about. "I forgot to checked that the trapdoor was latched."

Silas bolted into the darkness before they could stop him.

"Go, after your brother," Moira said. Lily could hear the fear in her mother's voice.

She chased her brother toward the prop room. "Silas, slow down," she called out. It was too late, though. Her brother threw open the door and disappeared into the room. Lily plunged into the room after him.

The prop room was a bazaar of costumes, masks, fake weapons and painted scenery. A red and white dragon costume hung the length of the room overhead. Silas was standing in the center of the room, holding a shaking candle in his hand. What used to be their father stood on the other side of the room. Thomas looked as though he had been dead for days. All of the color was drained from him. The gentleness was gone from his face, as well, replaced by a soulless hunger. His pupils shrank as Silas raised the candle. Their father looked at them the way a child looks at an ant. Something thumped on the other side of the trapdoor, and Lily saw that Silas had secured the lock.

"Father?" Silas asked, taking a hesitant step towards him.

The creature that used to be Thomas hissed. His clothes were muddy, and Lily saw spots of blood on them.

"Are – are you all right?" Silas asked. He stepped closer to their father.

"Silas, don't … that's not —." Lily got no further before a window shattered in the building. Silas turned toward the sound, and that was when their father struck. Thomas moved quickly, more quickly than a human could. In one movement he was on top of Silas, pinning him to the floor and ripping at his throat.

"Run, Lily!" Silas yelled thrashing about and trying to push their father away. Lily opened her mouth to scream. A spray of blood spurted across the room and then she was running for her life while her father gorged on the twitching body of her brother.

Somewhere in the theatre, Moira cried in pain. "By the Daughters, no." Another voice, a woman with a silken purr called, "Blackwood. Where are you? We have your mother."

"Hide," Moira yelled in the darkness. "Don't let them find you."

Lily hid behind curtains and ropes backstage, where sandbags were stacked for a performance that would never happen. The voices were close; they were coming from the stage. She peeked out and saw her mother and the shapes of three women.

"We will kill your mother if you don't come to us," another of the women said.

"Oh what great fun it will be," the third said. She sounded more like a demented child than anything else.

"Don't," Moira panted. Lily saw her mother on her hands and knees, crawling across the stage. *'They've hurt her. Who are they?'*

"We will give you one more chance," the first woman with the purring voice said.

'What choice do I have?' Lily thought as she walked out into the open. As she came onto the stage, Moira looked up at her through tearful eyes. "Oh no, oh no," she moaned.

"The last Blackwood," the purring voice gloated.

"How pathetic," the second woman said. "*These* are the ones that hindered us for so long?"

"Let me kill her, please," the third simpered.

Lily took a deep breath and tried to conjure whatever bravery she had. *'It's like acting,'* she thought. *'Maybe if I pretend hard enough, I'll actually be brave.'*

"The mother first and then her," the second one said. The three sisters stepped into a thin sliver of light that fell into the room. Lily saw their faces then, the smiles that stretched from ear to ear, frozen in the most horrific travesty of joy that she had ever seen.

"Oh Esmeret, you do take the fun out of it," the first said.

"Goody, goody," chortled the third.

Lily thanked the gods for her own screams, as they erupted from her throat, for they spared her from hearing her mother's.

"With you, dies hope," Esmeret whispered, as Lily felt her life draining away. *'Just give up and rest,'* Lily thought as their teeth fastened upon her again. *'This will be over soon. No more horror or nightmares. I can sleep at long last.'* Would it be over though? What about Pandora's Box? What about the Gardens? These thoughts came strange and unbidden. *'This isn't real,'* Lily thought. *'None of it is.'* She clutched at the thought like a drowning man as the room shimmered around her. *'I don't know what this is, whether it's a world that might have been or an illusion to frighten me senseless, but it's not real.'* The room shimmered again. This time she saw stone walls and a dark chamber around her. The theater melted away, and Lily was back in the Smiling Ladies' castle. The passage came to an end ahead of her. She looked back and could saw the women in white watching. *'They can't come here,'* she thought. *'They can come no further.'*

The third passage ended in a hall of dusty tapestries and stout oak tables that held candlesticks and other odds and ends, giving the appearance that someone lived here. *'They are just as much props as those in the Golden Bough,'* Lily thought. Where was she going? Surely, it must be dawn soon. It felt like she had spent days in the mad maze of illusions that she'd traveled that night. She walked through the hall and into another and from that into another. The castle seemed abandoned, like the largest mausoleum in the world.

How long she wandered the halls of the castle before she came to the final room, she did not know. Its door was heavy, oaken and sturdy. There was no mistaking the copper number that was nailed to its surface. She recognized the Roman numerals XXIII from Pandora's tomb and from the mural in the corridor of Nightfall Manor. Lily pushed the door and it creaked open on rusted hinges. A skeleton in a dress lay slumped across the flagstone floor in what appeared to be a bedroom, a body left dead where it had fallen. They hadn't even bothered dragging her out of the way. Dried, brittle black hair clung to her skull. Her bones were as small as those of a young girl. Lily bent to examine the corpse, knowing in her heart who this had been. *'Abigail. I don't know how they got you, but they did and they left you here like you were less than a dog,'* Lily thought angrily. She stroked the back of her great aunt's head. One of Abigail's arms was outstretched as if she were reaching for something. Lily looked up to where her aunt was pointing and smiled for the first time in days. It was here right in front of them all of this time and the Smiling Ladies never bothered to look. Scratched into the stone were the Roman numerals for 23, the same as on the door. *'What does it mean?'* Lily wondered. As she reached out to touch the numbers, she felt the stone move under her hand. She lifted the stone and revealed a hole just big enough to hold a cigar box. A tattered fragment of paper that looked as old as Ozy's Egyptian parchments lay on the ground in the hole. It showed a sketch of a maze, drawn in the heavy lines of squid ink with six words written in Latin at the top.

Lily slipped the paper into a dress pocket and replaced the stone. *'I must find out what this means,'* she thought. Then, she hoisted Abigail's skeleton gently in her arms and set off through the castle, determined to take her great-aunt with her. Each hall looked the same, dark and desolate. Nothing came near her, though she once saw one of the women in white crawling along the walls far ahead of her. She was on the verge of giving up hope that she would ever find her way back to the feasting hall, when she spotted a glimmer of light ahead of her and found herself walking back out of the entrance to the castle that she had come through when she arrived.

The darkness had lifted only imperceptibly, but enough for to Lily know that day must have arrived outside of the Shadow Garden. The carriage with the skeletal horses and the driver with the top hat waited for her. As she walked across the courtyard with relief in her heart, Vallia stepped from behind a column, careful not to stand in the daylight. The porcupine creature was at her heels as usual. "It seems you are a more worthy opponent than we thought. The Judge has ruled in your favor," she said in an icy voice. "But this game has not ended, it's only beginning. I promise you that. Soon, this place will open and we will pour forth to destroy the world."

"But not today," Lily said, giving her a tired smile.

"No," Vallia spat, looking as though she had eaten something repulsive. "Not today."

Lily rode back to Nightfall Gardens with the blinds pulled down and Abigail's body propped up on the seat across from her. Lily closed her eyes what felt like a second, and when she opened them, the door to the carriage was yanked open and Polly was standing there. "Oh, you came back, Miss, you did," she cried. And with that, the housekeeper wrapped her arms around Lily in a squelching embrace that coated her with slime from head to foot.

"Who's this, Miss, who's —," Polly started, and then her eyes rounded in surprise. "Well bless my ever-grubbing heart if it isn't Miss Abigail. Oh this is a happy day, a happy day indeed!"

After a long hot bath and a sumptuous breakfast, Lily found herself in the study that overlooked the Shadow Garden. A roaring fire crackled in the fireplace, melting away the chill in her bones and making her drowsy. *'What would have happened if she had chosen to stay in the imaginary Paris or had given up and married Gideon Wassum to protect her family, or if she had never realized that it was all an illusion?'* But she didn't care to dwell on that for long. *'I would never have left that castle,'* she thought. Yet, somehow she had made it out.

Polly and Ozy entered the room. The ancient housekeeper was carrying a tray of tea. Lily told them of the strange things she had experienced in the Shadow Garden and of the castle of the Smiling Ladies.

"A place of misery, Miss. Escaped from there I did," Polly said.

"I saw your sister," Lily said, remembering Justine and the threat she made.

"Never could stand a grub to be happy, she couldn't" Polly said. "But if she thinks it will be so easy to salt old Polly, she has another thing coming."

Lily grinned at that, saying, "I'm sure she does."

The two turned to depart and leave her in peace.

"Could I speak to you for a moment in private?" Lily asked Ozy.

"Of course. Anything that you'd like," Ozy intoned. The old butler creaked his way across the room and stood next to her chair. The liver spots on his bald pate seemed to have doubled in size since the day before, and his mummy bandages stuck up from inside his collar.

"Can you read Latin?" Lily asked, pulling the scrap of paper from her pocket.

"It's been a while, but yes," Ozy said. "At one time I was the cataloguer of the dead and had the best penmanship in the pyramids."

"I bet you did," Lily said, smiling and stoking his ego. "I need your utmost secrecy on this."

Ozy nodded his ancient head and pulled a pair of spectacles from his wrappings and examined the paper. "Hmmm," he muttered under his breath. "Fascinating. I don't know how this can be."

"What?" Lily asked, after waiting several minutes for him to speak.

"This parchment is old, very old," Ozy said.

"But what does it *say*?" Lily implored.

"Yes, of course. It says – it says, 'Under the golden god of the sun in the Labyrinth rests Pandora's Box.'"

'In the Labyrinth,' Lily thought. *'Pandora's Box is there and if I can destroy it then the Blackwoods will be free at last.'*

"Thank you," Lily said to the butler.

"If I may Miss," Ozy ventured. "Destroy this

paper. If the wrong person should get their hands on it, all of us will be doomed. If someone opens that box, far worse things than you can imagine will enter this world. The Shadow Garden and the White Garden and the Labyrinth, all of those are child play compared to what lurks within.

"I understand," Lily said. "Tell no one. And thank you, Ozy," she said, dismissing the butler. Ozy looked as if he wanted to say more, but then he sighed and began his long, slow trek out of the room.

When he was gone, Lily made some tea. She saw something move out of the corner of her eye. "Abigail," she said in recognition.

Her great-aunt was standing there on the other side of the sofa, her usually pinched and serious face grinning for the first time.

"You've come home now," Lily said. "I found what you were searching for. You can rest in the peace that you've long since earned."

The little girl nodded and smiled again. Lily sipped her tea, and when she looked back toward the sofa, her great-aunt was gone.

Lily looked out the window at the dismal light over Nightfall Gardens and thought she had never been happier. When Cassandra and Silas came back, they would find a way to enter the Labyrinth. Pandora's Box must be destroyed. She thought about what Ozy had said and shuddered. *'He's a worried old man who has lived longer than a person should,'* she thought. *'I'll keep the paper safe. No one will ever know about it.'* Dark clouds were brewing out over the mist. Lily saw purple lightning flash inside one of the clouds. She sipped her tea as the sound of thunder boomed a distant echo. *'But there'll be many hours before it gets here yet,'* she thought as the winds stirred the trees and she waited in silence for the storm to break.

ACKNOWLEDGMENTS

The Shadow Garden wouldn't be nearly as strange or mysterious without the help of the following people.

Kimberly, my love — no one has supported me through the writing of this novel as much as you. When the madness of life, threatened to knock me off stride or on those long days where there wasn't time for me to escape to Nightfall Gardens, you always encouraged me to take a deep breath and get back to work.

Frank Sentner, Paul Earp, Blaine Palmer, Matt Carson and Kristin Fayne Mulroy — you helped hammer a bloated first draft into a fine polish. Thanks for your friendship and encouragement.

To Lynn Sentner, I wouldn't have had those precious mornings at the coffee shop to write without you trekking down from Connecticut to help with the kiddo.

Every good book needs a great copy editor and Casey Ward, knocked it out of the park on this one. If there was a better word choice or more succinct way to say something, Casey found it.

And finally, once again to Tony Roberts for so perfectly capturing Nightfall Gardens with his cover illustration. Nightfall Gardens exists just beyond the shadows of the trees as dusk falls. It's available for all to see, but only a few, like Tony, can look for long, before flinching or turning away from what is waiting off of the path.

ABOUT THE AUTHOR

Allen Houston is a native Oklahoman who has lived in Japan and Indonesia. He has worked as a journalist at the *Dallas Morning News* and *New York Post*. He's currently city editor for *Metro New York*. Allen lives in Brooklyn with his wife, daughter and a menagerie of animals.

www.allendhouston.com @adhouston

Printed in Great Britain
by Amazon